LOVE OVERBOARD

Bev Dulson

Published in 2012 by FeedARead.com Publishing – Arts Council funded

A CIP catalogue record for this title is available from the British Library.

Also by Bev Dulson

BETRAYAL

Coming Soon

TWISTED SISTER

ACKNOWLEDGEMENTS

There are so many people I need to thank for LOVE OVERBOARD. Firstly it wouldn't even exist without the fabulous opportunity I got, to go on a Caribbean cruise when I worked in travel, so the first people to thank are my fab Thomas Cookers, Boss Man -Phil Nixon, Ian Rowlands, Claire Eccles-Cake, Jo Cooper, Helen Long and of course Helen Whitey-Burns (yes, Hels, there ARE Helenisms in this book –too funny not to use!) You were the best to work with and I miss you all lots! The second group of people I need to thank are the amazing entertainment team onboard Oceana, Adam Heppenstall & Richard Agg. You both took us under your wing and we had a ball! (Rich thanks for all the technical advice for Betrayal too!)

There are lots of other people who've given me inspiration, advice and helped me when I've had writers block. Thanks to Charotte Scott for reading the first ever rough copy, Gavin Scott for the name of my rugby team. Oldershaw rugby club for my mis- spent youth! Also my little (but taller) brother Will for the fluffy sheep song. My lovely Nanny Bill for being my no.1 fan – love you nan.

Cat Batty, Lynne Morley and Chris Thom my amazingly talented writer friends for their constant support and help. Helga Shoebridge for my amazeballs book cover. Everyone who supported Betrayal (and let me know how much they enjoyed it – you don't know what that means!)

Obviously, my amazing husband Mark for putting up with me wittering on about characters and spending hours tapping away on my laptop 'coz "I have to get this written down now." And our beautiful girls Rebekah and Faye, love you more than cake!

Finally the book would never have happened without one very special person, my shipmate and friend for life, Katie Pearson. That ship rocked babe, bottoms up...boobs out! Xxxx

Author's Note

Although this book is a work of fiction it's been my guilty pleasure, any coincidence to people living, is probably not coincidental. There MAY be some comparisons to real life people (especially Thomas Cookers!!!). I may have borrowed stories, character traits and popped them in the book. I'm sure none of you will take offence. (I have borrowed a lot of your names too as a little thank you for all the good times!)Love Overboard is a work of fiction with not so fictional characters!! The main reason I wrote this book was so that when I'm old and grey I will have this book as a souvenir of an amazing time in my life!

For my lovely Shipmate Katie –
That ship rocked!
Bottoms up, Boobs out
This one's for you
xxx

CHAPTER ONE

Lucie pulled the chairs out and looked under the tables in the bar, The Yacht and Compass. "Oh Zo, I can't believe I've lost my bracelet."

"You wore it last night. Sure you put it on tonight?"

"Yeah, I've worn it every night on the ship."

Zoey laughed. "Luce, it's only our second night."

Zoey glanced around the bar, with its Chesterfields, leather bound books and dark wood panelling, it reminded Zoey of something out of an old English manor. She spotted two of the cruise ship's entertainment guys on the other side of the room. One looked straight at them, whilst talking to the other.

She nudged Lucie. "Maybe we should ask him if anyone has handed it in."

"Ask who?" Lucie asked. She was still scanning the floor for the bracelet; she pushed her long blonde hair behind her ears to stop it getting in the way of her search.

"That one over there, he keeps looking at you."

Lucie looked over to the tall, hunky guy wearing navy trousers, a pale blue short-sleeved shirt and one of those funny white officer's hats.

Mmm, he's quite cute, she thought to herself.

"C'mon then let's go and ask him," Zoey headed over.

Lucie had no choice but to follow. The guy looked friendly enough and he was obviously staff, so hopefully he could help them.

"Hiya, sorry to interrupt but my friend has lost her silver Tiffany bracelet. Has anyone handed one in?" Zoey asked flashing her best travel agent's smile.

"Sorry girls, no one has passed anything to us, but we'll help you look. I'm Nick." He gestured to the other guy, now chatting to another passenger. "He's Steve. Saw you at the cocktail party. Virgin's right?" he winked "Cruise virgins."

Zoey grinned. "Is it that obvious? We work for 'BOOK IT!' We've got customers onboard. We're supposed to be looking after them, but the ship is so big we hardly ever see them. I'm Zoey and this is Lucie."

"Nice to meet ya both. Hope your customers aren't having too many problems."

"Not really, it would seem that life on this ship is pretty damn good," Lucie said.

By the time Steve had wandered back over, the pub had emptied out as the other passengers headed out of the bar, presumably off to the other various forms of entertainment. The four of them began to search again, but with no luck.

"Listen girls, try Reception in the morning," Nick shrugged. "Someone may have already picked it up and handed it in there."

"We're on duty there in the morning so we can ask then," Zoey said.

"Nick, we need to show our faces in 'Le Club'".

"Yeah, no rest for the wicked. Hey, why don't you come with us? Drinks on us to help cheer you up."

Lucie glanced at her watch. "Well, we have an early start..."

"Ah, c'mon Luce, it isn't all work, we're on holiday too."

Before Lucie could reply Zoey was heading out of the bar with Steve, leaving her with no alternative but to walk with Nick. Subtle as a brick, that was Zo, Lucie thought as she began to chat to Nick. He really was quite tasty.

'Le Club' was the small night club in the centre of the ship, as soon as she walked in Zoey loved it. The walls were different shades of purples and lilacs, with lots of silver furniture and mirrors. It was over the top and so camp, it looked like Laurence Llewellyn-Bowen had gone bonkers in there.

"How cool is this?" Zoey said.

"D'you think? It looks like a tarts boudoir," Steve laughed.

"Like you'd know," Nick joked.

The drinks flowed freely as did the banter, and as the evening wore on Nick and Lucie were oblivious to anyone else. Zoey and Steve were chilling out on one of the over sized purple sofas, getting drunk. 'Le Club' had the ambience of some kind of exclusive night spot; most of the older passengers probably didn't even know the night club existed.

"Those two are getting on well."

"It looks like your mate has bagged one of the few straight guys on board," Steve laughed.

"Just my luck, I don't want to be a gooseberry for the rest of the cruise."

"Don't worry lovely; I'll pretend I'm straight for the next two weeks if you want."

Zoey grinned. "You stick at being you mate; we'll have more fun that way."

"D'you reckon?"

"Hell yeah! Every girl should have a gay best mate."

"Why?" Steve asked looking confused.

"OK. I'll ask you some questions; you say the first thing that comes into your head."

"Shoot!"

"Manolos or Jimmy Choo?"

"Manolos, Jimmy's too over rated," Steve replied straight away.

"Friends or Sex in the City?"

"Always Friends."

"George Clooney or Jon Bon Jovi?"

"JB all the way," he laughed. "But what is your point?"

"My point is; Nick wouldn't have a clue about Jimmy Choo shoes. Those two are probably having a deep and meaningful conversation, and we're just having a laugh."

"They're playing my song, think those two would notice if we hit the dance floor?"

"They've only got eyes for each other," Zoey laughed as they headed off doing the 'dancing to the dance floor dance' to 'Dancing Queen.'

Not being a fan of Abba Lucie was happy to sit this one out and carry on talking to Nick, besides they'd danced earlier on and these shoes were killing her. She'd noticed when they were bopping away to "It's Raining Men" how tall he was, even in her heels he towered over her, she liked that. She was pretty tall herself so short blokes were a definite no no. Plus there was the uniform, he looked hot. They'd been chatting easily, she was aware they were both flirting with each other, he would lean in closer to talk to her and she'd mimic his movements although she was slightly concerned the more she moved forward the more boobage she was flashing!

"So, you're enjoying the ship then?"

"Yeah It's fab, but I keep getting lost. I have no sense of direction." She wrapped a finger around a few strands of her blonde hair and tilted her head to one side as she spoke.

"I'll just have to take you on a proper tour of the ship then." He winked at her as he lifted his drink to his lips.

She spotted Zoey waving them over. "Think we're wanted on the dance floor."

"C'mon then, let's go and show them how it's done," he winked again.

He looked even sexier when he winked, she let him take her by the hand and led her to the dance floor. He was having a very strange effect on her, the minute he held her hand her skin erupted in goose bumps.

It was the early hours of the morning when Zoey and Lucie finally headed off towards their cabin. The best thing about cruising, they decided, was that when it was time for bed after a night of partying there was no hanging around waiting for a taxi. You could walk back barefoot, which was great for Lucie's sore feet and then just fall into your cabin and stumble straight into bed. The guys had persuaded them to take a stroll round the deck and go the long way home.

Zoey and Steve were walking slightly ahead arms linked as they giggled away.

"How pissed are those two?" Nick laughed.

"Looks like they've had a good night."

Nick smiled. "Me too."

Lucie didn't know if it was the balmy, sultry Caribbean air or just being here with Nick that left her almost gasping for air. She decided to stick to safe topics of conversation.

"Yeah, Zo is a nutter alright."

"I can't believe you only met a few days ago, you seem like you've been friends for ages."

"We just clicked as soon as we met at the airport, some people just do," She replied.

"Mm, I suppose you're right."

They walked around the deck in a comfortable silence. Lucie didn't think she was too drunk, she could still walk in a straight line…or maybe the gentle rolling of the ship was making her think she wasn't swaying. She couldn't believe she was on this luxurious ship, in such an exotic location with this really, well, hot guy. Zoey and Steve had disappeared around the front of the deck. The ship carried on sailing into the darkness, the stars twinkling the way ahead. The air felt heavier and she knew it wasn't just because of the heat.

"So, back home, are you… are you with anyone?"

"Nope, Zoey and I are like a younger version of Thelma and Louise on this trip. Two single girls up for an adventure."

"So, who gets to be Brad Pitt?" he stopped, grinning cheekily at her.

"Got any suggestions?" She suddenly felt nervous. She knew he was flirting with her; they had both been doing it all night. But what if she'd gotten the signals wrong? She and Zo were a long way from home; maybe he was just being friendly.

Before she could question herself further he leaned across and gently kissed her lips. He pulled away and looked searchingly into her eyes; she couldn't tear her eyes away from him. Then without any words between them, just the look in their eyes confirming their desire, they found themselves in each others arms caught up in the moment. Nick pulled her even closer to him, his hands running through her hair, kissing her so hard that when they came up for air her lips were tingling just like the rest of her body. She gasped for air; he gently pulled at her bottom lip as she caught her breath. Then they were kissing again, he tasted like southern comfort and she certainly felt like she was getting drunk from his kiss. His hands were travelling down her back; he squeezed her bum and pushed her closer to him, pressing his pelvis against hers. Her skin felt clammy and sticky, both from the intense heat of the night and the passionate effect Nick was having on her. He pulled away and grinned. "I don't mean to alarm you Luce, but that isn't my mobile phone in my pocket."

She threw her head back as she laughed. "Didn't think it was, mobile phones are much smaller these days"

He grinned. "Knew you were my kinda girl."

The sunlight streamed through a gap in the curtains and straight into the cabin, waking Zoey up after what felt like only five minutes sleep. She tried to make the time out on the clock; surely it wasn't time to get up yet? She was positive she'd only just closed her eyes to go to sleep. The red numbers on the clock were blurred; she rubbed her eyes and looked at the clock again. This time she had no trouble seeing the time, it read 8.15am. She threw the covers back and jumped out of bed.

"Shit! Luce, we're late!"

Zoey began throwing clothes on, simultaneously dragging a brush through her chin length brown hair.

Lucie looked dazed after being abruptly woken from her sleep. "What?"

"We're on duty this morning; we should've been there fifteen minutes ago!"

After a quick brush of their hair and teeth, they looked about as respectable as could be expected after four hours sleep. They headed off towards reception.

"I don't know why we rushed so much; no one has had any problems yet," Lucie complained.

"Well, it'd be sod's law that the one time we weren't

here, someone had gone overboard or something," Zoey replied as she sat down on one of the comfy chairs at the foot of the staircase that led all the way to the top of the atrium. Once she'd gotten herself settled she turned to Lucie. "So, fill me in on all the goss from last night."

With all of the rush of the morning, Lucie had forgotten about the kiss. How could she have forgotten about Nick?

"Zo, it was amazing," Lucie couldn't keep the smile from her face. Just as she was about to tell Zoey about her romantic walk with Nick, they were interrupted by one of their customers. It was the bride of the honeymoon couple that Zoey had booked.

"Hi girls, I have a big problem," newlywed Paige Simpson looked worried.

"What's wrong?" Lucie asked concerned.

"Mike ordered the 'Special Occasions' package for us to start our honeymoon off in style."

Zoey nodded. She remembered adding it on as a surprise.

"Well, the thing is, the dressing gown is too big."

Zoey was about to laugh until she realised, by the look on the woman's face that she was deadly serious.

"Erm, I think one size fits all," Lucie explained.

"Well it doesn't fit me. It swamps me. It would even be too big for you Zoey."

Zoey opened her mouth to speak, but closed it straight away when she realised she had nothing to say.

Lucie could see the look of hurt flash across Zoey's face. How dare this woman be so rude. She sprang into happy travel agent mode, a huge grin across her face. "Mrs Simpson," she began cheerfully. "You're on your honeymoon, that's the one time you don't need a dressing gown," Lucie winked conspiratorially at her.

"Oh. Ok, yeah you're right. Thanks." Paige Simpson

turned and walked away. “Cheeky cow,” Lucie muttered under her breath to the retreating newlywed.

“Morning, ladies.”

Lucie turned round; Nick was perched on the arm of her chair.

“Hi... hi,” she stammered caught off guard and too busy being dazzled by his smile.

“How do you look so awake, when we’ve hardly had any sleep?” Zoey asked.

“My body clock is used to zero amounts of sleep,” Nick grinned as he absentmindedly began messing with Lucie’s long blonde hair.

“We obviously aren’t, we over slept this morning,” Zoey laughed.

“Yeah, we haven’t even washed our hair or anything,” Lucie added, then instantly regretted it. What a dozy thing to say.

Zoey began to tell him about ‘Mrs. My-dressing- gown’s-too-big’, to give Lucie a chance to get her composure back.

“What a freak,” Nick laughed. He glanced at his watch, “Oops, I’m gonna be late now. I’m on deck quoits duty in five minutes, can’t keep the old dears waiting. I’ll catch ya both later,” he winked at Lucie, she nodded and smiled. He dropped his pen on the floor, as he bent down to pick it up; he discreetly kissed Lucie on the cheek. It was that quick and intimate that even Zoey hadn’t noticed. As he walked away Lucie couldn’t take her eyes off him. That kiss last night had been the most passionate kiss she had ever experienced and God he was fit.

“What was that Luce?”

“Was I talking?” Lucie asked.

Zoey just nodded her head and grinned.

CHAPTER TWO

FOUR YEARS LATER...

You are cordially invited to the weddings of

Zoey Catherine Shaw
&
Adam Maxwell
****

Lucinda Scarlett Maxwell
&
Anthony Maxwell
Saturday 4th September 2008
Crabwall manor 2pm

Zoey Shaw was quite happy to be ditching her maiden name and becoming Mrs Maxwell in less than 17 hours and...she lifted her wrist to her face and squinted at her watch, forgetting she wasn't supposed to make any facial movements with the "miracle bride" face pack on.

"Madam, please don't move your hand, I've only just put the second coat of polish on."

Crap! What was she supposed to be? A statue? She was getting married in 17 hours and twenty two minutes, she wanted to dance around in excitement not sit like she'd been put on the naughty step. All this beauty treatment malarkey was all well and good, but it did get to be a bit annoying...she'd had some sort of weird wrap treatment that morning, she'd been covered head to toe in green algae, wrapped up in tin foil and left to bake for half an hour, listening to bloody stupid pan pipe music, all in the hope of losing that last extra inch off her body. Which was just fine and dandy till the bloody fire alarm went off. The therapist had seen the look of horror on her face and told her it was ok, it was only a test. Like she was really going to evacuate the building dressed up like a Christmas turkey. Still, it would all be worth it tomorrow, she so couldn't wait to be walking down the aisle and marrying Adam and not only that but Lucie, would be walking down with her marrying Adam's twin brother, Ant.

Who would've thought two weeks on a Caribbean cruise could result in a friendship for life and a happy ending for both of them? Not only had she and Lucie stayed in touch after the cruise but they had become even closer. They both still worked for 'BOOK IT!', and were now assistant managers, Zoey based in a town called Wallasey and Lucie in the next town along, Moreton. Both towns were coastal areas of the Wirral peninsula, which was just across the water from Liverpool. It was strange how their lives seemed to go in tandem. They were both doing well in their careers and now they were marrying twins. Some people might've thought it was cheesy but to the four of them, it felt like the natural thing to do. They were all so close it seemed mad not to.

They had met their future husbands a year after coming back from the cruise. Zoey's younger brother Ed was a rugby fanatic. Zoey would often join him at the local Rugby club. Rugby was practically a religion in their family when they were growing up, so the club was pretty much a home from home. The late night drinking and the fit rugby guys were always a bonus! Both she and Lucie had gone to the club Christmas party; they hadn't been there long when two guys caught their eye. Athletically built, tall, dark, handsome, fine specimens of a rugby player - and there were two of them!

"Who are they?" Zoey asked turning to her brother.

"Oh, the gruesome twosome?" Ed rolled his eyes.

"Yeah right, as if!" Lucie replied.

"You can't seriously be interested in those pretty boys?" Ed mocked.

"What's wrong with them?" Zoey asked.

"Well, they're backs for starters, not proper rugby players like me in the scrum."

"That's a bonus, they won't get cauliflower ears," Lucie laughed.

"I think my little bro's ego is being threatened."

"Hey, they might be gorgeous, but don't they know it. I'm gorgeous and haven't got a clue!"

The girls both burst out laughing. He was right he was good looking, but boy did he have a big head to go with it.

"C'mon Luce, why waste your time with those guys when you know you could have me anytime you want."

"Sorry Ed, but you'll always be my best friend's little brother," she shrugged her shoulders and grinned.

"Your loss babe, you've broken my heart, you know that?" he grinned back as he lifted his bottle of Bud to his lips.

"Oh you'll survive Ed. C'mon Luce let's go and introduce ourselves to those guys, it would be rude not to."

So they headed off, armed with their Bacardi Breezers. As they got nearer Zoey realised they looked even more gorgeous close up, it was kind of freaky seeing two identical hot guys. Normally never at a loss for words Zoey was struggling for something to say as she realised they'd also caught the lad's attention. She was struck by a mischievous smile that revealed a dimple in the right cheek and a dimple in the left cheek of his mirror image. Fortunately, they saved her from complete and utter embarrassment.

"We're glad you came over to us," handsome hunk number one smiled.

"It saved us the walk over to you," handsome hunk number two added. "We thought you might've been with Ed."

"We are, but he's my brother. I'm Zoey and this is Lucie." She gestured to her friend, who as usual, let Zoey do the talking; once she started you just couldn't shut that girl up.

"I'm Adam and this is Ant."

The girls looked at each other and couldn't help a giggle escaping. "Adam Ant? Guess you could be our prince charming."

They carried on laughing as if it was the funniest thing they had ever heard.

"Not heard that one before girls, honest!"

Before they had chance to chat some more the DJ decided it was "Geno" O'clock. The timeless classic by Dexy's Midnight Runners had been a time long tradition by the

Spartans Rugby team…whenever it was played you got yourself up on a table, on a chair, on somebody's shoulders and clapped along, pretended to play a trombone, generally just made a show of yourself. No sooner had the first notes of the song been played the girls found themselves hoisted up onto the lads shoulders, She was on Adam's gorgeously muscley shoulders and Lucie on Ant's matching pair. That was how they met their future husbands, the cute guys with the emerald green eyes, the cheeky smiles and their dimples – which were the only way to tell these other wise identical guys apart, Adam with the dimple in his right cheek and Ant with the dimple on the left.

As she waited for her nails to dry, not daring to move under the eagle eye of the beautician, Zoey idly ran through what was left to do, false tan, done, manicure and pedicure, almost dry, Christmas turkey wrap? She wasn't convinced she was the inch smaller that it promised. Massage, she shrugged her shoulders, yep relaxed, so that just left getting this facial gloop off her face then hair and make up in the morning. So all she needed to do was meet Lucie after she finished with her last treatment and they could enjoy their last night of freedom.

Lucie felt more than relaxed as she lay back enjoying her Indian head massage, the chilled out pan pipe music drifting effortlessly in and out of her mind. This time tomorrow she would be a married woman. She, Lucie Scott, was about to become a wife. She found the whole thing a little bit daunting to say the least, she loved Ant, but she was finding the wedding palaver quite stressful. To be fair, Zoey had taken on most of the arrangements, she'd turned into a proper Bridezilla, in the nicest possible way. On their hen night in Dublin Zoey had confided to her, after a few too many tequilas that she couldn't believe she'd landed a guy like Adam. She knew why Ant would be attracted to Lucie, but she would never understand why Adam wanted her. She knew Zoey had loads of insecurities, she didn't see herself how others saw her, the bright, funny attractive girl that always made people smile. Why wouldn't Adam want to be with someone like that? Zo couldn't wait to get down the aisle. So because of Zoey's ultra organization all Lucie had to do was to pick her wedding dress and remember to turn up on the day. The butterflies started to flit excitedly around her stomach, she really was getting married, such a grown up thing to do and something she'd never quite imagined herself doing. She was quite free spirited and the whole wedding, mortgage thing had never entered her head when she first met Ant. Working as a travel agent was perfect for Lucie, she got the chance to help make people's dreams come true, whether it be a first holiday for a loved up couple, a honeymoon, a flight half way across the world for someone who hadn't seen a loved one for years. The stories customers told her made her feel emotionally attached sometimes. It also gave her the chance to travel, she got a great discount and the chance to go on educational visits so she could come back into store and sell the location with more knowledge. She'd been to some amazing places, New York, Dubai, ski-ing in the Alps although, the best trip ever had been the Cruise. She'd had the time of her life on "Oceania", it had firmly cemented her and Zoey's friendship and of course it had brought Nick into her life, albeit briefly. She'd never admitted it to anyone, but she'd fallen in love with Nick. Well, he was a thing of the past now, she'd found herself in love again and this time everything was right, the timing, the place and the guy. What was that saying about you find love when you least expect it?

She and Ant had started off dating casually when Adam

whisked Zoey off her feet, it was nice to go out as a foursome, then they'd found themselves looking forward to being on their own. Without realising it Lucie and Ant were slowly falling in love. She liked his quietness, they could just sit and chat, whiling the hours away, there was no pressure. What started off as an easy friendship gave them the bond they needed for their relationship, that and their shared love of romantic comedies. One night in the rugby club whilst Zo and Adam only had eyes for each other she and Ant had been chatting about their favourite films. She assumed his would be some all-action film so she was surprised at the way the conversation had been going.

"I can't tell you my fave film," he smiled shyly.

"Why not - is it some dodgy porno?"

He shook his head laughing. "No. it's just embarrassing and it will totally crush my macho rugby player image."

"Lassie?"

"Nah. It's not THAT bad."

She leaned closer to him. "Go on," she whispered. "Your secret's safe with me."

He titled his head closer to her, weighing up whether he should tell her or not.

"Ok, but it's our secret, I've never divulged this info to anyone before and if I tell you, I may have to kill you," he smiled.

He didn't get a chance to tell her right there and then, they were interrupted by Adam and Zo sitting down with them. Later that evening as he walked her home, opting out of heading down to the King Street Tandoori for the usual late night curry with the rest of the guys, the conversation found its way back to films. They'd been talking away as they walked, they weren't holding hands, nothing had been said between them about any possible relationship, their arms kept brushing against each other as they staggered back towards the flat she shared with Zoey. She was very aware of how close her body was to his, they were relaxed in each others company but something felt different tonight, she wasn't sure what had changed.

"So go on, spill, what's the film?"

He stopped walking, he dug his hands in his pockets and grinned at her.

"Promise you won't laugh?"

"Cross my heart," she reinforced her words by crossing her chest.

"Love Actually."

"No way, that's one of my fave's too. I love the bit about Andrew Lincoln's character, always feel a bit sorry for him that he doesn't get the girl."

"Me too! Romantic comedies are my guilty pleasure. I'm not as confident with women like Adam is, he's always the one they notice first, the loud one. Girls think I'm the same as he is and are normally disappointed. So when I was younger I used to watch all these films to try and help me get pointers..."

She stepped closer to him. "I like that you're quiet, we can chat properly."

"I like that you listen," he moved closer to her "you don't expect me to be Adam."

"That's coz' you're Ant." Her voice was barely above a whisper as he took her hands in his, pulling her closer and kissed her lightly on the lips.

"Do that again," she murmured as he moved away.

She smiled as she reflected on their first kiss. Spending the rest of her life with Ant was something she was ready to do, she just hoped there was still room to travel and go on adventures together.

Lucie and Zoey were relaxing in the hotel bar, having a few cheeky drinks to calm the nerves slowly starting to build.

The hotel was beginning to fill up with family and friends who were staying over for the wedding. The girls had hidden away at a corner table of the bar to have half an hour or so to themselves before the madness of family started. Zoey's mum and dad were arriving from Cornwall anytime soon, they ran a little B&B in Bude.

"I see the future mother-in-law in law arrived about an hour ago," Lucie sighed.

"Only problem with gaining a husband, you gain the mother-in-law too."

"Have you seen her outfit? It's peach with shoulder pads."

Zoey almost spat her drink out as she struggled not to laugh. "What does she think this is? Dynasty? It's 2008 not 1988."

"At least we're in this together, safety in numbers and all that."

"Can you believe we're actually getting married tomorrow?" A dreamy look appeared on Zoey's face as she spoke.

Lucie smiled. "It's gonna be the best day ever." She lifted her glass. "Here's to us, bottoms up..."

"Boobs out."

Sharing a room with Zoey reminded Lucie of the cruise, despite her excitement Zo had managed to fall asleep and was now snoring away, yep it definitely took Lucie back to the ship! She lay back on her pillow and closed her eyes, the quiet beep of her mobile made her open them again. She reached out for her phone.

Hope ur asleep babe c u in church almost Mrs M...love you kiddo x

Her fingers flew over the keypad as she typed a message back. Putting the phone back, she snuggled back under her duvet, closed her eyes and fell asleep smiling.

Lucie hadn't believed people when they'd told her how quick the wedding day would go, but now she found herself half way through the evening reception, the vows had emotionally been taken, the photographer had told her at one point to stop smiling so much, he wanted an arty photo, speeches had been given and about half an hour ago she'd danced for the first time with her husband. The day was whizzing by, she never wanted it to end. Ant, who had been weigh-laid by a great aunt was on his way over to her, his smile just as big as hers. He reached out taking her hand in his.

"I am neglecting my beautiful wife already," he tilted his head in the direction of the door. "Come with me."

She followed him, still holding hands as they weaved their way across the dance floor, accepting well wishes as they went. Once they reached the door Ant led her outside onto a small balcony that looked directly into the ballroom. He pulled her into his arms, turning her so she could see through the window, her back leaning into his chest. He rested his chin on her bare shoulder.

"Look at everyone, they're having so much fun at our wedding."

She followed his gaze, Adam and Zo were in each others arms, oblivious to everyone around them. Her friends from work hadn't stopped dancing all night, her mum had been mingling all evening checking everyone was ok, her dad hadn't once got off the dance floor, his cravat loosened and shirt half undone. The rugby lads were gearing up to do one of their mad dances, everyone looked like they were having a great time. She nodded her head in agreement with Ant.

"D'you know what though, Luce? The person having the best time isn't even in that room, he's standing here with everything he needs in his arms."

She let her head fall against his shoulder. "Not like you to get mushy on me."

"Ah, if I can't do it on my wedding day, when can I? Was my speech ok? It's alright for Adam, he's used to speaking in public, he was really funny. I was dreading having to do mine."

"It was perfect, you even had some of your team mates crying so it must've been good."

"I meant what I said y'know, I'm gonna spend the rest of my life making you happy." He spun her round in his arms, lifting his hands up to her face. "I love you Lucie Scarlett Maxwell." He ran his thumb along her jaw line. She reached up putting her arms around his neck, pulling him closer.

"Love you too my brand new hubby," she whispered moments before his lips found hers and they shared their first proper kiss as husband and wife.

CHAPTER THREE

THEN

Lucie and Zoey were wandering around the picturesque port of the small island of St Maarten. Zoey had been surprised at how different the Caribbean islands were she had expected to be unable to tell one island apart from the other. Grenada was a very poor island, people living in shacks and St Thomas had been the exact opposite, red roofed houses and the American influence very apparent.

St Maarten was a small island of two cultures, the Dutch half and the French half. The island had been divided into two, centuries ago. Zoey had read the information sheet about the island that morning and discovered how all those years ago two Frenchmen and two Dutchmen were sent off round the island, they left from the same point and wherever they met up in the middle, the ground they'd already covered belonged to their country. In the sweltering heat the Frenchmen set off with plenty of water and the Dutch with the "local rum". Needless to say the effect of the rum and the midday sun slowed the Dutch down and when they eventually met the Frenchmen again they had only covered a quarter of the island with the remainder of the island going to the French, the triumphant winners – or maybe not. The French may have had three quarters of the island but the Dutch had covered the most fertile part for growing crops. Not bad for two drunken guys!

Lucie and Zo spent the morning wandering around the little markets but by the afternoon they were starting to flag, the late nights were catching up with them. They decided to head back to the ship and grab some lunch and then head out on deck for some serious sun bathing. The ship was fairly empty, it looked like most of the passengers were spending the day on the island. The girls found their usual sun bathing spot at the back of the ship.

Zoey settled on her sun bed to read her book and Lucie was listening to her mp3 player, she'd chosen some mellow rock tunes, it matched the romantic mood she was in. Her mind drifted back to Nick. That kiss had been amazing, he'd totally swept her off her feet. She wondered what he was doing right now, he was here on the ship, somewhere and all they could do was grab a few moments together here and there. He practically worked nineteen hours a day. A chill went over her, a cloud must've covered the sun. She opened her eyes. Nick grinned at her.

"Thought I'd find you two here," he grabbed a chair and pulled it between their sun beds. Lucie took out her ear phones.

"We're just recovering from last night, think I was pretty drunk," Zoey said.

"Yeah, just slightly, you sang all the way to your cabin."

"Oh God, I didn't do anything embarrassing did I?"

Lucie laughed. "Nah, just told us all how much you love us and told Steve it was such a waste he's gay."

"Oh that's ok, I love everyone when I'm drunk, I'm a very happy drunk!"

Nick turned to Lucie. "How about you, recovered yet?" he winked at her.

"I err, don't think so."

God why did she turn into a gibbering wreck whenever he was around? She knew exactly what he was talking about, was it so obvious his kiss had totally floored her?

"I've got to go and supervise the bingo now – those old dears get so competitive! I've got an hour spare about fourish...?"

She nodded her head, she didn't trust herself to speak.

"We need to be discreet, I'm breaking every rule in the book."

"Oh, I love it! It's so romantic, it's like Mills and Boon," Zoey grinned.

Lucie rolled her eyes but Nick just laughed.

"I'll leave you to it. I know your cabin number, I'll catch up with you later," he stroked her hair as he stood up. She watched him walk away, her stomach doing flip flops.

"Tell you what girl, that guy has fallen overboard for you," Zoey giggled at her own joke.

"What if he does this on every cruise? You know what they say about sailors, a girl in every port and all that."

"He doesn't strike me as the type to do that and if he is, well what the hell? We're only on this ship for two weeks, just enjoy yourself, live dangerously! Go and give yourself some damn good memories."

"Maybe you're right," Lucie sighed.

"Damn right I am. There's no one here to judge you, go and have a holiday romance."

"You know what? I think I will." The girls clinked their bottles of Bacardi Breezers together.

"Bottoms up..." Zoey started.

"...Boobs out," Lucie finished.

At five to four there was a knock at the cabin door. With butterflies in her stomach, Lucie answered it. She'd come back early to jump in the shower and get changed, leaving Zoey snoring away on the sun lounger. She wanted to look at least half decent. She opened the door fully and there he was, his sunglasses perched on his head, his tan bringing out the blueness of his eyes. He was dressed in his daytime uniform, knee length navy shorts and beige coloured polo shirt with "Oceania" written in small letters just above where she imagined his left nipple to be. Oh God she groaned inwardly at the thought of his bare chest.

"Are you inviting me in or what?" he smiled.

She reached out for his hand and pulled him into the cabin, letting the door fall shut behind him. He reached up, took his shades off and lashed them on the small cabinet in between the two single beds. He was still grinning at her. The excitement was rushing through her body. She'd never wanted anyone so badly. He didn't seem to move, but he must have done because all of a sudden he was there, right in front of her. He bent down and slowly began to kiss her neck. God that felt good, his lips felt so hot against her skin She bit down on her lip, screaming out yet would be far to embarrassing.

"Are you sure this is ok?" she whispered.

"Mmm." He carried on kissing her neck, moving up towards her face, pulling her too him.

"You won't get into trouble?" God she wanted to rip his clothes off right now.

"Mmm." He pulled at her bottom lip as he kissed her, running his fingers through her hair.

"I really wouldn't..." she began, and then gasped as his fingers trailed her collar bone. Who knew collar bones were sexy?

"Luce?"

"Mmm." She just about managed to make her voice audible.

"Shut up."

Before she could reply he silenced her with the most passionate kiss she'd ever experienced. Ah, what the hell, she quickly pulled her top over her head and did the same to him. He pushed her gently back onto the bed.

"This ship rocks babe, I promise you that."

She'd lost the power of speech as she looked into his eyes, she'd just have to take his word for it. He didn't disappoint, it was the most amazing sex she'd ever had. He was so passionate and he literally had her gasping for more and she had to admit that the knowledge that they were doing something they shouldn't was a huge turn on, after all she was representing 'BOOK IT!' and he was supposed to be entertaining guests in a very different way.

The following morning Nick was on his way to the office. He and Steve had told the girls they'd give them a tour of St Lucia as they both had a few hours off, but he had to clear it with his boss, the cruise director, Todd Knight. He had to be really careful about Lucie, but he knew he'd be able to blag his brash American boss into thinking it was a good idea. Normally there was a strict rule of no fraternizing with the guests, but he knew which route he was going to use to get his own way. Todd Knight was in his late forties and working on cruise ships had been his life. He looked younger than his age. Todd put that down to sea air and being "down with the kids."

When Nick entered the office he found Todd sitting behind his desk, feet propped up reading the new edition of "Oceania Today" that Nick had hastily put together after he'd used the time he was supposed to spend on the daily news sheet, locked away in Lucie's cabin.

"Yo Slater, Wassup dude?"

"Yo boss," Nick adopted Todd's friendly lingo. "Just checkin' off the ship for a few hours."

"Coolio, no problemo. What's the plan?"

"Well, I was thinking it would be good for err, relations, between our two companies if me and Steve kinda took the 'BOOK IT!' girls under our wing. Y'know show them how dedicated the staff are to the, err, job in hand. I thought it would be a nice gesture to show them the island."

"You and Steve hmm? I suppose that's ok. If it was just you Slater, I'd have to say no, I know you're a bit of a ladies' man."

"Ah c'mon boss, I'm not that bad."

"I noticed you had a lot of visits to the sick bay when the lovely Doctor Wilde was on board."

"Sea sickness boss!" he protested.

"Whatever Slater, just keep it in your pants from now on."

"No problemo boss, see you later dude," he grinned as he left the office.

"Laters' Slater."

Doctor Wilde had certainly lived up to her name and she'd had an excellent bed side manner, he smiled at the memory as he walked along the corridor. Walking towards him was Steve, they high fived each other.

"If I were you mate, I'd turn back round and go the long way round to get off the ship," Steve advised.

"What's the matter?"

"Tara's looking for you; apparently you were meeting her in the crew bar last night."

"Ah, shit..."

He and Steve had spent another enjoyable evening in 'Le Club' with Lucie and Zo. He'd totally forgotten he'd told Tara he might go to the crew bar. Tara was an acrobat in the gymnastic display show. They occasionally met up when the mood took them, the company didn't mind the staff getting it on, no one was going to sign up for a celibate life at sea. Lately Tara had started getting a bit clingy, but he'd put up with it, that girl was bendy! He hadn't really given Tara a second thought since Lucie had arrived.

"I'll sort Tara out later."

"Bet you will," Steve grinned.

"Oh c'mon dude, it's not like me and Tara are together, you know how casual it all is."

"Maybe you better tell her that, 'coz from where I'm standin' looks like you've fallen big time for the lovely Lucie."

"Maybe dude. C'mon, let's go and find them, before Tara finds me."

"Ok, but stop calling me dude, you're not talking to Todd now."

Nick and Steve hired a car and were now heading across the island towards the drive-in volcano.

"Hey girls, keep your eyes open as we go round this bend," Steve said.

"Wow."

As they turned the corner the view was breath taking. The Pitons, two identical mountains and St Lucia's highest point rose majestically out of the water, dominating the vista.

"That's just beautiful," Lucie whispered.

The winding road took them round another corner, temporarily blocking the pitons from view, when they came back into sight two clouds had appeared at the peak of the mountains.

"Wow, those clouds have come from nowhere," Zoey commented.

"We'll pull over here and take some photos," Nick suggested.

"This is amazing," Lucie was in awe as they got out of the

car and could take in the full view that was in front of them.

"It's one of my favourite views in the whole of the Caribbean," Nick sighed happily as he pulled Lucie closer.

Zoey began to snap away with her camera, both at the stunning views and her new found friends. Lucie was laughing at something Nick had said and flung her head back in laughter. Zoey had caught the moment on her camera. She turned back to the Pitons and took some more photos. She was about to suggest a group photo but could see that Lucie and Nick were far too busy taking advantage of being off the ship and not having to watch who saw them kiss.

"C'mon guys, lets head up to the volcano," Steve suggested. He leaned in towards Zoey. "Can't stand the volcano, it stinks like bad eggs, but it's better than watching those two getting all lovey dovey with each other."

Zoey nodded and grinned as she glanced back at Lucie and Nick who were still kissing. "Think the rotten eggs are deffo a better option."

Steve flung his arm around Zoey's shoulder. "C'mon lovely, let's go."

Nick and Lucie followed slowly behind them.

"Nick..." she began.

"Mmm," he replied.

God, there was that sexy 'mmm' again. "Y'know yesterday?"

"The bingo or the deck quoits?" he teased.

"You know what I mean."

"You mean that fabulous sex in your cabin?"

Despite herself she blushed, yet again he'd rendered her speechless and all she could do was nod until she regained her composure.

"I just wanted you to know that I, well I don't just jump into bed with every guy I meet... we don't really have the time to..."

"What? For me to wine you, dine you and all that?" he grinned. "Look if we were back on dry land, then it would be different, but you've found yourself on the love boat honey." He reached for her hand as they carried on walking. She smiled to herself, this was turning out to be better than she could have ever imagined.

CHAPTER FOUR

PRESENT DAY

SUMMER 2009...Almost one year since the wedding

"So any ideas if the guys have anything special planned for Saturday night?"

"Haven't a clue, its rugby season though so I wouldn't expect anything too romantic," Lucie laughed.

"What about prezzies?" Zoey asked.

"No idea, but if past experiences are anything to go by, then we've probably got the same presents."

"Ah well, that's what comes of marrying twins. If you find anything out let me know, you know what I'm like!"

"No probs honey. Oh gotta go, customer," Lucie replied.

Zoey put the phone down with a confused look on her face. She loved surprises when that was what they were – a surprise, but when she knew something was going on it drove her crazy. She'd always been like that, ever since she was a little girl and she'd rummage under the Christmas tree, feeling the presents. On Sunday it would be her first wedding anniversary and on Saturday night she was pretty sure her husband had a surprise up his sleeve and it was infuriating the hell out of her.

"You look deep in thought there, Zo," Suze, one of her colleagues commented.

"I'm just trying to work out what Adam and Ant have planned for our anniversary."

"Isn't it weird being married to twins? What if you get them mixed up?" Callie the modern apprentice asked. She was only seventeen and always had questions about everything.

"It was strange at first, we made them wear name badges for the first six months."

"Did you?" she asked shocked.

Zoey laughed. "No, I'm just joking!! They may look alike but they have totally different personalities and are completely individual."

"But, isn't it just like fancying your best mate's bloke?"

"Nah. Like I said they are both totally different, you fall in love with the person, not just their looks. Look at me and Luce, we are both so different but were married to guys who are identical."

Where as the lads were carbon copies of each other, she and Lucie were polar opposites. Lucie with her long legs, slim figure and flowing blonde hair, in contrast although she was slightly taller than Lucie, Zoey was more curvaceous. She hated her big boobs, wobbly tummy and a backside that could put J Lo to shame. But for some bizarre reason, known only to Adam, he loved her and all her imperfections. She knew whatever Adam had planned for their anniversary would be special, she just hoped that the pregnancy testing kit sitting in her hand bag would give Adam the best anniversary present ever. They had been trying for a baby for nearly six months, how perfect would it be to tell Adam on their wedding anniversary that he was going to be a dad?

"Just nipping to the loo girls." She may as well go and put herself out of her misery.

In Lucie's branch of 'BOOK IT!' she was also taking a trip down memory lane, however she wasn't thinking about Ant. She had just booked a couple onto "Oceania". It invariably led her thoughts back to Nick. He popped back into her thoughts every now and then, probably more frequently than she'd like to admit. When she'd first got back from the cruise they'd emailed regularly, but after a while life got in the way. It got to the point when she did get the odd email, it just brought back the painful memories of leaving him. The connection that had once been so strong was broken. She could never comprehend how two weeks of her life had affected her so much. She could feel long-forgotten thoughts trying to creep back into the forefront of her mind. She was with Ant now, had married him and if she let herself think about Nick too much, it would lead her to think about what might have been if she had be brave enough to follow her heart.

Lucie was still in a reflective mood later that evening as she sat on Zoey's sofa. The lads had rugby training on a Wednesday night, so she always came round to Zoey's after work for tea. Zoey loved having people in her home, the more the merrier, she enjoyed being the hostess. She liked to try new recipes out on her. This week it was Spanish Chicken, with spicy potato wedges. Zo was in the kitchen putting the finishing touches to her culinary masterpiece. Lucie could hear her singing loudly and out of tune to what she thought was Bon Jovi. There was a hell of a noise coming out of the kitchen, her singing was so bad.

"Woah, We're half way thereee woah, livin' on a prayerrrr."

Lucie wasn't being unkind, Zo was the first to admit she couldn't sing, the poor girl had failed her school choir auditions five times! She got up from the sofa and started to look through Zoey's bookcase for any new books she could borrow. Adam and Zo's house was full of books, DVD's, CDs, mementos from holidays and photos. She wandered over to the mantelpiece, in pride of place was a picture of Zoey and Adam on their wedding day, next to that was a picture of the four of them and on the other side was a photo of the two of them on "Oceania", the start of a beautiful friendship, Zo always said. She picked up a photo of the two tanned smiling girls, their arms around each other, the camera capturing the essence of the cruise. She knew exactly who had taken the photo – Nick.

They were on their way to dinner and had taken a walk along the deck to take some pictures of the beautiful sunset and bumped into Nick and Steve.

"Hey, fancy bumping into the two most gorgeous girls on the ship," Nick greeted them and gave them both a kiss on the cheek.

The first thing she'd noticed about Nick was how comfortable he made her feel whenever he was around, she never felt that if he touched her he was invading her space it just seemed natural that he should greet them with a kiss or a gentle touch of the arm. The front door slammed shut, she replaced the photo back on the mantlepiece. Adam walked into the living room, followed by Ant. It amazed her how even now she was still taken by surprise at how alike they were. Obviously that's what happens with twins, but it did freak her out sometimes when they were standing side by side, like now. Zoey came in just behind them with a huge plate of wedges.

"You're back early."

"Training was cancelled, so we thought we'd come and sample my wife's fabulous cooking," Adam grinned as he pinched a wedge and landed a kiss on her lips.

"Hey you, hands off," she pretended to chastise him as she placed the wedges on the table. He grabbed her by the waist and hugged her to him. She giggled. Ant wandered over to Lucie and gave her a kiss on the cheek. Adam and Zo were still hugging and caught up in some private joke. Lucie looked over to them, they seemed genuinely happy. She thought she and Ant were too, but sometimes she felt something was missing. She was probably just being silly. Thinking about Nick out of the blue was making her feel nostalgic about the wrong guy. She reached over and squeezed Ant's hand.

"Hey kiddo." He smiled showing off the dimple she loved so much. Yeah they were fine, everyone felt a bit insecure every now and then didn't they?

* * *

The plane banked left, away from the island and giving Nick Slater his last view of "Oceania", the ship that had been his home for the last seven years. Now at twenty eight he felt he should be grown up enough to set down some roots and do something with his life. He'd miss the ship and the friends he'd made, but lately he'd been thinking about other things. The emails he was getting from friends back home were all about them getting married, buying a home, becoming a grown up and it suddenly seemed like something he should at least attempt to do.

Whilst he was having these thoughts about his future one person from his past kept popping into his head, Lucie Scott. He hadn't heard from her in ages, but it hadn't stopped him from thinking about her. He wondered if she ever thought about him, he hoped she hadn't forgotten him. He could never and would never forget her and the pretty intense two weeks they'd spent together. He remembered the first time he'd seen them, it was at the captain's 'Welcome Aboard' evening. The captain stood at the peak of the atrium, giving him a bird's eye view of the decks below as he surveyed his adoring public.

"Is this anyone's first cruise?" The captain boomed.

There was a cheer of "Yes," from a number of the passengers.

"Mine too," Captain Walshe grinned.

The crowd erupted in laughter. Nick groaned inwardly, every welcome aboard speech started the same. As he switched off to the rest of the captain's "impromptu" monologue he took the opportunity to people-watch. That's when he saw them, two girls dressed in glamorous ball gowns, gazing up open-mouthed in awe of the captain. They looked out of place, not the usual purple rinse brigade. They also appeared to be on their own, they intrigued him. The next night after a pub quiz in the Yacht and Compass the two girls had come up to him and that was the start of a heady and passionate two weeks. Lucie had lost her bracelet...but they had found each other. That bracelet never did turn up.

Both the girls had been so much fun and up for a laugh, he enjoyed spending time with them. Zoey was completely nuts and he'd connected with her straight away, but Lucie was something else, she had totally blown his mind. Where was she now? What happened to the girl he stupidly let go?

CHAPTER FIVE

THEN

It was tropical night on board Oceania, Zoey and Lucie were out on deck by the main pool and bar. The sun loungers had been cleared away to make room for dancing. The ships' band were playing songs that sounded like they were straight from the film Cocktail. The band were all dressed in Hawaiian shirts, ironic as they were in the Caribbean. The girls were sitting on a bench at the edge of the pool, dressed up in their glad rags and drinking their usual Bacardi Breezers. They watched Nick and Steve dancing with the old dears. The guys were dressed in their evening attire of a tuxedo, with a bell boy style jacket.

"This is amazing. I love all of this," Zoey sighed happily.

"Mmm. Me too," Lucie grinned unable to take her eyes off Nick. She burst out laughing as she watched him spin an old dear around the dance floor.

"It's such a shame Steve's gay, he's too gorgeous," Zo complained.

"I know what a waste. Guys that fit should not be allowed to date guys, it should be like a law or something."

"Trust you to bag the only straight guy on the ship."

"There must be others, it's a big ship."

"I bloody hope so."

Nick and Steve were on their way over.

"What are two beautiful girls like you doing sitting in the corner?" Steve grinned.

"Waiting to be whisked off our feet on to the dance floor," Zoey smiled.

Nick held his hand out to Lucie and Steve did the same to Zoey. She watched as Nick and Lucie glided across the dance floor, they made it look so easy. Suddenly Zoey felt nervous, what if she was too much of a klutz or too heavy to be "whisked". Steve seemed to pick up on her sense of unease.

"Just follow my lead, you'll be fine."

She did as he said and found that she was practically dancing on air, she'd never felt so light in all her life. It felt amazing.

"Oh my God! I love this!"

"You're not a bad dancer."

"I might take this up when I get home."

"I wouldn't go that far," Steve joked.

"Well go and dance with that old dear over there, eyeing you up. She'll be over here in a mo and stamp on my foot or something."

"Eurgh, B.O. Barbara no way! She masks the B.O. with white musk, she stinks! She cruises three times a year and always wants to dance with me and Nick."

Zoey giggled.

"What's so funny?"

"I'm just having the time of my life."

"And I owe it all to you," he sang. "Looks like we're not the only ones." He spun her round.

Nick and Lucie were gazing into each others eyes as they danced, oblivious to everyone around them.

"Hardly hiding the obvious are they? Oops, there's Todd the cruise director, if he sees that he'll flip. Steve and Zo to the rescue!"

Before she could ask what was happening he'd waltzed her right across the dance floor and straight into Nick's arms, he carried on with Lucie in his arms.

"Wow, cool move. Sorry to butt in, but Steve didn't want you to get in trouble with your boss. You and Luce looked kinda loved up there."

"God Zo, cheers mate. Todd would go berserk if he knew what was happening with me and Lucie, but I can't help getting carried away when I'm with her," he sighed.

"Sounds like you've got it bad."

As the song neared to an end Nick and Steve danced them into the centre of the dance floor.

"We hate to leave you girls. But we're getting evil looks from the coffin dodger brigade over there," Steve explained.

"Stick around, we definitely want the last dance."

"Hey Slaz, it's your turn to dance with B.O. Barb."

"No way Stevie, I danced with her at the last ballroom session."

The girls laughed as the boys argued.

Steve groaned. "Sometimes I hate this job."

Nick squeezed Lucie's hand and winked. "Catch ya later, Babe."

Zoey and Steve rolled their eyes as they watched Lucie practically melt.

Once it got to midnight Nick and Steve were "off duty", but most nights didn't end at 12 o'clock. They headed off to 'Le Club' to meet up with the girls. The girls were already on the dance floor dancing to Girls Aloud when they got there.

Nick bought a bottle of champagne. As soon as the girls spotted them, they headed straight over. Steve handed them both a glass.

"Ooh, I feel like I'm in a James Bond film, being handed champagne by guys in a tux," Zoey giggled.

Nick and Steve both struck what they assumed was a sexy pose and raised an eyebrow. "The names Bond, James Bond."

The girls raised their glasses. "Bottoms Up."

"Boobs out."

Nick and Lucie found some seats while Steve and Zo hit the dance floor. They were laughing watching Zo and Steve doing air guitar impressions to Guns and Roses.

"I cannot believe Zo is doing a rock chick routine in her posh dress."

"I can," Lucie laughed.

Steve and Zo were so busy laughing they almost fell over.

"Fancy a walk out on deck? We can talk properly then."

She nodded and smiled.

They wandered out on deck in silence for a few minutes. There was a slight breeze in the air, but it was refreshing after the heat of the day.

"It'll rain soon."

She started to laugh "Ok Michael Fish, how d'you know?"

"It's in the air. It won't rain for long though," he stopped, put his hands on the rail and turned round to face her.

"D'you think Zo and Steve will be ok?" she asked.

"Those two will be fine, they're as mad as each other."

"It's a shame he's gay, they'd make a great couple."

"Steve did actually say that if he was straight she'd be just the kinda girl he'd go for, but as he's gay the only problem is she has boobs"

"Poor Zo."

"You two have been have become really close on this trip haven't you?"

"God, yes. I can't believe how well we've got on."

"Will you still stay in touch when you get back home?"

"Yeah, we actually don't live that far away form each other. We'll be shipmates for life."

He reached for her hand. "Hope we will be too. You have no idea how amazing this cruise has been for me. You're so special Luce."

"Oh Nick..." she couldn't get the rest of the sentence out.

The heavens opened. He pulled her towards him and they began to run along the deck, laughing amidst huge blobs of Caribbean rain.

"Wait!" she screamed with laughter as she stopped to pull off her high heels. They carried on running until he pulled her into a doorway. They were completely soaked, but still giggling.

"I look like a drowned rat."

"The sexiest drowned rat I've ever seen."

He pulled her close kissing her hard as the rain continued to fall. He reached up, scrunching her wet hair with his hands. He never knew until that moment what a turn on kissing could be. He pulled away from her.

"I need you right now," he whispered.

"Me too."

They eventually returned to her cabin in the very early hours of the morning to find Zo and Steve fast asleep on her bed.

"Oh God... you don't think..." Lucie began.

Nick began to laugh. "Don't be silly for starters they're both fully dressed and secondly there is a half eaten bag of crisps between them. They've obviously just drunkenly passed out."

"I was worried there for a second."

"Best wake Stevie up, it would be ironic if he got the sack for spending the night with a female passenger," he grinned.

By the time they had managed to get a very drunk Steve out of the cabin it had gone four am. Nick had to be up at six am, but when he finally fell into bed he couldn't sleep, his mind was buzzing with thoughts of Lucie.

The following morning, despite only having a few hours sleep, the girls made it to Reception on time and positioned themselves at the usual two comfy chairs they sat at to start their hours work. On time they may have been, completely with it, they weren't.

"God, Zo, these late nights and early mornings are killing me."

"I always knew there was a reason I wasn't a rock star, I just can't burn the candle at both ends."

Lucie laughed. "It's only been a few days, we are such light weights."

"Ah, but don't forget, our body clocks are already a few hours behind."

"Yeah that'll be it."

"I'm just glad the ship is at sea today, we can just find a sun lounger, catch up on some sleep and top up our tan."

"Yeah, that sounds like a plan."

"Nick got anytime off today?"

Lucie shook her head. "He said sea days are really busy, he has to keep the passengers entertained."

Zoey snorted.

"Zo, you have such a dirty mind," Lucie laughed.

"Can you blame me for having my mind in the gutter after the things you and Nick have been getting up to?"

Lucie couldn't help smiling at the memory. "Well, as much as I would like to be shacked up in the cabin with

Nick, he's busy doing poolside games and quizzes."

"Looks like it's just you and me then chick."

Nick was in the crew bar going over his schedule for the day. He knew he had a hectic day and night ahead. When the ship was in port he could relax a bit more. He'd just grab a quick coffee, he probably wouldn't get chance to eat properly till tonight, it was a formal evening and he was down to host one of the tables. He was trying to swing it so that he was on Lucie's table. Just as he took his last swig of coffee he spotted Tara walking in.

"Ah, Shit," he mumbled. He'd been avoiding her and he could see her eyes blazing from across the room.

"Hello stranger," she greeted him coolly.

"Tara! You're looking lovely this morning," he grinned.

"Hmm. I'm surprised you even remember what I look like. I've seen you chasing round after that tarty travel agent."

His eyes narrowed and he glared at her. "I take it back Tara, you look like shit. Don't let me hear you refer to Lucie like that again."

"Lucie is it? You'd just better be careful Todd doesn't find out."

"If that's your attempt to threaten me and tell Todd, then let me remind you, I am your senior officer. You have no claim over me Tara, we've never been exclusive and we never will be."

"Well let me remind you Nick Slater, she'll be off this ship after this cruise what are you gonna do then? 'Coz I tell you what Slaz, this ship has sailed."

"Whatever Tara, Whatever."

She spun on her heel and stormed out of the crew bar.

After a crazily busy day Nick was now standing by the entrance of the restaurant for the evening meal. He'd managed to get himself on Lucie's table. He was just waiting for the girls to arrive. He could see them over the other side of the atrium, they were just about to get their photos taken by the ship's photographer. They were laughing, in fact, when he thought about it, that's what those two always seemed to be doing. They were always having fun. They headed over in his direction.

"Ladies. Let me escort you into dinner."

They stood either side of him and linked arms.

"I could get used to this," Lucie smiled.

So could I, he thought inwardly.

He was sitting opposite her at the table for dinner, unfortunately he was next to B.O. Barbara, who was trying to monopolise his attention. Still it gave him a good excuse to pretend to listen to her when really he couldn't take his eyes of Lucie. Tara's comment about Lucie being gone after this cruise kept popping into his head, he kept trying to push it out. He really didn't want to think about Lucie not being here.

Lucie was so aware of Nick and his intense gaze, the room may have been full of people, but to her it felt like it was just the two of them. She could hardly eat her meal, it looked absolutely wonderful, but her stomach was doing flip flops. Is that what happened when you fell in love? She'd never been in love before. Oh God she couldn't be? How could she have fallen in love with a guy who in a week or so she was never going to see again?

CHAPTER SIX

PRESENT DAY

By the time Saturday night came around Zoey was beyond excited about her anniversary. She'd finished work early, gone to the hairdresser's and now she was dressed in her new black dress with white polka dots. She still had no idea where Adam was taking her, all he'd told her was to be ready at seven o'clock. She'd already sent Lucie a text to see if she knew what was happening yet. Lucie said she was meeting Ant at the Rugby club at eight. Zoey was just fastening her purple killer heels as she heard Adam's key in the door. She gave herself a quick final glance in the mirror; well at least her hair looked good if nothing else. She sighed as she turned her back on the offending mirror and headed out of the bedroom and down the stairs.

"Hey babe," she called out.

"Hey sexy," he grinned at her; he was standing in the hall and watched her come down the stairs. "Looking good Mrs Maxwell," he added.

"Not too bad yourself," she smiled unable to thank him

for his compliment. He was still dressed in his chinos, pale blue shirt, navy blue blazer and club tie. It had been a league game today and the lads always wore their club suits after these game. Zoey thought he always looked gorgeous in his rugby suit.

"All ready?" he asked, pulling her close.

He smelled so yummy, she loved the smell of Ralgex. "Yep, where are we meeting the other two?"

"We're not. It's just you and me tonight babe."

Zoey wasn't quite sure what the plan was when they pulled up outside the Mersey ferry terminal.

"You don't know how much I've been hoping it wouldn't rain today!" Adam grinned.

"I'm intrigued."

"Well, let's get out of the car and I'll tell you." He led her over to the railings so they could get a good view of the river and over to Liverpool. A ferry boat was just about to dock.

"I know how much you love cruises honey; my budget wouldn't quite stretch to a Caribbean cruise so I thought I'd do the next best thing, a river cruise on a ferry across the Mersey."

She burst out laughing. "You are nuts!"

"That's not all, I've booked us a table at the Panoramic."

Her gaze automatically turned to the tallest building on the skyline where the Panoramic was at the top. "Then I've booked a room at the Malmaison."

Zoey was almost speechless. All she could say was "Wow."

He ran back to the car to get the over night bag he'd hidden in the boot.

"Come 'ead babe, let's go. We don't want to miss the boat!" Lucie sat in the Rugby Club chatting to some of the other wives and girlfriends, she kept glancing over to the door every time it opened looking for Adam and Zo, it wasn't like them to be late. She felt like she was all dressed up with nowhere to go, not that she knew where they were going. She was wearing her new pink maxi dress. Ant was still at the bar chatting to one of his team mates. She let her mind wander and drift away from the conversations around her. Despite herself she found herself thinking about Nick again, she didn't know why he kept popping back into her conscious thoughts. It wasn't bad thoughts in her mind, she wasn't wishing he was here or anything like that, she just had lots of lovely memories of her romance with Nick. She'd just assumed that once you were married you stopped thinking about past loves. Just then she spotted her present love heading over to her, big beaming smile on his face, automatically flashing that cute dimple of his.

"Sorry kiddo, I got sidetracked," Ant apologised.

"No worries, I was catching up with the girls, she replied. Well that sounded better than saying she was day dreaming about an ex-boyfriend. She wondered if she could really class Nick as an ex-boyfriend when they had only spent two weeks together? Probably not, but it didn't feel right to class it as a holiday fling either.

"Cool, c'mon let's get going."

"Aren't we waiting for Zo and Adam?"

"Nah, those two have gone on a bloody ferry! I've booked us into the Wallasey Chinese."

"Great," she grimaced. Who said romance was dead?

"I sometimes take it for granted living by the sea," Zoey mused as the ferry began it's short trip across the Mersey.

"I know, you can't beat sea air."

Zoey leaned against the railings of the ferry, Adam stood behind her, his arms wrapped around her.

"Sailing around the Caribbean was amazing, but right here, right now, crossing the Mersey with that gorgeous sky, being in your arms is the best feeling ever. I'm so glad you asked me to marry you."

"I'm just glad you said yes."

She turned round to face him. "I did a pregnancy test this morning."

"And?" he asked hopefully.

She couldn't bring herself to tell him so she just shook her head. He pulled her tightly to him and kissed the top of her head.

"Babe, it'll happen for us, I promise. No being sad tonight." He held her face in his hands and brushed away the tear that began to fall down her cheek.

She nodded her head. "I just love you so much Ads and I thought it would be perfect to tell you tonight that we were finally having a baby."

"Well, maybe it's the perfect night to make a baby." he grinned at her, she smiled back. "I love you too Zo, you mean the world to me and tonight is going to be amazing and you better get drunk 'cos tomorrow ma is doing a special anniversary dinner."

"Oh God, no," she groaned. "I can't face your mum at the best of times, never mind with a hangover!"

"Hey, she thinks you're great."

Lucie and Ant called at Zoey and Adam's the following day before the "anniversary dinner." Ant was helping Adam to finish off the decking in the back garden. Lucie and Zo took the chance to catch up before heading off to old ma Maxwell's.

"So, how was your ferry across the Mersey?" Lucie asked, she watched Zoey's face light up immediately. Her friend was positively glowing.

"It was so romantic. I never realised how lovely it could be sailing off into the sunset to Liverpool."

Lucie knew only too well how romantic ships and sunsets were.

"Sounds lovely, Zo."

"It was amazing, the suite in the Malmaison was decorated in different shades of purple, totally co-ordinated with my shoes and bag. We had champagne and chocolate covered strawberries waiting for us and the Panoramic was out of this world, views right across to Wales and the tables were heated, how nuts is that? This morning we had individual hampers delivered with our breakfast in ... ooh and there was fluffy white bathrobes."

Lucie couldn't help smiling as Zoey got more and more excited with each thing she told her.

"What about you, where did Ant whisk you off to?"

"Rugby club then Wallasey Chinese."

"Oh." Zoey didn't know what to say and from the look on Lucie's face she didn't seem very impressed with Ant's anniversary surprise. "Well, you know what blokes are like..." she added.

"Yeah, yours planned a river cruise, posh meal and luxury hotel."

"Maybe it'll be my turn for the Chinese next year," Zoey laughed. Lucie just sighed.

"What's the matter chick?"

"I don't know I just feel a bit funny at the moment."

"Why?"

"Nick keeps popping into my head."

"Nick? Nick Slater? There's a blast from the past."

"Yep, the one and only! I did a booking on "Oceania" the other day and since then I keep thinking about when I was on the ship," Lucie explained.

"God, I wonder what he's up to now. We haven't heard

from him for years. D'you think he's still on the ship?"

"He always said it would take something special for him to leave," she answered quietly.

"Do you ever wonder what would have happened to you two if things had been different?"

"Sometimes, but you know those two weeks were the best and I'd have rather have had that than nothing at all. It was the romance of the ship that made it what it was, it probably wouldn't have been the same away from the sultry, sexy evenings and the Caribbean heat," Lucie sighed, aware that she was drifting back to memories again she quickly changed the subject. "So how's things on the baby front?"

Zoey pulled a face. "Not good, yet another month of trying."

"It'll happen soon and I hope it is sooner, get old ma Maxwell off my case. I swear if I hear my biological clock is ticking and how wonderful it would be for Adam and Anthony's – full title obviously – children to start school on the same day, I'll go ballistic. What does she want us to do? Conceive on the same day?" Lucie ranted.

This was how it started over the wedding she and Ant were quite happy just living together, but old Ma Maxwell disapproved of her son living "over the brush". Then Adam went and popped the question to Zo and before she knew it she also had a sparkling rock on her finger and was down the aisle. According to her new mother-in-law (or smiling assassin being more appropriate) it was just "perfect" seeing her two boys married on the same day. She wasn't saying she never would've married Ant, it had all just been a bit quick. Now with all this baby talk, she was worried it might just be before she was ready, too. She hoped Zoey did get pregnant, but she just hoped it wouldn't put extra pressure on her and Ant, they hadn't even talked about kids yet, they weren't ready.

"Talking about our delightful mother-in-law, we'd best make a move and get this over and done with."

"Zoey! Lucie! How lovely to see you both," old Ma Maxwell exclaimed as she opened the front door. She kissed the air next to both of her daughters'-in- laws cheeks, nearly knocking the girls out with her over usage of Vanderbilt perfume. She was in her usual attire of a twin set, tweed skirt and disgusting brown brogues. Lucie was convinced that she was the only person since about 1997 to get her hair permed and if she was going to go to the bother of going to the hairdresser, she should really ask them to do something about the grey too.

"My boys!" she squealed. "Adam, Anthony, come and give your old mum a hug."

"She'll squeeze them to death," Lucie muttered. Zoey stifled a giggle.

"Dinner's ready, come and sit down," she ushered them into the dining room. "Anthony, I've done carrot and turnip just the way you like it." She patted his arm. Lucie groaned inwardly, how patronising could one person be? She resigned herself to playing happy families around the dinner table.

"There's apple pie and custard for those with clean plates. I've got low fat for you Zoey dear, I know you're watching your weight. Lucie dear, do have another roast potato, you need more weight on you."

Lucie gritted her teeth, she wanted to knock her out with a roast potato. "I'm fine thanks...mum." That was the one thing old Ma Maxwell insisted on, the girls calling her mum as they were one big happy family. Lucie hated it, she had her own mum. She didn't need another one. Adam and Ant's dad had passed away when they were very young and as a result old Ma Maxwell found it hard to let go of her boys. She may pretend that she loved her daughter's-in-law, but what was that saying, keep your friends close and your enemies even closer? Their mother-in-law was the queen of put-downs, hidden by the false saccharine grin, hence the name smiling assassin. Well Lucie could play her at her own game. Zo said she let the comments go over her head, but Lucie knew the barb about the custard would've hurt her feelings.

"Oh boys, I need your help next week, I'm having a table delivered. Your poor old mum won't be able to move it."

Poor old mum, my arse, Lucie thought.

"No probs mum, but what's wrong with this table?"

"Oh nothing Anthony dear, it's just too small, we only just fit around it. I'll never get you lot and the grand children around it for Christmas and the Sunday roasts."

"Oh don't worry about that – mum. My mum's table is big enough for us when Ant and I decide to have kids."

Old Ma Maxwell's eyes narrowed. "Well I don't want to miss out on my boy's children, which is why I've planned ahead and got a new table. I'm sure Zoey will be more than happy to provide me with grandchildren soon, even if you feel it's a bit beneath you to give your husband a child."

"Err, we haven't talked about kids yet mum," Ant tried to diffuse the situation seeing the blazing look in Lucie's eyes.

"Well dear, Lucie's biological clock IS ticking, I would suggest you'd need to get cracking soon."

Lucie looked down at her plate. Damn. She'd eaten all her roast potatoes, could she do serious damage with a gravy-filled Yorkshire pudding? Somehow she doubted it, but she was sorely tempted. She would be glad when this "anniversary meal", with the evil mother-in-law, who could've been Hyacinth Bucket's long lost sister, was over.

CHAPTER SEVEN

THEN

Nick was out on deck getting ready for that evening's sail away when 'Oceania' would say goodbye to the island of Tortola which had been its home for the last twelve hours. He was there to help get the passengers into the carnival atmosphere although they normally didn't need it. The mix of the early evening heat, sunsets that made the sky look like it was on fire and the cocktail of the day made sure everyone was in high spirits. Even so, he was dispatched with his mic and the steel band just to enhance the mood. Usually there would be other ships in port and the passengers would be waving to each other. It only added to the party. He plugged his mic into the PA system and messed around with the tuning and his music in preparation to get the party started. He would be instructing the band to start in a few moments. So many people had said to him over the years that the sailaways made them feel emotional. He could understand that, it was one of those one off experiences that you don't get anyway else but on a cruise ship, sailing off into the sunset with a fantastic view of an island that may have just become your favourite place on earth, off onto the next adventure.

The icing on the cake was if you were experiencing it with someone special. He nodded to the band and they started off with the cricket world cup theme. Instantly he saw the passengers react to the music, hips swaying, arms waving and cheering. He was aware he'd hardly been able to take his eyes off Lucie since she and Zo appeared out on deck while he was helping the band to set up. They were drinking sex on the beach – now there was a thought, he smiled to himself. The gentle breeze was blowing their hair and as usual they were giggling, soaking up their surroundings. He was desperate to go over to her, take her in his arms and kiss her, but he couldn't. Still at least he could legitimately go over and chat, he was after all supposed to mingle with the guests. He headed over, she watched him walk towards her, never once breaking his gaze and smiling her shy smile.

"Evening ladies," he reached out and gently touched Lucie's arm. "You cold Luce?"

"Err, must be the night air." Or the fact that every time he touched her she got goose bumps. Zoey just grinned at her, knowing exactly what she was thinking.

"So what did you get up to today?"

"We found the most amazing beach, I've never seen sand so white. Each island we visit, I leave thinking that's my favourite and then we get to the next one and I'm just spoilt for choice. I just don't want this to ever end," Zoey sighed happily.

Nick squeezed Lucie's hand. "I know what you mean Zo."

"I think Tortola is definitely my favourite," Lucie agreed.

"Are you guys watching the show tonight?"

"What is it? I forgot to read the newspaper thingy," Zoey said.

"D'you know how long it takes me to write them? No bugger reads them," he laughed. "It's Chicago at the theatre tonight, it's amazing, you'll love it."

"Yeah I'm up for that, what about you Zo?"

"Sounds like a plan and all that jazz," she sang the end of her sentence, complete with waving jazz hands.

"Then," he lowered his voice. "Instead of heading off to 'Le Club', Steve and I have something in mind, but you'll have to wait till later."

"Sounds intriguing," Lucie smiled.

"Sorry, it's short and sweet, but I better go and talk to some other passengers. Even though I'd rather stay here and drink cocktails with you guys, still there's always later." He winked and headed off back over to the other side of the deck.

Lucie sighed and lent against the rail, watching him.

"You ever been in love Zo?"

"Thought I was once, but it turned out to be a false alarm."

Lucie burst out laughing. "God, you make me laugh."

"However. If you are asking me are you in love, then I would say a big fat yes."

"I can't explain my feelings, but it's amazing, like nothing I've ever felt before, when he kisses me, my feet don't touch the floor and the sex, my God I've never had sex like it."

"Alrite, calm down, now you're just boasting! As much as I find Steve adorable in a cute puppy dog way, I don't think I float his boat, so stop bragging about all this fab sex you're getting." Zoey was laughing so Lucie knew she wasn't really mad.

"Sorry chick, if it's any consolation I think Steve is gutted you're not a bloke."

"If there is a compliment in there somewhere, I'm not quite sure how to take that."

Lucie's giggling carried on. "I think all this sex on the beach is going to my head."

"I told you stop bragging!"

The combination of the alcohol and possibly being in love had sent Lucie into hysterics, tears of laughter streaming down her face.

A waiter appeared with a tray full of cocktails; he took one look at Lucie and instantly looked confused.

"Sorry, but she's already had enough sex on the beach."

Dinner was yet another enjoyable meal, in fact it was more than enjoyable it was fabulous. Every evening Zoey would tell herself she wasn't going to have a dessert, she remembered the cruise training they'd done in staff training back at the shop. One of the little "funny facts" had been for every day you are on a cruise ship you put a pound on in weight. Funny my arse, she thought, well it would be if it wasn't her arse that was seeing the benefit of fourteen days on a cruise ship, that was a bloody stone, she'd get charged for excess baggage on the way home. So she thought she'd skip dessert and felt really proud of herself when the waiter asked what dessert she would like and she said in a big loud voice "No Thank you."

"But madam, we have your favourite, chocolate cake."

"Oh go on then, just a small piece."

If the waiter carried on trying to shove food down her face then he wasn't going to get his tip at the end of the cruise. The chocolate cake arrived, it was so beautiful she took a photo of it.

"See, I'm not the only one who has found love on this ship," Lucie laughed as Zoey took a bit of the cake and pulled an expression that could only be described as orgasmic.

After dinner they headed off towards the theatre to watch Chicago. Nick and Steve were at the theatre doors, ushering people in. Their faces instantly lit up when they saw the girls walking towards them.

"Are you two a sight for sore eyes," Steve grinned. "I keep getting my bum pinched by randy old ladies."

The girls laughed.

"Could be worse mate it could be randy old men," Nick grinned

Steve pulled a face. "Even I have age limits!"

"Listen, after the show meet us by the lift next to the 24 hour café," Nick told them.

"Sounds all very cloak and dagger," Zoey laughed.

"We'll be there."

Zoey was still singing Chicago songs as they walked towards the lift two and a half hours later. Lucie hadn't really been able to concentrate properly she was too busy thinking about being with Nick later on.

The lads were already waiting by the lift when they arrived.

"Right girls, it's time for something really special," Nick smiled.

They got in the lift and Steve pressed the button for the top deck.

When they arrived on deck fourteen it was deserted, they walked up a small flight of stairs taking them to deck fifteen, the highest and smallest deck, it was deserted. There was a small bar in the far corner of the deck, Steve headed over to it and got some drinks. Nick pulled out four sun loungers and arranged them in a cross like shape so that their heads would all be next to each other when they lay down.

"Mizz Scott, Mizz Shaw, please take your loungers for 'Movies under the stars!'"

Steve handed them both Bacardi Breezers as they lay down. Steve and Nick took the loungers in between them.

"Wow," Lucie breathed.

"Amazing," Zoey gasped.

"That my dear's is possibly the best view of the night sky you will ever get," Steve announced.

"I've never seen so many stars," Zoey commented. The navy sky was literally glittering and twinkling, she could see the constellations, even though she couldn't name them.

"So beautiful," Lucie sighed.

"I agree, although I have seen more beautiful sights," Nick turned his head towards her and grinned.

"Leave all the romantic slushy stuff, till we've gone Slaz," Steve joked.

"Ok, ok."

The four of them lay there in silence, just taking in the sight before them. Steve reached out for Zoey's hand, she did the same to Nick who was already holding Lucie's hand, with her other hand she held Steve's.

"Ship mates for life guys."

"We just wanted to give you one of the best memories we could think of," Steve said.

Nick couldn't wait any longer, he broke the chain of friendship to reach across and kiss Lucie.

"Right, that's it, we're outta here, if you two can't get a cabin then I'm taking Zoey gambling," Steve declared.

"Ooh I've never gambled before, well I played strip rummy when I was about seventeen does that count?"

Their laughter rang out straight into the darkness.

"No honey it doesn't count, but it sounds much more fun," Steve laughed.

"Zo why doesn't that surprise me?" Lucie asked.

"If we start losing tonight. We may have to resort to that."

"No way, I'd scare the passengers quicker than you can say abandon ship."

"We'll have none of that Zoey, you are one sexy, hot, diva."

"You're gay Steve, you can't possibly comment," Zoey laughed.

"Hey girl, you could turn me yet."

"Err, I think it's you two that need to get a cabin," Nick laughed.

Once Steve and Zoey had gone Nick moved onto Lucie's sun lounger. She rested her head on his chest.

"This is just the most beautiful and romantic place ever."

He kissed the top of her head. "Luce, there is no one else I would want to be sharing this with."

She lifted her head off his chest and tilted her face towards his. He leaned closer, she felt his lips on hers, and the mere touch of his lips was like a jolt of electricity through her body.

"You feel it too huh?" he murmured.

She couldn't answer, he really did render her speechless whenever he touched her. He slipped his hand beneath her top and gently trailed his fingers across her skin, her goose bumps reappeared.

"You cold babes?"

She shook her head. "It's just a reaction to you," she breathed.

He lifted her further up his body and kissed her hard. They pulled at each other's clothes. She didn't want to stop, but she didn't want him to get into trouble either. As she pulled away from him the breeze blew her hair away from her face, the moonlight lit up the raw passion in her face, her heavy breathing moved her breasts rhythmically. Nick thought it was the most erotic sight he'd even seen. He went to pull her back down.

"Wait, are we ok here? I don't want to get you into trouble."

He grinned. "We're fine. Security doesn't check up here for another half an hour."

He was kissing her collar bone as he spoke. "Now, get back down here and let me give you a memory that you really won't forget."

He pulled her close and with one swift move he undid the clasp on her bra strap, the force of the electrical current between them sent the bra flying across the deck. She lowered herself so that her bare breasts were against his naked chest. Just like the air his skin felt hot, sweaty and sticky and things were about to get even hotter.

CHAPTER EIGHT

PRESENT DAY

It took Nick Slater exactly two months to get himself settled back in the UK. He spent a few weeks catching up with family and friends in Shrewsbury, and then set about relocating himself to Chester. He'd picked Chester for one reason and one reason only, as far as he knew Lucie still lived on the Wirral. A place called Wallasey, which was about a thirty minute drive from Chester. He had enough savings to live on for a least a year while he got himself sorted. That was the beauty of living on the ship for so long, wages going in, no bills going out. He'd rented an apartment over looking the River Dee; it was nice to have a view of water, if you couldn't be on it. He didn't want to get a permanent job as yet, he'd wait and see what happened with Lucie first before he tied himself down to one place. He knew he was taking a big risk, she may not even live here anymore, she might have a boyfriend or worse still she might just want him to stay a memory.

He headed out on to the small balcony with a cup of tea. His little balcony, over looking the river was like a creature comfort, the balcony had swung it for him when he first came to view the apartment. He was more than ready to try life back on dry land and make an attempt at being a grown up. He watched the boats meandering up stream, it was a warm September day but it was taking him some time to get used to the English weather again. Yep. England could definitely do with some Caribbean heat. He smiled to himself as he remembered the hottest nights he'd ever had in the Caribbean with the lovely Lucie. He knew she'd been slightly suspicious that he seduced passengers on every cruise, but he'd been telling her the truth when he'd told her he'd never done anything like it before, not with passengers of course. Staff were a bit different, that came with the territory. It wasn't worth risking his job to start sleeping with passengers that was until Lucie came along, she was so worth it. They had partied long and hard on that particular cruise. After he had finished his duties for the evening he and Steve would join Lucie and Zoey in the nightclub. The staff weren't really supposed to be in there, but as Lucie and Zoey were "working", he could get away with it and say that he and Steve were "working" too.

He wandered back in the apartment and put his cup down next to his PC. He clicked the screensaver to reveal the screen underneath. Since his return home he'd been introduced to the world of Facebook. Using the internet on the ship was expensive, so it was usually a quick obligatory group email home every few weeks, there wasn't time for wasting hours on social networking sites, which is what he'd found himself doing the last few days. It was great for looking up old shipmates, he'd found Steve on there, who also happened to be friends with Zoey, he noticed she'd had gotten married as her name was listed as Zoey Maxwell was Shaw. He thought this might be a good starting point for finding Lucie. So he and Steve had become friends on Facebook. He'd had no luck tracing Lucie, so he thought the best option was to get in touch with Zoey. He was still getting to grips with Facebook, he wasn't sure what would happen if he "poked her" – although that sounded fun, so the safest option would be to send a friend request, but the big question was should he send a message about trying to find Lucie? He didn't want to lay all his cards on the table just yet, but then again what did he have to lose? He clicked on Zoey's picture from Steve's page and clicked on the add friend button, now, what to type in the message box?

Every Saturday night from September through to April was spent the same – at Spartans Rugby Club. Zoey and Lucie would get home after a busy day selling people their dream holidays, get changed then head off to meet the lads at the club. By the time they got there the lads were usually well trollied by then having spent the aftermath of the game on the beer. The girls found the lads propping up the bar with a couple of their team mates. Zoey glanced around to see if Ed was about. She spotted him across the bar deep in conversation with the club captain, no doubt sussing out the competition she thought to herself. Ed always had to be top dog at everything he did.

"Here she is – my woman!" Adam grinned, announcing the arrival of his wife as if she was some A list movie star. Zoey blushed, but still flashed him a huge smile as he pulled her close for a kiss.

Ant, the more reserved twin greeted his wife with half a smile. It wasn't that he wasn't affectionate; he just didn't tend to do it in public. Sometimes Lucie wished he would.

Physically identical, personality wise, totally different. Adam at nine minutes older was the more confident out going one. He and Zoey were perfectly matched with their mad crazy sense of humour, they were opposite sides of the same coin. Ant was a lot quieter, he didn't mind Adam taking centre stage all the time. Despite their differences they were extremely close. They had that whole twin thing going on, when one would know if there was something wrong with the other one. They even managed to break the same leg in the same game of rugby when they were nineteen.

The guys got the girls their usual Bacardi Breezers.

"How was the game today?" Lucie asked Ant.

"Great, we won 27-12. I scored twice," he grinned.

"Me too!" Adam added.

"Well, you might score again honey, I peed on the stick this morning and we're good to go!" Zoey smiled.

"You have got to get pregnant soon. The amount of baby making you two do," Lucie laughed.

"Well, that's the plan," Zoey replied.

"Best make it an early one tonight then," Adam grinned.

"If I don't get you out of here before the singing and the silly games start then I haven't got a hope in hell," Zoey said.

For a Monday morning Zoey was feeling quite chirpy as she walked to work. She'd stopped off at the twenty four hour chemist to stock up on more folic acid and called into the newsagents for 'Mother and Baby' magazines. She wanted to make sure she was doing everything conceivably possible to conceive. It was quite an exciting time and she and Adam were definitely having fun trying for a baby. A baby! It made them sound so grown up. She just wished it would hurry up and happen. She was starting to worry that it was taking too long. Any tips she could get from these magazines would come in useful.

By ten am the girls had caught up with the weekend gossip and dissected Saturday nights X Factor, disgusted in Simon Cowell's latest controversial decision, which thanks to Sky plus Zoey never missed out on. Their manager Larry, who bore a striking resemblance to Harold Bishop from Neighbours, was upstairs on a conference call and would no doubt come downstairs huffing and puffing that he'd wasted forty minutes listening to a load of bollocks. At nearly fifty, Larry was old school, he'd been threatening retirement for the last few years – but he was still hanging on!

"Zo, are you sure you never get Adam and Ant mixed up?" A curious Callie asked. She was always asking questions about the twins, she was fascinated.

Zoey shook her head laughing. "Course we don't get them confused, they're like chalk an cheese."

"Yeah, chalk an cheese who happen to look the same," she pointed out. "I mean, could you pick Adam out if he was in a line up with Ant?"

"I hope to God he never would be, but if he was, well, he's my husband so I'm pretty sure I could pick him out. Besides which, when they smile they have dimples on opposite sides of their face."

"You're not allowed to smile in a line up," Callie said

Zoey laughed. "Cal, you nutter! I promise you I can always tell Adam and Ant apart."

"Well, I suppose if you're gonna make two guys identical, they may aswell be Adam and Ant. They are far too hot for there just to be one of them," she continued.

"Callie! That's Zo's husband you're talking about, give it a rest!" Suze interrupted.

Zoey just laughed. "Just reminds me of how lucky I am."

She logged onto the internet, she'd just have a quick look at Facebook before she found some window offers. She was addicted to checking her news feed. Larry came bursting into the shop from the back office.

"Bloody waste of time! What a load of old bollocks! Bushy hasn't got a clue what he's talking about," he ranted, referring to their regional Manager - Roger Bush, who came in for a lot of stick with his unfortunate name. Zoey stared at her screen, it couldn't be. Not after all this time. She was aware of Larry waffling on, but she was drowning out what he was saying. She clicked on the message and read it twice before she could speak.

"Holy Guacamole."

"What?" Suze asked.

"I er, got a message, a blast from the past. That's all."

"Friend Request or message?" Callie asked.

"Oh bloody hell girls, how many times have I told you to stay off facepad in work?" Larry sighed.

"Facebook Larry, Facebook!" Callie corrected.

"Who's the message from? You look shocked," Suze asked.

Larry shock his head in exasperation. "I give up with you girls," he headed off in the direction of the foreign exchange. "Manager in name badge only, that's me."

"Not shocked, surprised. It was from a guy called Nick. Me and Luce met him on Oceania. Lucie had a bit of a fling, well more than a fling really... we haven't heard from him in years."

"So what does he want now?" Callie asked.

"I'll read the message... Hey me old shipmate, Nick

Slater here. How are you? Hope you're ok. I can see by your name you got married – congrats!! I'm back on dry land now for the foreseeable future. I would love to catch up with you, talk about old times. I'm based in Chester at the moment, not far from you. I lost touch with Lucie, but still think about her loads.... Anyway hope to hear from you soon! Nick x"

"So, are you gonna let Luce know that lover boy has been in touch?" Callie asked.

"Oh God. What a dilemma not only do I not know whether to tell Lucie about this, but I don't know whether to accept Nick or not. I accepted Steve's friend request, so it would look funny if I didn't accept Nick's... Oh God."

"Zo, stop rambling, there is nothing to stress about, they're just old mate's catching up."

"It's not as simple as that, it wasn't just a holiday romance, they fell in love. I don't think Luce has ever gotten over him."

"The way I see it, if you tell Lucie that this Nick has been in touch, then it's down to her what she does with that information, the pressure's off you," Suze suggested.

"If Nick and Lucie get back in contact and something happens, people will get hurt and it will be my fault."

"You can't be responsible for other people's actions Zo," Callie advised sounding all serious. "Besides if your husband is as fit as Adam and Ant why would you bother swapping?"

Suze gave Callie a look that suggested she keep her mouth closed. Then gently she said to Zoey. "You're probably worrying about nothing; they might not even fancy each other anymore."

"Yeah, like I said you wouldn't swap Adam for some guy who has just rolled in off the last ferry would ya?" Callie added.

"We're not talking about me and Adam; we're talking about Luce and Ant."

"Tomato, tomatoe," she shrugged.

"Oh for God sake, Callie," Zoey snapped as she picked up the phone and speed dialled Lucie's shop.

"Good morning, thank you for calling 'BOOK IT!' Jake speaking how may I help you today?"

"Hey J, it's Zo. Is Lucie free?"

"Sorry hon, she's with a customer, any message or shall I get her to call you?"

"Er no, it's nothing important, I was just calling for a chat," she sighed as she put the phone down. What would she have said anyway?

She ran her hands through her hair, this was a problem she could do without. She glanced over to the foreign exchange, Larry was ranting to some poor unsuspecting customer "...so the regional manager expects me to be in the Foreign Exchange and out on the counter serving, can't bloody do both can I? They haven't got a clue... 50 Euros wasn't it mate? Are you a member of the local golf club? Think I've seen your face there... it's commission free if you are mate, managers discretion..." The poor customer looked like he didn't know what he'd walked into. She tuned Larry out and could hear Callie and Suze talking.

"No, I'd rather have five roast potatoes and have less meat, I love me roasties me, in fact if I can get away with it I'd have six."

"I'm quite happy with four cos I do love me meat."
How many times did they have a conversation about how many roasties made a 'perfect' roast dinner? That's the type of problem she could deal with, not the return of Nick. She had a very bad feeling about this.

CHAPTER NINE

THEN

"Can you believe we've been on this ship for over a week already?"

Lucie shook her head in response as she stood in front of the mirror pulling her hair into a ponytail.

"I don't want to go home. I could stay here forever," she sighed as she put her hairbrush down.

"You mean you could stay with Nick forever."

Lucie turned and grinned at her and shrugged her shoulders. "Maybe I do. I just feel like I'm living in a fairy tale."

"Mills and Boon, more like," Zoey laughed as she got up off the bed and took a whole three steps to get to the cabin door, it was just as well that she and Lucie had become good friends. Zoey couldn't think of anything worse than spending two weeks in such a confined space with some one that she didn't get on with.

"What ya doin?"

"Just gonna get the daily news sheet – don't want to be accused of not reading it again." Actually, Zoey liked reading the daily sheet, she was saving them all up, along with the menus to take back to the shop to show customers.

"You only want to see what the chocolate of the day is," Lucie laughed.

"You are so right."

On the top right hand corner of every edition was a picture and description of a chocolate which could be bought with afternoon tea at the Ritz lounge bar.

"Mmm, Milk chocolate with a soft praline truffle centre; with a dusting of chocolate shavings on the top. You see this is why the papers are so depressing back home, they don't have a chocolate of the day on the front page."

"Oh to live on planet Zo."

"Hey, there is an envelope for us as well." She passed it to Lucie while she carried on scanning the paper and reading about the delights of the beautiful island of Antigua.

"The lads have a few hours free, they said to meet them at the beach bar by the welcome to Antigua sign at 10.30am and to bring beach stuff."

Zoey checked her watch. "Lets head off to Reception now and we can go straight to breakfast after we've been on duty."

"See you're still getting evils off Tara," Steve commented as he noticed Tara glaring at Nick from across the crew room.

"Ah, she'll get it over," Nick shrugged.

"Anyway Slaz, what I want to know is how the hell have you managed to get us a half day off the ship again?"

"Well I've sold my soul to the devil, and I promised Todd that I'll host the ballroom classes for the next month."

"Rather you than me mate, I hate getting felt up by the old dears. Lucie must be special."

Nick just grinned. There was no need to tell Steve yet that he'd also volunteered his services for the old ballroom dancing.

"You got it bad mate."

"Maybe, maybe not. C'mon lets go and sort out hiring the jeep."

Two hours later they were zipping along the Antiguan costal road in an open top jeep, the breeze whipping at their hair, reggae music pumping out of the radio, heading for a secluded beach. Lucie and Nick were in the front, Zoey and Steve in the back. Lucie felt like she was in some Hollywood movie, with Nick as her handsome co star. She looked at him out of the corner of her eye, so he wouldn't know that she was looking at him. His fingers tapped the steering wheel in time to the music, she let her gaze wander up his bare, tanned, muscular arms. Lucie tilted her head slightly so she could look at his face. His eyes were hidden by his aviator shades. His jaw line was set in concentration as he drove the jeep around the bends. She obviously wasn't as discreet as she though as a few moments later Nick turned to her and flashed his sexy smile at her.

"You ok Luce?" he asked.

She nodded as she beamed at him. He turned his attention back to the road, but he casually let his hand rest on her leg in between changing gear. Lucie was sure it must be something to do with heat because every time he touched her, the feel of his skin against hers seared like a flame through her body.

Nick swung the jeep around a corner and announced their arrival.

"This is the best beach you will ever find."

"D'you know Antigua has 365 beaches, you could spend a whole year here and never visit the same beach twice," Steve added.

They clambered out of the jeep. Before them was a small cove, totally deserted. The sand was white and unspoilt. In fact it looked like no one had ever set foot on this stretch of sand before. It was stunningly beautiful.

Steve grabbed the bags out of the boot. "C'mon guys, race ya!"

They all ran down the slope to the small beach. Once they'd got their things settled they started playing a game of volley ball, girls vs. boys. Nobody seemed to be playing by the rules as the girls were trying to make the lads run all over the place and the boys were just trying to get the girls into the water. The volley ball game was quickly abandoned once all four of them were in the water. The shrieks of laughter continued as a water fight began. This time it was Lucie and Nick against Zoey and Steve.

"C'mon Zo, let's get them," Steve laughed as he pushed at the water with his hands in Nick's direction. Zoey immediately joined in. Nick and Lucie did their best to fight back until Lucie hid behind Nick, she didn't want to get any wetter. Nick turned round, picked her up and dunked her in the water.

"Nick!" She squealed as she came up for air.

"Luce, you're letting the side down," he grabbed her round the waist, pulled her close and kissed her. She wrapped her arms around his neck, pulling him in even closer. The waves crashed against them, pushing them slightly off balance, they went tumbling into the water.

"Ha! Serves them right," Steve laughed. "Public displays of affection like that are far too sickening."

A little while later Zoey and Steve were sun bathing and letting Lucie and Nick have some time together.

"Look at those two, still frolicking in the water like loves young dream."

Zoey propped herself up on her elbows to get a better look. "Ah, they remind me of Scott and Charlene in Neighbours."

"You're showing your age there love."

Zoey threw her head back and laughed. "So are you Stevie boy."

"Sorry you're getting stuck with me whilst those two are far too busy being all loved up," Steve commented "I'm hardly the type of guy you were hoping to meet."

"Hey, Firstly, stop going all serious on me and secondly I am having so much fun with you. Ok it would have been nice to come away and have a quick holiday shag, but I'm really not bothered. I'd rather be having a laugh with my new gay best friend than having a big romance like those two."

"Really?"

"Hell yeah. If I'm not mistaken our two friends have fallen for each other big time, which is all well and good until..."

"...the cruise is over."

"Not going to be pretty."

"Now you're getting all serious on me, stop it," Steve grinned

"Sorry, I do have one more serious note to make... where the hell is the ice cream van?"

Steve laughed. "Never mind those two being gutted at being separated, I'll be heart broken when you go."

"I bet I only will have been gone five minutes when some cute sailor turns your pretty little head," she grinned.

Lucie and Nick were walking hand in hand along the waters edge.

She sighed happily. "I never expected any of this, I never

thought when I was told I was coming on this cruise that this would happen."

"What? That you'd be walking along a beautiful beach, hand in hand with a handsome, sexy, funny ents officer," he teased as they disappeared out of view from Zo and Steve behind some rocks.

"Exactly, although you missed over inflated ego off the list," she laughed.

"Just as well I know you're joking," he stopped and turned to face her. He reached up and gently stroked her cheek with one hand and pushed her hair behind her ear with the other. He then lifted his shades up onto his head so he could look into her eyes.

"Lucie, you blow my mind," he leaned closer to kiss her, she wrapped her arms around his broad back, minimising the space between them. She loved the scent of his skin, a mixture of heat and sun lotion. As he kissed her he pulled her slowly to the ground. He gently pulled at her bottom lip, then moved his mouth to her cheeks and trailed kisses all down her neck, talking to her in between kisses.

"I... Want... You...So...Much..."

She ran her fingers through his hair, knocking his shades straight onto the sand yet again he'd turned her into a quivering wreck.

That evening was the Captain's exclusive cocktail party, pre dinner drinks out on the sun deck. Nick had made sure the girls were on the guest list. The girls had spent the afternoon being pampered in the salon after getting back onboard earlier in the afternoon. They left their cabin and headed out towards the casino to take the glass lifts at the atrium up to sun deck.

"Luce, you look positively glowing hon."

"Ah thanks Zo, the girl in the salon has worked wonders."

"I think it might be Nick who is working wonders."

Lucie blushed. "Am I that obvious?"

Zoey just grinned. "I think it's fab."

Lucie's face became serious. "I think I've fallen for him Zo."

"I think you have too."

"What do I do?"

"Just go with the flow chick." The lift pinged open.

Nick and Steve were already out on the sun deck attending to the guests. Every time the door opened Nick's gaze went straight to it, looking for Lucie.

"I'm sure she'll be here in a minute. In the mean time chill, Todd's wandering round, stop being so obvious."

"Sorry dude, I'm just..." he stopped mid sentence. Lucie and Zoey walked out onto the deck, their arms linked and as usual, they were laughing. It gave him such a warm glow inside, what it was he couldn't explain.

Steve waved them over, Nick couldn't take his eyes off Lucie. She had a knee length pink prom style dress on, which looked lovely against her Caribbean sun tan, her blonde hair hung poker straight. She looked amazing.

"Girls, you both look stunning," Steve complimented them as they reached the boys.

"Well, we've got to look our best for the Captain," Zoey smiled.

Nick winked at Lucie. "You look amazing babe," he whispered and discreetly ran his hand across her bare back. Again the goose bumps appeared at the softness of his touch.

Lucie hoped one day she might actually feel in control when he touched her. Although somehow she doubted that.

The waiter had given the girls a glass of champagne and Steve introduced them to the captain. He was now back at Nick's side who had been joined by Todd.

"Yo. Slater, I don't know what's going on with you and that travel agent girl, but I've got my eye on you dude."

"Todd, honestly...ow," Steve elbowed Nick in the ribs, he glared at his friend.

"Boss, you don't need to worry, look at those girls, they only have eyes for the captain."

Nick followed Steve's gaze. Lucie and Zo were throwing their heads back in laughter at something the Captain had said. He frowned slightly as he saw the captain put his arm around Lucie's shoulders.

"I don't know, put a bloke in a captain's uniform and it makes women go weak at the knees," Steve laughed.

"Tell me about it; see that brunette in the red dress over there?" Todd asked. The guys nodded. "That's the Captain's mistress, as she disembarks next week, his wife will be boarding."

"Womanizer hey!"

"Well Slater, you know what they say about sailor's, girl in every port. See ya later y'all." With that Todd headed off.

"What the hell did you elbow me for?" Nick hissed.

"I was trying to cover your arse."

"Leave my arse out if this. I'm happy to share a cabin with you, but when you start talking about my backside you make me feel uncomfortable."

"Oh you flatter yourself. You're too much of a Casanova for me," Steve laughed with ease at their usual banter.

"Who's a Casanova?" Zoey asked as the girls appeared behind them.

"Err, the Captain," Steve replied.

"Ok maybe I do need my arse covering," Nick whispered as the girls attention was distracted by a waiter and yet more champagne.

"Girls, Karaoke in the pub tonight, catch you there after dinner."

The Yacht and Compass was already busy by the time Lucie and Zoey arrived after yet another seven course meal. No sooner had they stepped into the pub, a bar steward appeared.

"Usual ladies?" He asked. The girls nodded.

"I love how they remember everyone's drinks order."

"I love karaoke."

"Oh my God, Zo, no one likes getting up to sing."

"No, I'd never sing, I can't sing to save my life. I just like watching people being stupid."

Nick and Steve were already on the small dance floor part of the pub getting people to sign up to sing.

"Ladies and gentlemen, next we have two lovely ladies. Lucie and Zoey," Nick announced.

The girls shook their heads. "No way."

"Ah come on girls, don't be shy," Steve began clapping and chanting their names, the audience joined in. Zoey could see a few of their customers clapping away, great total embarrassment. Steve came over and dragged them up to the dance floor, whilst Nick cued up a track. Steve gave them a mic each and stood in between them.

"Don't worry girls, we'll all sing together."

Zoey was truly petrified, she wedged the mic in between her ample cleavage in the hope of drowning out her terrible voice. Lucie was equally scared, she actually had a great voice, but she hadn't had enough Bacardi Breezers to show it off.

"Ladies and gentlemen, as the girls are up here under duress, it's only fair that Steve and I give them a bit of a hand. I'll start off, girls join in when your ready."

The music started, Nick winked at Lucie.

"Ooh, it's ok Luce, I know this one," Zoey sounded slightly more confident than she felt.

Steve began to bop along to the intro, then Nick turned

to Lucie and sang...

> *"You're just to good to be true, I can't take my eyes off you..."*

The audience sang along. Lucie was mesmerised by Nick, he was singing to her, his blue eyes twinkling mischievously. She tried to sing, but nothing really came out of her mouth. Fortunately Zoey and Steve thought it was danceaoke and were flinging each other around the floor, so no one was really taking any notice of her. Nick was by her side, his arm around her shoulders as he sang...

> *"Let me love you baby, let me love you..."*

Every one was up on their feet, dancing and singing along. Lucie got that feeling again, like she was in a movie and she was dreading the moment when someone shouted "Cut," and it would all be over.

After the madness of karaoke, the four of them took a walk out on deck on the way to 'Le Club.'

Nick pulled Lucie in close.

Steve and Zoey were slightly ahead of them, keeping watch for any of the senior officers wandering around.

"Can't believe you got me and Zo up to do karaoke."

"I had an ulterior motive, I was looking down the song list earlier in the evening I saw that song and I thought of you."

She was hoping he couldn't see her blush in the darkness.

"I love how you do that."

So that answered that.

"Have you ever seen the film Ten things I hate about you?"

Nick shook his head. “Sounds lovely,” he pulled a face.

“It’s a girly film. Anyway, there’s a bit in it where Heath Ledger, he’s like the main bloke in it, is trying to show this girl that he really likes her, so when she’s playing football he gets the brass band on the pitch to play that song, the one you sang tonight, and he sings it to her from the stands. It’s really well, y’know, romantic,” she knew she was blushing again.

Nick could hear Todd’s voice from the deck above, he knew he was on his way down the stairs.

“Quick, in here.” He pushed her into a door way, they were in a linen room.

She was giggling, he pulled her close to him, kissed her and ran his hands through her hair. She pulled away breathlessly.

“Sorry,” he apologised. “I’ve been wanting to do that all night. What were you telling me about a romantic film?”

“It doesn’t matter, I think I’m in it.”

He flicked the lock on the door.

CHAPTER TEN

PRESENT DAY

Lucie was stuck with the 'Martini' family – Anytime, Anyplace, Anywhere – all for under £200 each. This was part of her job that she hated. Trying to extract information from some customers was like pulling teeth. She was sure they thought she was some kind of secret agent, not a travel agent. So questions like,

"How many nights would you like to be away for?" Were met with, "Just tell us what you've got love."

So she would try to narrow down the 'Anywhere' with a few suggestions;

"Turkey?"

"Oh no love, it's full of Turkish people."

"Greece?"

"Oh no love, too many Greeks and the food is funny."

"Ok, so lets start with you telling me the places you don't want to go to then maybe I can find you somewhere you would like to go on holiday."

At times like this she wished she had the balls to take a leaf out of Little Britain and say "Computer says No," but she was supposed to 'lead by example' so that was that!

Nine times out of ten these type of people ended up in Benidorm, it was just exotic enough. Full of English people, English food and a pub called the Red Lion. Lucie despaired of these people, there was a whole world out there and yet year after year these people would end up going to the same place, still at least it kept her in a job. These particular customers were getting on her nerves, no matter how hard she tried she couldn't pin them down to somewhere. Suddenly a bolt of lightening must've struck 'Mrs Martini' because she finally found her voice.

"Ooh, what about Benidorm?"

"Great idea, what have you got in Benidorm love? We went last year, had a ball. Lovely people, great food and we even found a smashing pub...what was it called love?"

"The Red Lion."

Lucie groaned inwardly as she tapped the code for Alicante airport into her computer. At least this wouldn't take too long now, she had to pop down to Zoey's shop and pick up a spare cartridge for the printer, and she could definitely do with escaping from the shop for half an hour and tonight was movie night, Ant had texted earlier to say he'd been into Tesco on his lunch and got The Proposal. She'd text back saying "Good choice, Ryan Reynolds is hot." He'd replied saying he's just got a refund on it and chosen a Jennifer Aniston film instead. Fortunately she knew he was joking.

Zoey couldn't concentrate properly, she was trying to work out next months targets and the figures were just swimming in front of her eyes. She knew she'd have to tell Lucie about Nick getting in touch, but she was worried what Lucie would do with that information. What would happen between Lucie and

Nick and where would that leave Ant? Maybe she was over reacting, it was a long time ago, and they were all older and wiser, weren't they? She sighed loudly.

"Zo, I don't know why you're stressing so much. It's not your problem, tell Luce about Mr Lover man and leave her to it," Callie advised.

"It's not that simple."

"It's all in the past though isn't it? Luce and Ant are happily married now. I'm sure you're worrying about nothing," Suze said.

"I really think Luce thought Nick was The One. When we got back off the ship she just wasn't interested in any other guys, until Ant came along and I know she loves Ant but..."

"But what?" Callie asked excitedly clearly enjoying the drama and an alternative conversation to the usual 'Roast Dinner' one.

"It was the passion with Nick, I've never seen anything like it. They were practically smouldering every time they were together."

The shop door opened, Lucie walked in.

"Luce! What are you doing here?" Zoey asked. Her voice came out in a funny high pitched squeak.

"You ok, Zo?" Lucie frowned. "Larry said we could take one of his spare cartridges, as long as we give him two back."

"That's our Larry, always wheeling and dealing," Suze laughed.

"Seriously, Zo, what's wrong? You look like you've seen a ghost."

"The ghost of lovers past," Callie said attempting to put on a spooky voice.

"What?" Lucie asked.

"Oh it's nothing," Zoey mumbled.

"Tell her, Zo."

"Tell me what?"

"Your Mr Lover man has been in touch, shabba," Callie giggled.

"Callie, butt out, it's got nothing to do with you, stay out of it." Suze told her.

"Right, I'm well confused, will somebody tell me what is going on?"

"Nick's been in touch, on Facebook."

"Nick? Nick Slater? Slaz? My Nick?" Her voice got higher with each word as she sank down onto the chair opposite Zoey.

"Yep, all four of them, the very same."

"On Facebook? I'm not on Facebook."

"He messaged me on Facebook, me and Steve are friends and he must've found me through Steve, hoping to find you. I looked on Steve's wall and he'd written a message on his wall asking if you were on Facebook."

"What wall? I got in trouble for writing on a wall when I was a kid. You just can't go round writing on people's walls." Lucie was babbling and quite possibly delirious.

"Lucie, you seriously need to drag your arse into the 21st century. Now is not the time to give you a lesson in Facebook so let's just say Nick sent Steve a message to see if you were on Facebook. He can't message me properly yet cos I haven't accepted his friend request. I wanted to speak to you first."

"He's already your friend, why would he ask you to be friends again? I just don't get it," Lucie was clearly getting hysterical.

"Right, let's just forget the Facebook thing for now. We'll go in the back, I'll get you a cuppa and we'll work out what to do about Nick."

Once the girls were in the back office, Lucie was slightly calmer after a few slurps of tea. She breathed out slowly as she settled down on the small sofa in the staff room.

"OK, lets start this again."

"Nick's back, he's in Chester and he wants you to get in touch."

"CHESTER? Chester? As in twenty minutes down the road Chester?"

"Luce, chill honey. Yes it appears he's not that far away."

"Oh God, Zo. D'you know how many times I wished he'd come back? Every night before I went to sleep he was always the last thought on my mind. I'd imagine him coming into the shop in that Tuxedo uniform of his, sweep me up into his arms and kiss me like he used to."

"Yeah, I'm getting the whole officer and a gentleman thing."

"Oh it wasn't just the officer and a gentleman thing, it was Dirty Dancing too, I'd be in a pub and I'd imagine him coming in, making his way over to me and saying "Nobody puts Lucie in a corner."

"Is there any film that hasn't been re enacted in your head?"

"Well, not Titanic, that wasn't a happy ending, was it?"

"Chick, you already have your happy ending, you've got Ant."

"Ant? Oh God yes Ant. My husband."

"D'you need some Whisky in that tea? Larry has a bottle in the draw."

"No, I'm fine. It's a shock obviously, but I haven't thought about Nick in....I don't know... must be weeks, err, months."

Zoey raised an eyebrow.

"Honestly, Zo it will be fine. I'm married now, he may be for all we know. It really will be fine, nothing to worry about."

Zoey wasn't sure who Lucie was trying to convince, but now wasn't the time to lecture her. Nick hadn't said much in his message, but Zoey would bet a years supply of Wispa bars that he wasn't married and she was pretty sure he would be hoping to pick up where they left off.

"So...should I reply to him? What do you want to do?"

"I don't know yet; think I just need to sleep with him... NO, I mean sleep on it, yeah sleep ON IT, that's what I need to do."

"Luce, you are seriously worrying me girl."

"Maybe I do need some of that whisky."

By the time Lucie walked up her road that night she was slightly more together. So what if the one true love of her life was back? He had his chance and he blew it. Who did he think he was coming back after five years, five bloody years? Did he expect her to be waiting for him like she had nothing better to do? She was very happily married and her Ant was one hot rugby playing guy with fabulous thighs, better thighs than Nick. This was just one of those things that threw you a bit, she was sure in a few days she'd be thinking Nick who? She noticed Ant's car was already outside the house. He normally didn't get in before her. Right, time to get her head out of the shed and go and chill with Ant. She could tell he'd already put the tea on as she walked through the door, she could definitely smell sausages.

"Hey babe," he shouted from the kitchen.

She walked straight through to him and dumped her bags by the kitchen table.

"I am no Nigella Lawson, but I can cook a mean sausage, mash and peas complimented by a glass of your favourite rose wine." he grinned.

"You are certainly not Nigella Lawson, but that sounds wonderful," she was now by his side and gave him a kiss on his cheek.

"How was your day, kiddo?"

She sighed. "Oh the usual, people wanting to go away for two weeks all inclusive for about fifty quid." And an ex boyfriend or whatever he was, popping up again.

He handed her a glass of wine. "Well, I've run you a nice bath, so by the time you've relaxed and had a nice soak the sausages should be done to perfection and the mash should be nice and...mashy all ready for movie night"

She smiled "What have I done to deserve this?"

"Absolutely nothing, oh and there's something for you pinned on the fridge door."

She turned round and under a fridge magnet that said "You can touch the dust, just don't write on it" – given to her as a 'joke' by the out law, were tickets to see Pink in concert at the Echo Arena. She jumped up and down screaming and laughing, she flung her arms around Ant, nearly soaking him with her wine.

"Oh my God!"

"Happy Anniversary kiddo."

"But...but... that was days ago."

"I know, and I may not be all flash and romantic like Adam is with Zo, I just like to show you in my own quieter way and when you're least expecting it that I love you Lucie Maxwell, have done since our Love Actually conversation in the rugby club and will do forever."

She couldn't speak, she was totally stunned. Ant was pretty much the strong and silent type; he didn't do mushy and romantic. Still she wasn't complaining. She felt tears well up in her eyes, God, what was the matter with her? She quickly blinked them away.

"Listen, how about we forget the perfect sausages and the mashy mash... come and join me in the bath and we'll celebrate our anniversary again," she suggested.

"Yeah, we can always dial a pizza later," he grinned.

She laughed as he took her by the hand and they headed upstairs.

Nick who?

Zoey was unusually quiet as she got ready for bed that night.

"You ok, Zo? You don't seem yourself," Adam asked.

She yawned. "I'm fine, just tired. Stressful day that's all." God, she hated this already, she couldn't tell Adam what had happened today 'coz she would bet that years supply of Wispas again that Lucie hadn't mentioned any of this to Ant. She hoped she wasn't wrong or she wasn't going to be eating Wispas for a hell of a long time. That thought depressed her too.

"You're not worried about the pregnancy thing are you?" he asked, breaking her thoughts.

"No babe, I know it'll happen, we just need to be relaxed and laid back about it."

"I do prefer it when you're laid back," he grinned.

She flung a pillow at him. "Ads!" she laughed.

"That's better."

He always managed to put a smile on her face and make her feel better. She looked over to him and grinned.

"What?" he asked.

"Nothing, just thinking how amazing you are."

"And she says that before she gets me into bed."

"You are crazy, do you know that?"

"Crazy for you," he knelt on the bed leaned over and pulled her onto the bed with him.

"Are you going on top or am I?" she asked.

"Hadn't really thought that far ahead babe. Wild idea I know but I was just gonna see how things progressed and just go with it."

"That's cool honey. Just don't forget, if you are on top..."

"I know, shove a pillow under your bum and lift your legs up afterwards," he sighed.

"Exactly, need to give your swimmers the best possible chance to get to my eggs."

"If I didn't love you so much and wasn't as horny as hell I'd tell you exactly where to shove my..."

She grabbed him and silenced him with a kiss, she ran her hand down his bare back and slipped it inside his boxies. He groaned as she touched him, instantly forgetting any of the pre sex instructions she'd given him.

The next morning Lucie was waiting for Jake outside 'BOOK IT!' she may have forgotten all about Nick last night as she snuggled up on the sofa with Ant watching The Proposal, but he was certainly on her mind when she woke up this morning. She knew she had to deal with the situation. She'd sent Jake a text and asked him to meet her at the shop, earlier than usual. She could see him crossing the road.

"Ok, Mrs Maxwell, what was sooo important that you had to drag me from my bed at stupid O'clock?" He clearly wasn't happy.

She had a real soft spot for Jake and in turn he would always help her out. He was the only one to volunteer to stay late if a customer kept them after half five and could always be relied upon to have good gossip. He was in his early twenties with dark spiky hair and far too skinny, she always wanted to feed him up.

"Thanks for getting here early, I promise your next Maccy D's is on me."

"This better be worth it."

Once they were in the shop and sitting behind Lucie's PC, she told him what she needed to do.

"Ok J, I need you to set me up on Facebook."

"You dragged my arse in early for that? We could do that anytime during the day."

"I know, but I don't really want anyone else to know."

"Luce, the whole point of Facebook is that people know you are on there."

"I know, I just need to make contact with someone first..."

"I'm intrigued."

"D'you remember the guy I told you about from Oceania? Nick?"

"That guy? Oh yeah, THAT guy," he nodded his head.

He'd joined "BOOK IT" about a year after Lucie got back from the cruise and she was still hung up about him then.

"Well, he wrote on Zo's fence or something, wanting to find me."

"Yeah, that would be the wall, God this is gonna be on long Facebook lesson," Jake sighed.

"Look, all I wanna do is message him and maybe arrange to meet up and hopefully get some closure and shut the book on the chapter of my life that was Nick."

"What do Ant and Zo think about this?"

"They don't know," she replied quietly.

"You're sure this is what you want? You might say you want to put an end to it in your mind, but it might not work out the way you want it."

"Yes. I need to do this."

"Ok, let's get started. Type your name in."

"Do I have to be Lucie Maxwell? Can I put Lucie Scott in, he won't recognise my married name."

Jake raised an eyebrow. "You can be Lucie Locket or even Lucie in the sky, whatever."

She began to type.

The first thing Nick did when he logged onto his pc was to check Facebook, it was almost becoming part of his morning routine, wake up, have a pee, brush teeth, make a cuppa, check out Facebook. This morning he was glad he'd logged on, 'coz the first thing he saw was a friend request. When he clicked on it and saw the name Lucie Scott, to say his heart soared was an understatement. Suddenly, leaving the ship and settling in Chester seemed like the best idea he'd ever had. He clicked his mouse to accept his new friend.

CHAPTER ELEVEN

PRESENT DAY

"Crap."

"What?"

"I've only just sent the friend request to him and already he's written on that wall thingy. I wasn't expecting it to be that quick."

"Luce, if you wanted him to take his time over it then maybe you should have sent a letter," Jake sighed.

"Maybe that might have been a better idea."

"What does he say?"

"Just that he's glad we're back in touch, am I ok? He still thinks about me and he's sorry it's been so long."

She stared at her computer screen wondering what to write in return. She found it all very strange knowing he was probably sitting in front of his computer waiting for her response, or maybe he wasn't maybe he'd gone back to bed where his girl friend (if he had one) was waiting for him, or maybe he was chatting to other people on line. She typed the first thing that came into her head and hit the send button before she could chicken out.

Hey Slaz, am new to all this Facebook thing, was really surprised to hear that you are now in Chester, is that permanent or are you just passing through? It's lovely to hear from you again. How's life? X x

Ok, maybe she should have read it before she sent it, did she sound desperate asking if he was sticking around? Why hadn't she told him she was married? And what was with the kisses? No only had she put one kiss, which could've been accidental, everyone put smiley faces on the end of messages by mistake these days didn't they? But two kisses? She only ever put two kisses on the end of messages to Ant and Zo.

A message came straight back. By the time she was supposed to be opening the shop messages had been flying back and forth. She apologised and said she'd have to log off, but she'd be in touch before the weekend.

"So, are you feeling any closure yet?" Jake asked.

"Err, no not yet, but maybe after I've met him on Sunday then I might," she mumbled.

"WHAT?"

"Zo, are you feeling ok? You've put the ski brochures in the far away section and the summer sun brochure in the winter sun section," Suze commented.

"Canada is featured in the ski brochure, that's long haul and the summer sun..." she sighed. "Ok, since you ask, no I'm not ok. Guess who I found on Facebook this morning? Lucie and Jake are now friends, it told me. She hadn't requested me so I clicked on her to send her a request and what do I find? Lucie Scott and Nick Slater are now friends.

Lucie bloody Scott, seems she has forgotten a certain husband and she obviously didn't want me to find out that she was in touch with Nick. So what does that tell me? Yep, that I was right to worry. Not only that, I accepted his request and it looks like they had a lovely chat this morning and are meeting up on Sunday! What the hell is that all about? So that is why the summer sun is in the winter sun section 'coz I am confused.com. End of rant." She spun back round the face the brochures and moved them to the right section.

Suze and Callie exchanged a worried look.

Callie cleared her throat. "Y'know you may be worrying over nothing, these days it's ok to be mates with an ex," she spoke with a voice that she thought was wise an authoritive. It only succeeded in making Zoey feel older than her twenty six years.

"The problem is, if they meet up again, it might just reignite the spark again."

"If it does, there's nothing you can do to stop it," Callie added.

Lucie stared at the phone, she knew she was gonna have to call Zoey and she knew she wasn't going to be very happy, especially when she asked her to come with her on Sunday. The lads had an away game on Sunday and they never expected the girls to trek out across Cheshire to watch them. So when Nick had suggested lunch on Sunday it seemed perfect, she wouldn't even need to mention anything to Ant. It wasn't that she didn't want to tell Ant, she just didn't want to go over everything that had happened between her and Nick. She wasn't interested in any of Ant's exes, well apart from that Sasha one he used to go out, she was the only one who did her head in. Why would he want to know about this? He wouldn't. She knew she would be asking a lot from Zo when she asked her not to tell Adam, those two never had secrets from each other. If Adam knew then he would definitely tell Ant.

"You ok, Luce?" Jake interrupted her thoughts.

"Oh yeah, just miles away," on a ship in the Caribbean...

"Penny for them?"

"They're not even worth that much," she sighed as she picked the phone up and dialled Zoey's number.

"Hey Zo, it's me,"

"Would I be speaking to Lucie Scott or Lucie Maxwell? I'm a bit confused at the moment."

"Look, Zo, I'm sorry. I had to use my maiden name, Nick wouldn't have realised it was me otherwise."

"I'm sure he would have done. So you and him are having a nice little lunch date on Sunday then?"

"I just need to get him out of my system, you know I've always wondered *what if* and this is my chance to end it properly."

"*What if* it turns into a romantic meal for two?"

"Actually, that's what I was ringing for, he wants to meet up with you as well, you see it really is just old friends meeting up and you can be our chaperone," she tried to laugh.

"Luce, I'm not sure about this."

"Listen, it'll be fine. There is just one other thing. Please don't tell Adam, I don't want Ant to know."

"Now you're havin' a laugh, if you want to lie to your husband that's fine, just don't ask me to lie to mine," Zoey raised her voice.

"I'm not asking you to lie, just leave out certain bits of information," Lucie pleaded.

"I don't know Luce, we'll have to talk about it. I've got stuff to do, call round later," Zoey sighed as she put the phone down, like she didn't have enough to worry about, she'd gotten her period that morning. Just to add to her problems Larry's booming voice was coming from the foreign exchange booth.

"Zo, have you got last months figures?"

"Right here, boss man."

"Right good, now all I need is a cup of tea while I go through them."

The girls put their heads down and became engrossed in their work.

"Every thing ok, Luce?" Jake asked.

"Yeah, it's something and nothing."

"Must be serious for you and Zo to be having words."

"She's just worried about me and Nick meeting up."

"Should she be?"

"God, no, me and Nick were over a long time ago."

He just smiled, seemed to him she'd just protested too quickly. Lucie might think she was just catching up with an old flame, but sometimes those flames of passion never really died out. Judging by how nervous she seemed to be at meeting Nick again maybe those thoughts had been running through her mind as well.

After work Lucie headed over to Zoey's. The lads had gone for a run, so she knew they could talk undisturbed. She had butterflies in her stomach. It wasn't often that she and Zo argued but she knew Zo would have something to say about the secret lunch meeting with Nick. As it was Zoey seemed to be pre occupied with a huge tub of Ben & Jerry's cookie dough ice cream.

"Zo, hon. This may be a weird question but what's with the ice cream?"

"I read an article in the paper today, scientists have discovered that ice cream can help you to conceive."

"I thought sex helped you to conceive. So I suppose you have five tubs of Ben Jerry's in the freezer?"

"Six," she replied amid a mouth full of ice cream.

"You really think this will work?"

"According to the scientists it will. Anyway, we need to discuss a certain person and this lunch you've arranged." Lucie sighed, before she could even start her argument for why she had chosen to keep this a secret they heard the front door open.

"Cooee, Zoey."

"Oh shit, it's the out law. Caught red handed," Zoey muttered as she looked down at her ice cream. Could she get rid of it before old Ma Maxwell got to the kitchen? She looked up at the door, too late there was the evil mother in law. She looked at Lucie who knew exactly what she was thinking.

"Oh hello Lucie dear, I didn't know you'd be here, well that saves me an extra trip."

It was then Zoey noticed the huge Tupperware boxes that the mother in law was carrying. She also clocked old Ma Maxwell looking at her ice cream like it was the dreaded weed.

"Oh, hi, err mum, I err wasn't expecting you."

"So I see." Another cursory look at the ice cream.

"What's in the box?" Lucie stepped in. Zo threw her a grateful look.

"Home made pies, steak, chicken and apple. They're all labelled so you girls don't mix them up. Apple pie wouldn't taste nice with gravy," she laughed at her own joke.

"You didn't have to do that," Zoey protested.

"Nonsense dear. I know my boys miss good home cooking. There's a box in the car for Anthony as well Lucie dear."

Lucie rolled her eyes.

"I'll just pop them into your freezer for you Zoey, I can see you're busy."

Zoey shot up. "NO! I mean, it's ok I'll do it later," six tubs of Ben & Jerry's flashed through her mind.

"Don't be silly dear, I'll do it."

Lucie could see the look of shame in Zoey's eyes. She hated her mother-in-law for making Zo feel bad about herself.

"Actually," Lucie began as she stepped in front of the freezer to block old Ma Maxwell. "What Zo meant was that she'll do it later because she had to empty the freezer, the fuse in the plug has gone and Adam needs to replace it."

"Ah, I knew there must be a reason why you were eating all that ice cream Zoey dear. I know you're trying to diet."

"Actually, I read that ice cream increases fertility," Zoey mumbled.

"Really? Well I look out for some BOGOF's next time I'm in Sainsbury's. Anything to help bring on the grand children! Although Zoey, my Boys come from fine stock so with Adam's genes and your child bearing hips I'm sure you won't need much ice cream to get pregnant. Now Lucie dear, you do need some help in the hips department so maybe I should get some ice cream to help you."

Lucie knew who she'd like to see BOG OFF.

It wasn't long after old Ma Maxwell's cheery visit that the lads came back from their run. Adam and Ant came bounding into the kitchen, full of too much energy. A bowling tournament on the wii began, beers and Bacardi Breezers were produced and the fun began. Zoey, who was just ever so slightly competitive danced around the room when ever she got a strike, then stamped her foot when Adam or Ant took the lead (freakishly the lads ended up with the same score as each other on every game they played.) Zoey was fighting a losing battle. It just made Lucie laugh even more. Especially as Zoey's competitiveness made her temporarily forget that she was supposed to be mad at Lucie.

Later, as Lucie lay awake in bed, Ant already fast asleep beside her, she reflected on her strange day. She couldn't believe she was back in touch with Nick after all this time and she was actually going to see him on Sunday. Would she still go if Zoey refused to go? They hadn't actually had time to discuss the Nick situation tonight. As she turned her back on Ant, she knew without a doubt that nothing would stop her keeping her lunch date with Nick.

CHAPTER TWELVE

THEN

'Oceania' was at its penultimate port of call, the island of Dominica. Tomorrow she would be sailing back into Barbados to offload her current lot of passengers. Lucie was in her usual sunbathing spot at the back of the ship, it was funny how in the space of two short weeks thing's became habit; such as her sunbathing location, what time she and Zo headed off to get ready for dinner and of course Nick; although he was more of an addiction than a habit. Despite the sun, the heat and the beautiful surroundings she couldn't help but feel a bit sad. This time tomorrow she and Zo would be at the airport on their way back to Blighty. No more cocktails of the day, no more sail aways. Before she could think about it anymore Zoey appeared.

"Oh my God Luce, can't believe you missed the choc-a-holics buffet."

"Was it any good?"

"Good? I was in heaven. There were at least twelve tables full of chocolate desserts, there was even a replica of the ship. Took loads of photos!"

"What did you have?"

Zoey sighed. "Nothing. There was far too much to choose from."

Lucie shook her head. "Only you Zo, only you."

Zoey just shrugged. "I was just spoilt for choice. So what have you been up to while I've been gone?"

"Not much, just taking the opportunity to grab as much sun as I can."

"I know, can't believe we're going home tomorrow. I wonder how many of our Bacardi Breezers I can claim on expenses?"

"Larry's cool, he probably wont bat an eye lid."

"This has just been the best time of my life." Zoey sighed happily.

"Me too," Lucie agreed, but her sigh wasn't quite as happy.

"At least you've had a fling. I have a real soft spot for Steve, but that's as far as that's ever gonna go."

"I think you and Steve would make a fab couple, I think you could make him swap teams Zo."

"Let's just leave Steve how he is."

"Yeah, you're probably right. I'm really gonna miss Nick though."

"Hey, I know you will, but that's holiday romances for you. Just think of all those amazing memories you've got AND you've got me, we'll be ship mates for life now....there is no getting rid of me."

Lucie laughed "As if I'd want to get rid of you."

"C'mon we better go and start getting ready; it's posh frock night tonight."

Back in the cabin Lucie was sitting at the dressing table drying her hair. Even over the hair dryer she could hear Zoey singing in the shower, whatever it was, was definitely off key. Lucie couldn't help but smile. She'd really miss Zo when they got home. They had become so close and found the same things funny. Zo was, too quote Peter Andre, *Insania* you only had to be with her for a few minutes and she'd have you laughing about something. They'd even gotten sharing this tiny cabin off to a fine art when it came to getting ready. Lucie would shower first, dry her hair while Zoey showered. When Zo was drying her hair Lucie was getting dressed, then she'd do her make up while Zo was getting dressed, leaving the mirror free for Zoey to do her make up. It was like a military operation.

Nick and Steve were in the atrium which was a hive of activity. Passengers getting their last minute photographs and others were enjoying pre dinner drinks. Nick wasn't paying much attention, he was too busy looking at the staircase, waiting for Lucie. He watched her glide down the staircase, totally unaware that he was taking in every movement, every expression on her face as she searched the room looking for him. Then finally her eyes locked with his, she gave him a dazzling smile and he felt like he'd drunk a whole bottle of champers in one go, bubbly, light headed and woozy. What was that feeling?

"Ow," Nick said a little too loudly as Steve elbowed him in the ribs. He glared at him, he was starting to make a habit of that.

"Nick, mate. Barbara was just asking if you had room on your dance card for her tonight."

Nick plastered his "entertainer's" smile onto his face. Trust B.O. Barb to interrupt his day dream.

"Ah Barb, poor Steve is missing out, he loves doing the foxtrot with you."

"Nick, you know you're her favourite," Steve grimaced. B.O. Barb was standing in between them; she reached up and pinched their cheeks. "You boys, fancy you both fighting over me. You know how to flatter a girl. I'll just have to dance with you both. I shall be looking for you in the ball room later."

She grinned at them both, flashing off her yellow teeth. As she walked away Steve muttered. "Surely she must realise I'm gay."

"Surely she must realise that I wouldn't go near her with a barge pole!"

"I know exactly where you wanna put your barge pole Slaz. There is the object of your desire, floating like a mirage down the stairs," Steve said theatrically. Nick followed his gaze back to Lucie, she totally took his breath away. The girls had obviously saved their best dresses till last. They looked stunning.

"Wow, they scrub up well for two travel agents' don't they," Steve grinned.

Nick was oblivious to anything Steve was saying. He couldn't take his eyes off Lucie. She was wearing a long black ball gown with little silver flowers embroidered along the bodice and down one side of the dress. He couldn't believe this was their last night. He knew he'd be looking for her tomorrow night, but she'd be on a plane. She walked towards him; he was convinced that the crowd parted especially to let her through.

"Hey you," she smiled up at him.

"You. Look. Beautiful."

"This old thing," she laughed nervously.

"I'm on ballroom duty later, so I'll catch up with you in 'Le Club'?"

She nodded. "Looking forward too it."

Zoey's raised voice distracted them.

"They really threw all that chocolate away?"
Steve nodded. "There were tonnes of it left."

"Oh man, what a waste," Zoey sighed.

"C'mon Zo, let's go and enjoy our last dinner."

"Too right, no one's chucking my food away."

The evening was racing on far too quickly for Lucie. She was in the loos waiting for Zo, and then they'd be heading over to 'Le Club.' She quickly reapplied her lipstick and ran a comb through her hair. She hadn't wanted to admit to Zoey earlier that this holiday romance may actually be more than that, for her at least. She couldn't be sure of Nick's feelings and she was far too scared of the answer, either way. If she really had fallen in love with Nick, which she thought was a real possibility... but having never been in love before she couldn't be too sure. She was going round in circles, so if she told Nick she loved him and he said it back...well that would just break her heart because she was on a plane out of here tomorrow. If he said he didn't love her, that would be just as bad and she'd look a fool. That left a third option, not to say anything at all, which seemed like her only choice.

Zoey came out of the cubicle, she quickly rinsed her hands and then hooked Lucie through the arm. "C'mon me hearties, let's go and enjoy our last night."

As usual Zoey and Steve were on the dance floor. Nick turned to Lucie. "Let's escape for a bit."

She nodded above the loud music and followed him. They got in the lift, Lucie fully expecting to get out at the top deck was surprised when they stopped on deck twelve. As far as she knew it was just cabins on this deck. Nick grabbed her hand.

"C'mon," he winked at her and began running along the passageway. She was totally confused and had no idea where they were going. Half way down the corridor he stopped running; pulled her to him and pressed his lips against hers. She begrudgingly pulled away and glanced around. "Someone might see."

He just smiled. "Don't worry its' fine." He pushed her up against a door and carried on kissing her. She felt the door open behind her, but she didn't fall, he had his arms around her and manoeuvred her into the room, she finally broke away from the kiss to see where she was.

"Wow," she breathed.

"I wanted our last night to be really special."

Lucie looked around the cabin; it was a million miles away from her pokey one. This one had a grand piano inside, a spiral staircase up to what she assumed was the bedroom, a Jacuzzi and a...she squinted, not quite believing what was in front of her eyes... a butler, holding a tray with a huge bottle of bubbly.

She looked at Nick in disbelief.

The butler stepped forward. "Good evening madam. Champagne?"

Lucie was speechless. Nick took the glass and gave it to her. He turned to the butler. "That'll be all Jeeves."

Lucie found her voice "Jeeves?" She laughed.

"Aren't all butlers' called Jeeves?"

"You are crazy d'you know that?"

"Absolutely,"

"How did you get a suite? What if the guests come back?"

"They had to leave yesterday, urgent family business or something and I've paid Jeeves' to keep an eye out. So..." he stretched out his hand to her and pulled her close, gently planting a kiss on her bare shoulder. "...We have all night." He moved his kisses up her neck and eventually found her lips.

By the time Lucie got back to her own cabin it was 5.30am. She'd have to be up in two hours, but she was too excited to sleep. Zoey was snoring away, should she wake her? She flopped down on the bed. That night had truly been the most amazing night of her life. She'd lost count of how many times they'd had sex; there was the Jacuzzi, the balcony, the piano...

"There you are," Zoey yawned. "I thought you and lover boy had jumped ship."

"Oh my God, Zo, I've just had the best night EVER. He took me to one of the suites, it had a piano, a butler, and we had sex everywhere!"

"With the butler?" Zoey asked sleepily.

"No, he was just there to give us champagne."

Zoey sat up in bed, sleep would be boring compared to this. "Go on, I want details."

"You know that scene, in Pretty Woman...the one with the piano?"

"Oh my God! Oh my God!" Zoey screamed

"I know! I know! It was so sexy and romantic and I really think I'm gonna wake up in a minute and all this has been a dream."

"You're confusing the love boat with Dallas," Zoey laughed.

"I have never felt like this before, he touches me and it's like he sets me on fire, damn he gets me all hot." She flopped down onto her bed, she'd give anything for this adventure not to be over.

"C'mon Steve, finish your coffee. I want to get down to reception. They'll be calling the girls deck for disembarkation soon." Nick was standing in front of Steve, moving from one foot to another impatiently.

"I'll only be a minute, you go on ahead if you want mate."

Tara glared at him from the other table. “Didn’t realise you and Steve had to be permanently joined at the hip.”

“Oh shut it Tara, I’m not in the mood for you today.” Nick stormed off. As he went off in the direction of reception he tried to get his head together. No girl had ever had this effect on him before. The thought of not knowing when he’d see Lucie again was horrible. He’d thought about asking her to stay on board and work on the ship, but he wasn’t sure what her answer would be.

Nick could already see them standing by the main staircase, they were dressed in their blue “BOOK IT” uniforms ready to escort their customers’ home. Zo was doing her usual talking ten to the dozen and doing a head count. Lucie had her head down, busying herself with a clip board. He snuck up behind her.

“Hey,” he whispered into her ear, although to her it may have appeared to sound like the ships fog horn as she jumped almost a foot away from him. When she realised it was him she smiled. He noticed her smile didn’t reach her eyes.

“Can you all make sure you have your passports in your hand luggage please?” Zoey’s voice boomed over the passengers. “No Mrs Thom, that’s your bus pass.”

Nick laughed. “This ship won’t be the same without you two.” He turned to face her, trying to commit every detail of her face to memory. Her soft blue eyes, the freckle just above her left eyebrow, her shy smile. He reached out and gently touched her cheek; he pushed a loose strand of hair behind her ear. They’d said their goodbyes last night, but he couldn’t believe that this was the last time he’d see her till…well, who knew when? She was nervously biting her bottom lip. He ran his fingers down her arm, setting off a trail of goose bumps. It made him smile. He reached for her hand and bent down to kiss it.

"God Luce, I can't believe this is it."

"Well. It's like Zo says, holiday romances are short and sweet."

"Don't say that, this is more than some holiday fling and you know it."

She nodded her head. "Course I do, I'm just trying to make it easier to leave that's all."

"We will see each other again – I promise."

She looked doubtful.

"Trust me Luce, I won't let you down, I lo..."

"Zoey, Lucie." Steve interrupted. "So glad I caught you guys." He gave Lucie a big hug. Nick stepped back. He wasn't entirely sure what he was about to say to Lucie then and he wasn't sure if Steve's appearance was good timing or not.

Steve spun Zoey round. "Ah, my disco diva, so gonna miss you."

"You too, wish I could put you in my suitcase."

"Passengers with purple disembarkation cards are asked to move to the security point on deck five, port side."

"Guess that's us Luce."

Another quick round of hugs. Lucie smiled that shy smile of hers again and that was it they were gone. Just like that.

It was a while before Nick and Steve caught up again, turn around day was always hectic.

"So did you tell her?" Steve asked.

"Tell her what?"

"Oh c'mon mate I thought that'd be stating the bleedin' obvious."

Nick still had a blank look on his face.

"That you love her."

Suddenly it dawned on him. The warm fuzzy glow, the feeling like he'd drunk far too much champagne...why hadn't he realised before? He loved her, he bloody well loved her.

Steve saw the look of shock on his face. "You didn't know? Me and Zo talked about it all the time."

"Why the hell didn't you tell me?" Nick shouted.

"Well, obviously, we thought you knew," Steve replied sarcastically.

Nick looked at his watch. Her plane would've already taken off. Why the hell didn't he realise sooner? Why didn't he ask her to stay? Why didn't he tell her he loved her...?

CHAPTER THIRTEEN

PRESENT DAY

It was Lucie's day off, she and Zo normally tried to get their days' off together, but this week she had a day to herself and she had no idea what to do. It was only a few days till she was meeting up with Nick, she was brimming with nervous energy. She'd tried doing the ironing whilst watching Phil and Holly to take her mind off it all. She knew it wasn't working when she realised Phil wasn't saying,

> *On today's show we have Lucie Maxwell, she thought she was happily married until her one true love sailed back into her life.*

And Holly hadn't really said,

> *What would you do if that happened to you? That's the subject of today's phone-in.*

All she'd managed to do was burn a hole in one of her work shirts and possibly sent herself insane. She kept pacing the floor, wandering round the house trying to find something constructive to do. Finally she dug out an old photo album. Zoey, being as organised as she was had gotten duplicates of their holiday photos and put them in an album, complete with little funny quotes. Lucie sat on the edge of her bed as she flicked through the album. The first picture was of the girls in front of the Oceania when they first arrived, in their uniforms and not a hint of a suntan, or of the adventures to come. Zoey had written underneath:

Oops, what a fashion faux pas, wearing the same clothes.

Lucie smiled to herself, as she carried on flicking through. She stopped at a picture of her and Nick in St Lucia. Zoey had caught the moment perfectly. She and Nick; gazing into each others eyes, about to kiss. Just looking at it gave her goose bumps. That wasn't a good sign. If she was like this over a photo what would she be like on Sunday?

Thursday morning was staff training in Zoey's shop, meaning the branch didn't open till 10 o'clock. If head office hadn't sent any compulsory training through then Larry would lock himself in the foreign exchange booth to verify the till and take the opportunity to shout "Super cash does it again!" when everything balanced. The girls used the time wisely, doing the window offers without being disturbed by customers and more importantly...discussing their love lives. Although at the moment Lucie was the hot topic of conversation.

"I really don't know what to do girls." Zoey sighed.

"I think you should go with Lucie to meet Nick," Suze advised.

“I don’t know if I want any part of this…”

“I think you should go, if they meet up on their own, there’s more chance of them nipping under the restaurant table for a quickie and if you are there, well that wont happen will it?”

Zoey pulled a face at Callie.

“She’s got a point Zo,” Suze started as she idly coloured in the word –FLORIDA- in red felt tip on her window card. “You’ll be able to see any little sparks re lighting and put them out.”

“Maybe,” Zo sighed. “I just don’t like not telling Adam, it feels wrong.”

“Lucie said she wants to met him to get closure, so if that happens, then there’s nothing to tell. If it doesn’t, well, we’ll cross that bridge when we come to it,” Callie advised.

Sensing that Zoey could do with a change of subject, Suze stepped in.

“Hey guess what I read in HEAT this week?”

Zoey and Callie looked at her expectantly.

“Richard Madeley said when he and Judy were trying to conceive he dunked his balls in freezing cold water.”

“Urgh, why does he think we need to know that, think I’m gonna puke.”

“Are you telling me this as a suggestion to improve my chances of getting pregnant?” Zoey laughed.

“Well, if it worked for Richard and Judy…”

“Think I would have trouble convincing Adam.”

“Is that baby talk going on out there?” Larry was temporarily distracted from counting the euros at the possible mention of one of his staff going on maternity leave. “I’ve told you girls, I need twelve months notice.”

Zoey rolled her eyes. “Boss, I’ve already given you twelve months notice. Just hope it doesn’t take that long.”

"Take some advice from someone older and wiser kid, stick to watching T.V. love, it's more fun."

"He gets worse," Callie groaned.

Later that evening Lucie and Ant met Zoey and Adam in the local pub, The Nelson, for the pub quiz. Zoey had just finished telling them about the Richard Madeley incident.

Adam nearly choked on his pint. "Where did Suze get that nugget of information from?"

"HEAT magazine."

"I have to confiscate that from my year nines."

"Ooh, bring it home then, it'll save me buying a copy," Zoey grinned.

Lucie just shook her head and rolled her eyes at Zo. She felt more like her normal self tonight. When the guys had been at the bar earlier Zoey had told her that she would come with her on Sunday, but she'd made it clear to Lucie that she wasn't happy about keeping it from Adam. Lucie couldn't really blame her, it was a big ask.

"Right guys, we need to improve on our dismal effort from the last quiz. We cannot come last for the third month running," Ant tried to rally the troops.

"We would have done ok last month if they hadn't confiscated my mobile, I wasn't really cheating. I was only asking Suze if she happened to know who the youngest member of Take That was."

Zoey shrugged her shoulders.

"Yeah, and managed to get ten points deducted from us."

The quiz began:-

What is the currency of Vietnam?

"You girls should get this easily," Adam smiled.

Zoey and Lucie nodded at each other and grinned. Zo

wrote the answer down, careful not to let any of the other teams in on the answer.

"You are so lucky you missed out on that conference call today. As usual Larry pretended he was too busy so I had to go on it..."

What song knocked Wet Wet Wet's Love is all around off the top spot in 1994?

"...Old Bushy was having a right rant; fortunately our shop escaped the wrath. I did a big cruise booking yesterday morning so he was pleased with that."

"No doubt I'll have the notes from that to look forward to tomorrow," Lucie pulled a face.

Adam and Ant exchanged a look, this was the real reason that they did so crap on the quiz, the girls just couldn't stop talking.

In Friends, what is Joey and Chandler's favourite TV programme?

The lads grinned at each other; at least they knew the answer to that one.

Lucie was in bed alone, Ant was downstairs. He always liked to catch the headlines on sky sports news before he came to bed. She lay looking up into the darkness. She had really enjoyed this evening. Zoey didn't seem to be in too much of a knark with her, which was a relief. Despite Ant's motivational chat at the beginning of the quiz they had yet again come last, but that was half the fun. They strolled back from the pub, hand in hand, making the ten minute walk more like twenty minutes.

"Do you really think Zo will make Adam dunk his balls in freezing water?" Ant had laughed.

"Well, if she doesn't get pregnant soon, maybe."

"Just don't ask me to do stuff like that when it's our turn."

Lucie hadn't really known how to respond to that, they'd never really had a conversation about babies, when to have them, did they actually want to have them... surely when you were married, that type of conversation was normal. It didn't come easy to her. She thought of Zo and Adam, they were so relaxed together and they clearly adored each other. Why was it so different for her and Ant? Things seemed to be getting slightly too serious at the moment and she didn't like it.

Ant came into the bedroom. He was trying to be quiet, thinking she was asleep, but even if she had been, by the time he'd banged into the wardrobe... *"Shit"*.

Stubbed his toe on the end of the bed...

"Shit".

She would have woken up anyway.

"Its ok babe, I'm awake."

"Sorry, kiddo, would've been up earlier, but there was some breaking news on sky sports, Gerrard's fit for the match on Saturday."

Lucie laughed. "Thank God for that, I thought I'd be up all night worrying."

He got into bed and pulled her close.

"You may mock, but it's been worrying me this week," he grinned as he leaned over and began to kiss her neck. She tilted her head as his kisses trailed from her neck along to her throat. She let out a moan, she turned her head to his and kissed him. He let his hands run through her hair. Their kisses became deeper, more urgent. She pulled him nearer. In her mind she was transported back, back to a night out at sea, out on deck, with Nick.

"Luce," Ant moaned through his kisses.

Oh. My. God. What was she thinking? She was in bed with her husband, fantasising about somebody else. Lucie pulled away from him.

"What's wrong?"

"I, er, I have really bad stomach cramps... I think I'm due on," she mumbled.

"Hey come here," he moved over so that she could cuddle against him. He lay his hand on her stomach and gently stroked it. "Does that help?"

"Yes," she whispered. Now she felt terrible, he was being so sweet and loving and she was thinking about an amazing sex session she'd had. The sooner she met Nick and got him out of her system the better.

Nick was out on the balcony. He'd gotten into a habit of having a coffee out there before he went to bed. He probably wouldn't be able to do it for much longer, there was a definite nip in the air tonight. It was almost bringing him out in goose bumps. That brought a smile to his face and made him think of Lucie. He always loved how much the affect his touch had on her. Steve had been right, she was so worth it. If only he'd known at the time. It was only after she'd gone that he realised for the first time and only time in his life, he'd fallen in love. He had been so tempted as they said goodbye to ask her to stay. He could've easily gotten her a job on the ship. Still maybe it wasn't too late, maybe he hadn't missed his chance. He only had two days to wait to find out.

CHAPTER FOURTEEN

Saturday morning in Zoey's branch of BOOK IT! And she was still stressing about the meeting with Nick tomorrow.

"You just need a plan that's all," Suze advised.

"Ooh, I've got it. Make an excuse to go to the loo..." Callie started all excited.

Zoey pulled a face "D'you think they'll fall for that? It's a bit far fetched."

"No, listen. About half way through lunch, go to the loo. Take your time, apply more make up, check facebook on your phone, send a text, whatever. When you come out tell them you got a call while you were in the loo to explain the length of time you were away."

"All this because...?" Suze asked.

"Because, when Zo leaves them on their own, their true feelings may come out and if they do, they will act differently. Zo will therefore notice any change in their behaviour." Callie grinned.

"Elaborate plan." Zoey said sarcastically.

"You may mock, but I've watched the psychologists on Big Brother."

"'I may as well give it a whirl. The sooner this whole Nick palaver is over the better."

"Girls? Any chance of any work getting done out there today?"

"Yes, Larry." They chorused.

The following day Zoey was driving her little purple Corsa along the M53 toward Chester. Lucie was sitting in the passenger seat, fidgeting nervously.

"You ok?"

"Why wouldn't I be?"

"Well, it's a big thing for you seeing Nick after all this time."

"It's no big deal. We're just catching up with an old friend that's all."

"Yeah that's why you're in your Sunday best and you had your hair done yesterday."

Lucie didn't reply. She knew Zoey was still mad at her for making her keep this little rendezvous from Adam. "Look I'm sorry ok. I know you're still pissed off at me for asking you to keep this quiet, but this is just something I need to do on my own – well with you."

"It's only 'coz it's you. I wouldn't do this for anyone else."

"I know. I appreciate it." Lucie turned to look out of the window.

Zoey tried to distract herself with the radio. She felt uneasy about the whole thing. She knew how intense Lucie and Nick's romance had been and she didn't know if they'd be able to resist each other second time around. Poor Ant was oblivious to the whole thing. She turned the radio up and began to sing along;

Can't read my, can't read my; no he can't read my poker face...
...p, p, p p, p, poker face my p,p,p,p, poker face.

Nick tapped his fingers nervously on the table as he waited in the Slug and Lettuce on Bridge Street for Lucie and Zoey. He glanced at his watch, five to one. The door opened, he glanced up. It wasn't them. He took a sip of his Budweiser.

"Nick?" He looked up, there they were. Zoey with her usual happy smiling face and Lucie... God she hadn't changed, still as beautiful as ever. He pushed his chair right back as he stood to greet them. The three of them ended up in some kind of group hug, with a lot of laughter going on which resulted in some strange looks from other diners. The trio sat down noisily as the excitement of meeting up again hit them.

"Oh my God. I can't believe we're finally all together again, you both look fantastic," Nick grinned.

"Life at sea certainly agrees with you, you've still got those boyish looks, and probably still the charm to go with it," Zoey laughed.

"Too right," he smiled and winked at Lucie.

Lucie was aware she was staring at him. Here she was, finally with Nick. It all seemed so unreal, like if she reached out and touched him; he'd disappear. Zo was right he hadn't changed, he was still totally gorgeous and he still made her heart leap. It was like the last five years hadn't happened.

"So, c'mon girls, fill me in. Tell me what you've been up to since those crazy two weeks in the Caribbean."

This was the bit Zoey felt uneasy about, how much was Lucie gonna tell Nick? Surely she'd tell him she was married, course she would. Lucie looked over to her, looks like it was down to her to start.

"Well, we're still sending people on holiday..."

"Oh, and you're married now aren't you? He's a lucky guy Zo," he smiled warmly.

"I think it was me that got lucky."

“She’s not the only one who made it down the aisle.”

“Don’t tell me someone finally made an honest woman of you?”

Zoey tried to read Nick’s face as he digested this information, but whatever he was thinking didn’t betray him.

“Yep. Old married woman now,” Lucie smiled, albeit awkwardly

“Wow. Well congratulations you two.”

“We’re married to brothers’, twins in fact.”

Nick grinned. “That’s so typical of you two; you don’t do anything by halves.”

The conversation flowed as they caught up on memories of “Oceania“. They laughed as they remembered B.O. Barbara’s infatuation with Nick and Steve and all the mad dancing Steve and Zo had done. Things were going well but Zoey was a little concerned that neither of them had mentioned their romance. She decided it was as good a time as any to put her plan into action.

Zoey sat in the cubicle. Lucie and Nick hadn’t seemed at all suspicious when she’d told them she was popping to the loo; she’d have been more surprised if they had. She sent Suze and Callie a text.

Operation oceania in2 action ;-0

Right, she’d sent a text, time for a wee. She glanced at her watch. Only two minutes had passed. Ok, she could waste another minute washing her hands then time to check out Facebook.

Lucie felt the atmosphere change the minute Zoey left the table. Right up until that moment it had been really relaxed between the three of them. Now it had all changed. She was staring at Nick.

He was doing the same to her, he couldn't take his eyes off her taking in every little detail about each other. Even down to the little freckle above her left eye. Nick spoke first.

"I can't believe you're here, sitting opposite me and looking even more beautiful than I remembered."

She blushed. "It's been a long time Nick." Oh My God, what a cliché. She seriously couldn't believe she'd just come out with that.

"Right now five years feels like five minutes." He reached across and took her hand in his. She didn't pull her hand away; she just gazed into his deep blue eyes. They were so familiar; she could feel herself falling under their spell again.

"I've thought about you so much, wondered what you've been doing all this time and now it appears I've let you walk out of my life again..."

"Again?"

"I knew the minute you left the ship that I shouldn't have let you go. I could've easily gotten you a job on the ship, but I couldn't ask you to give up your life back home for me. Now I've lost my chance a second time."

He fiddled with the diamond on her engagement ring. "Now I'm in the same boat! I can't ask you to give you life up," he sighed. "I was stupid to think that after all this time you'd be waiting for me, we'd lost touch. Of course some guy was gonna come along and sweep you off your feet."

"I would've stayed. On the ship. If you asked, I would've stayed," she whispered.

"Don't tell me that. Not know I know I can't be with you."

"I loved you."

"I love you," he murmured.

Lucie instantly felt the hairs on the back of her neck tingle. He was stroking her hand as he spoke. How the hell did you get goose bumps on your hands?

She was still lost in his eyes. How could he just walk back into her life after all this time and still manage to have this affect on her. She was older now, wiser, married....

"So. Where do we go from here?"

Even if Lucie knew the answer, she couldn't reply. She spotted Zoey coming back across the restaurant. She pulled her hand back across the table. All she had to do was act normal.

"Sorry I was so long guys, would you believe my mobile went off when I was in the loo. Typical eh?"

Lucie just shrugged her shoulders and smiled.

Zoey sat down, discreetly eyeing them both for any changes to their behaviour. The problem was, she didn't know what she was looking for. Lucie kept giggling, but she had worked her way through a bottle of Blossom Hill. So she was bound to be a bit tipsy. Nick was charm personified. Which was exactly how she remembered him; although he seemed to have outgrown the cheesy lines, which could only be a bonus.

The laughter and the chat continued. Lucie's phone beeped at the same time as Zoey's.

"The boys." They grinned at each other.

Zoey was first to her phone. "Yep, they're on there way back from the match and they want us to meet up at the club for a quick drink."

"Yeah, heard that one before, we'll be there all night."

"We best make a move."

They quickly exchanged mobile numbers with each other. Nick stood up first, pulling the chairs out for the girls. He gave Zoey a big hug and a kiss, and then he turned to Lucie. "I can't tell you how amazing it's been to see you again." He leaned closer to her and gently kissed her cheek. Lucie was hit with a mixture of emotions and senses. He still smelt like sun tan lotion and heat (they really should bottle that stuff it was an amazing aphrodisiac), his kiss was like a switch turning something on deep inside her. She knew she could never see him again. It would be too dangerous. She really couldn't trust herself to be alone with him. She could feel the fire in her belly, she knew it would be working outwards and she'd be blushing again.

"I'll be in touch."

She nodded. What was that conversation she'd just had with herself?

As it happened the quick drink at the club really was that. Adam had an early meeting at school the next day and he didn't think it was a good idea to be hung over. Lucie and Ant stayed a bit longer. The team had won their game that day which meant they were now in the semi final of the Cheshire Plate.

The singing had already started. Ed was standing on a table:

"Oh Fluffy Sheep," he began to the tune of "When the Saints."

"Oh Fluffy sheep." A chorus of drunken rugby players sang back.

Oh fluffy sheep are wonderful,
Coz they're white and they're fluffy.
Oh fluffy sheep are wonderful.

The lads all cheered and the singing got louder and ruder.

Zoey was driving home. Although not drunk, Adam had downed far too many "celebratory" pints to drive. As she drove he leaned across and squeezed her thigh.

"Missed you loads today babe."

"How can you miss me when you're running around a rugby pitch?"

"'Coz you're my lucky mascot. I always play better when you're cheering me on. Anyway, how was the shopping trip? You and Luce went to Chester didn't you?"

"Err yeah. It was interesting."

"Sounds ominous."

"Well, Luce made me keep something secret. I had a row with her about it 'coz I never keep anything from you, but it's all sorted now so I can tell you. Which is a relief."

"Zo, what the hell are you talking about?"

"Remember when me and Luce were on the ship and we met that guy Nick?"

"How can I remember? I didn't know you then."

"You know what I mean. I've told you about him."

"Oh yeah, Luce had a bit of a thing for him didn't she?"

"Yeah something like that." She indicated and turned the car into their road.

"Well anyway, after all this time he finally got in touch and we met him for lunch today."

"For lunch? Why did you have to keep it a secret?"

"Lucie didn't want Ant to find out and she thought if you knew, you'd tell Ant."

"Damn right I would've. Does it not strike you as strange that she wanted to meet up with some guy she had a fling with and not tell her husband? Is that what marriage is all about? Would you do that to me?" He was getting irate.

"Of course I wouldn't. Look all she wanted to do was put an end to that part of her life and she didn't feel it was worth worrying Ant about it." She tried to explain.

"What if it isn't the end?"

"It is. I saw it with my own eyes, there is nothing

between them anymore. They're just friends." Zo swung the car into the space outside their house.

"You're an expert all of a sudden?" He jumped out of the car and went straight into the house.

"Adam! Wait!"

"So you would've just let her have an affair with this guy and kept it from me and Ant?" he shouted as they got into the hall way.

"Of course I wouldn't. That's exactly what I was trying to stop. If there had been something between them then I could've tried to nip it in the bud."

"Saint Zoey are we now?"

"Oh Ads, don't be like that. All I wanted to do was stop anyone getting hurt. Mainly Ant and you're making out that I'm the bad one in all of this."

"I can't even talk to you at the moment."

Lucie and Ant were still at the rugby club. The atmosphere was buzzing and neither of them were in a rush to get home. They wanted to squeeze every last minute of the weekend in before they had to start thinking about the working week.

"You look lovely tonight Luce," Ant grinned at her as they stood at the bar. He slipped his arm around her waist.

"Do I?"

"Yeah, you have this glow about you."

"It's being with you, you mean so much to me."

"Not as much as you mean to me," he swayed slightly. "I know I only tell you when I've had a few, but I mean it y'know."

She looked at the floor. She felt awful. Nothing had happened between her and Nick today, but the fact that if it had, she probably wouldn't have been able to stop it, made her feel guilty. She looked back up to Ant. He had that drunken glazed look in his eyes. It made her smile, when he was like this he was so open, nowhere near as quiet as he was normally. She leaned over to kiss him, standing on her tip toes to reach his lips. She did love him, maybe not as passionately as she loved Nick, but Ant was special to her.

He kissed her back, encircling her in his arms.

"Oi, Mr and Mrs Macca, get a room." One of his team mates shouted.

He pulled away and grinned at her. "Sounds like a plan, I think I should take you home."

Zoey was having trouble sleeping and she wasn't the only one. As she lay awake in bed she could hear Adam next to her, she could tell by the way he was breathing that he wasn't asleep. They never went to bed on an argument and she knew that would be why he was still awake. This was stupid. He might be happy to huff and puff all night long but she wasn't. It wouldn't look very professional if she was yawning her head off in front of customers. If they didn't sort this out now it would set a precedent for future disagreements.

"Adam?"

He didn't respond so she whispered his name again.

"What?"

"This is silly, we're lying here awake, neither of us able to sleep. We should talk."

He sighed and turned on his side to face her. "I just can't believe you'd lie to me Zo."

"I was just trying to do what I thought was best that's all. If I'd told you about Luce meeting Nick it would've put you in an awkward position with Ant and I didn't want to do that to you. It wouldn't have been fair. Obviously if things between Luce and Nick looked like something could happen, then I would've told you."

"It just seems weird, you and Lucie going off to meet some guy she used to go out with and wanting to be so secretive about it."

"I know, I wasn't comfortable with it and she knows that. She just wanted to get some closure."

"I suppose it's stupid for us to fall out over something that doesn't really involve us."

"Exactly. Honestly Adam, I just want to forget about this."

"Come here babe," he pulled her close. "I hate it when we fight."

"Me too." She snuggled closer to him, loving the feeling of being in his strong arms. It sounded stupid but she felt thinner when she was being held by him.

"I love you so much Zo."

"Don't know why, but I'm so glad you do."

He manoeuvred himself up onto his elbows. "How many times do I have to tell you babe? You are everything to me." He lowered his lips onto hers and took her back into his arms.

"I love you." she whispered in between kisses.

"That's better, that's what I wanted to hear."

She could hear his smile in his voice. She was so relieved they were talking again and she was happy that Lucie could put all this Nick business behind her. Which was just as well because if it had gone in an other direction things could've gotten awkward for all of them.

Lucie and Ant had barely got through their front door before they started kissing passionately and pulling at their clothes. They didn't even make it up to the bedroom. They had mad, frenzied sex on the stairs. It was quick and urgent, like it was the most important thing in the world right then. They lay panting on the stairs, sweaty and hot.

"God Luce, that was amazing," Ant stroked her damp hair.

He was right; it had been pretty damn hot. Not like their normal sex life. It was like something had awakened in her. Now what could've caused that she wondered? She heard her phone beep somewhere by the front door where she'd dumped her clothes.

Ant was in danger of falling asleep on the stairs, the alcohol and sex a heavy sedative. She nudged him. "You go up babe, I won't be long."

She went over and picked up her clothes and grabbed her phone. There was only one number that wasn't stored by name in her phone.

Sweet dreams x

A little smile spread across her face.

CHAPTER FIFTEEN

"So…. How did it go?" Suze asked Zo as they settled down to work on Monday Morning.

"It was actually ok. It was great to see Nick again and it was totally fine. Lucie and Nick were like two old friends. It's such a relief."

"See I told you people could be friends with their exes these days," Callie butted in.

"Well it seems in this case you were right. So it's all over and done with now, which is just as well 'coz me and Adam had a huge row about it."

"You and Adam argued?" Suze asked, shocked.

Zoey grinned. "Yep, it does happen every now and then."

"Keeps things fresh doesn't it."

Zoey rolled her eyes at Suze. "Yes, Callie, it does."

"It's all sorted now though. I think Luce spent a lot of time wondering, what if…. now she can see it for what it was, just a holiday romance."

"At least you don't have to worry about it anymore."

"God, I know. Could you imagine the hassle it would've caused if there had still been something between them? Not just with Lucie and Ant but me and Adam would've ended up getting dragged into it too."

Callie smiled. "Well, it's all well that ends well."

Lucie had spent most of the day in the back office sorting out the piles of brochures. The next edition's had just been launched, so they'd been inundated with them. It was a job they all hated doing, but she had far too much nervous energy so she may as well put it to good use. Also, she didn't trust herself to concentrate a hundred percent on her customers today. Her head was in the shed, totally all over the place. It had taken her ages to fall asleep last night; the mad frenzied sex with Ant obviously hadn't worn her out. When she eventually fell asleep, she dreamt about Nick. At that moment the lack of sleep hit her. She looked around at the stack of brochures still left to move and sighed. Her mobile beeped, she pulled it out of her pocket and pressed the button to open the envelope.

> gr8 2 bump in 2 u ystday need advice on cruise hol can u help? Meet for coffee?

Lucie smiled to herself, he obviously wanted to make it sound business like. If David Beckham could *allegedly* get caught out by a mobile, anyone could. Not that she had anything to feel guilty about. All she'd done was meet Nick for lunch, hardly the crime of the century and they'd been chaperoned! She returned the text straight away.

> coffee would b gr8 when r u free? ;o)

They sent various texts and coffee had changed to a quick drink in Wetherspoons, round the corner from her shop after work. She then sent a message to Ant to let him know she'd be late home as she was going for a drink after work. Technically she wasn't hiding anything but she knew he would assume that it would be with the guys from work. She brushed the sense of unease to one side, just as she'd been trying to forget all day that Nick said he loved her. She looked at the brochures again; suddenly they didn't seem so bad.

Nick arrived early at Wetherspoons, as he was new to the area he wasn't sure how long it would take him to get from place to place. He stood at the bar drinking a pint of Fosters. It had just gone five o'clock; he knew Lucie would be another half hour or so. He felt even more nervous today than he did yesterday. Although today was different, it would just be him and Luce and he'd also laid his heart on the line yesterday. He'd never felt like this about anyone except Lucie, was it love? He thought so, or to quote Prince Charles, "What ever love is." He pulled a face, not a good comparison, that didn't end well. On the one hand he was excited about meeting up with her again, but on the other hand she may have only agreed to see him again so she could tell him face to face that she didn't want to see him anymore. He couldn't believe she was married, if she'd just had a boyfriend then maybe he might've had a slim chance, she might've been prepared to end that relationship and be with him. But marriage was a whole different ball game; literally, her husband was a bloody rugby player. Nick liked to keep himself in shape, but he didn't fancy his chances against a rugby player.

He saw Lucie before she saw him; she strode confidently through the pub. He smiled, she looked very businesslike in her uniform and with her hair pinned back and her black rimmed glasses, she had that whole sexy thing going on. She scanned the room looking for him; he raised his pint glass to her. As she got nearer he noticed she was carrying cruise brochures under her arm. He couldn't help but laugh.

"What's so funny?"

"What's with the cruise brochures?"

"Just in case I bump into anyone…it'll look like I'm talking shop."

"Or, it looks like your planning a romantic break with your mysterious lover," he grinned.

She pulled a face, but couldn't help blushing at the same time. It made him smile.

"Sorry, Luce, I didn't mean to tease you. Let's start this properly. Can I get you a drink?"

"The usual."

"One Bacardi Breezer coming up," he winked at her.

They sat at a table in the corner, the cruise brochures stacked, unopened between them.

"So, where were we?" Lucie asked nervously.

"I think we were at the point where I told you that I love…"

"Don't," Lucie interrupted. "Don't tell me that."

"It's true."

"Nick, I'm married now. You can't just expect us to take up where we left off," she smiled sadly.

He ran his hand through his hair. "So what you're saying is if you weren't married it would be all systems go?"

"What I'm saying is, I've only been married a year. I owe it to Ant to not give up on my marriage at the first hurdle."

"You owe it to Ant? Strange choice of words Luce…"

"Nick, stop it. This is hard enough as it is." She was

unable to take her eyes off him, particularly his lips. How easy it would be just to lean across and kiss him, to be in his arms again, to...

"Luce!"

"What?" she had gotten lost in her day dream.

"You were miles away."

"Thousands of miles away, a long time ago," she sighed.

"I wish we could go back in time, I never should've let you go."

"Doesn't matter how much we wish that, we can't and y'know maybe that was our time maybe that was all we were supposed to have."

"Look Luce, I'm not gonna give up on you, yeah, yeah I know you're married...but I just don't think this is it for us. I'm not gonna put pressure on you, I just want you to know that I'm ready when you are."

Lucie didn't know what to say, she wished she could just say to him there would never be a Lucie and Nick, but deep down she wasn't sure. When did everything get so complicated? She glanced at her watch, she better get home soon...to Ant.

"It's ok. I know you have to leave. I'll run you home."

"Thanks Nick. Look, maybe its best if we don't see each other for a while. I need to get my head together and I don't now if I can trust myself around you."

"Well, that's a good sign," he winked.

Despite herself she couldn't help but smile.

"C'mon then you, I best get you home."

She asked Nick to drop her off at the bottom of her road. Ant would be home, she didn't really want him to see her getting out of a strange blokes car. Nick brought the car to a stand still, he turned to face her.

"I will be in touch," she said.

"Like I said, I'll be waiting."

She looked down, not wanting to get lost in his eyes again. "I'm sorry."

"What for?"

She had to stop herself from saying, being married. "For not waiting for you."

He reached out and put his arm around her shoulders. "Well in that case, I'm sorry for not asking you to wait." With his other hand he gently stroked her cheek, turning her face to his. She knew what was coming; she couldn't have stopped it, even if she wanted to. His lips were on hers, their tongues dancing around together. He pulled her closer to him; she sunk into his kiss, her body responding as if it was making up for lost time. She moved her head slightly, breaking the kiss up. She licked her lips, tasting him on them.

"We have to stop," she whispered.

He nodded his head slowly as he nuzzled her neck.

"Nick," she breathed.

He pulled back; lifting his hands up to show he wasn't touching her anymore. "Hey I'm sorry, I can't help it. I see you, I wanna kiss you, touch you..."

"Right. I really have to go. I can't do this now."

"Until next time," Nick said as she opened the car door to get out.

Lucie opened her front door, attempting to put a look of normality on her face. She knew she'd done the right thing telling Nick she needed some space, but God that kiss... it wasn't just a thanks for the drink kiss, it was a, I haven't seen you in five years and I still fancy the arse off you kiss.

"Ant?" She hung her jacket on the end of the stairs, the house seemed strangely quiet, no TV or music on. She called out again, still no reply.

Ant was always home by this time. She headed off into the kitchen, opening the fridge and cupboards trying to decide what to have for tea.

Spag Bol? Nah she wasn't in the mood.

Jacket Potatoes? Hmm, maybe.

"Hey babe," Ant was walking through the door. "Didn't feel like cooking, too hung over from last night, really am getting to old to drink on a school night. I thought we'd have a take away, just timed it right hey." He plonked the take away bags down on the worktop, kissing her on the cheek.

Lucie's heart plummeted through to her stomach. He had no idea how good his timing had been, five minutes earlier he'd have walked past Nick's car and witnessed his wife snogging another guy. What was she doing? She leant against the cupboard to steady herself from the nausea that was sweeping through her.

"Hey," Ant steadied her. "You ok kiddo? You've gone really pale."

"I'm fine, just haven't had time to eat much today, you know what it's like when you get stuck with customers for four hours at a time."

"Get this down you; I've got your favourite, sweet and sour chicken. Then go and relax in a nice hot bath." He enclosed her in his arms, pulling her to him and kissed her softly.

Could he tell that five minutes earlier she'd been kissing someone else? Evidently not, he was smiling at her as he pulled away.

"While you're in the bath, I can watch the Liverpool match."

Lucie pulled a face. "There was me thinking you were all concerned."

"Always, kiddo."

Ant was settled in front of the telly cheering as Gerrard slammed the ball into the goal. “You beauty!”

Lucie decided it was time for that bath, she didn’t mind watching footie, but watching it with Ant was a nightmare. He couldn’t keep still. She headed out of the living room, her phone beeped in her pocket.

Check ur bag :-)

She went back into the kitchen, grabbed her hand bag and started searching through it. Inside she found a rectangle box, wrapped in silver paper. She wondered how he’d managed to put that in their without her knowing. She dropped it back into her bag and took it upstairs. She sat on the edge of the bed, reopened her bag and took out the box. She started to pull at the paper, but her fingers were shaking. She took a depth breath. What was she getting all worked up about? She counted to five in her head and then started on the paper again. As soon as she saw the pale blue box, she knew what was inside. She opened it slowly; there it was... a silver Tiffany bracelet.

CHAPTER SIXTEEN

"Good afternoon, thank you for calling BOOK IT! Jake speaking."

"Hey Jake speaking, it's Zo."

"Hiya honey, how ya doing?"

"Fine. You sound cheerful; shouldn't you have a hang over?"

"A hangover? Why?"

Lucie's head immediately shot up in his direction.

"Thought you lot went for a drink after work."

"We went for a drink after work?"

Lucie was nodding her head furiously.

"Sorry Zo, I must've been so drunk that I forgot. You know what I'm like."

"Hmm, yeah. Is Luce free?"

"Is Lucie free?"

Lucie shook her head.

"D'you know what Zo, a customer's just sat down with her. I'll get her to ring you."

He put the phone down and glared at Lucie.

"Lucie Maxwell, in the back now."

She followed him through the secure line door and into the brochure room.

"Why would you tell your best mate that you were out with work, when you obviously weren't?"

She plonked herself down on a stack of Turkey brochures. "There's no point me trying to lie is there?"

"Not in the slightest, Luce."

"You can't tell anyone, especially not Zo."

"Let me guess, Nick?"

She looked shocked. "How d'you know?"

"Let's just say I was waiting for it to happen. You can so tell you're not over him."

"Oh my God. Is it that obvious?"

"So spill, where were you last night?"

"Spoons, and yes I was with Nick. We were just catching up, but well, we ended up having a bit of a kiss."

"A bit of a kiss?"

"Well a lot of a kiss."

"So that's it? Is he out of your system?"

"Well that's just it, he's never been out of my system and I think I might've made it worse."

"Where does Ant figure in all this?"

She put her face in her hands. "Oh God J, I don't know. I love Ant, I really do, but I have feelings for Nick too. We're supposed to be giving each other some space…but we haven't stopped texting all morning. He wants to meet up again on Sunday. Ant has an away match. I know it's wrong…"

"You've surprised me, Luce."

"Why?"

"I thought you'd have more respect than to mess with people's feelings like this."

"Look, it's my life and my mistakes."

"You're right, but it's Ant's marriage too."

"I know, I know. I just need time to sort it out."

"So are you meeting him on Sunday?"

Lucie stood up and nodded. "Yep. I'm gonna tell him it's over. Right now, I need to get back to work."

"Wish I could believe you Luce," he sighed as she disappeared back into the shop.

Lucie was in Zoey's kitchen watching her cooking and waiting for the lads to come back from training. Lucie poured two glasses of wine.

"So how was your day?" Zoey asked as she lifted a spoon to her lips to taste her cooking.

"Oh the usual, people wanting to go away for next to nothing, but expecting five star hotels."

"Gets you down sometimes," Lucie sighed.

"Anything else bothering you? You seem really quiet tonight."

"I'm fine, just tired that's all."

They heard the front door go, kit bags dumped in the hall, chattering and laughter as the lads came down the hall.

"Hey babe, we've brought a reprobate home with us," Adam shouted from the hall.

"Hey sis, what's for tea?" Ed bounded into the kitchen like Tigger on speed.

"Just as well I've made extra, it's only scouse."

"How is the gorgeous Lucie?

"Looking forward to seeing her gorgeous husband," she replied as she looked past Ed to where Ant and all of his six foot two solid rugby player's body filled the door frame. He smiled, flashing off that cute dimple of his.

"Damn you Anthony Maxwell, if you hadn't arrived on the scene, I would've been in there."

Zoey snorted. “In yer dreams Ed.”

“I tell ya Zo, if these two pretty boys hadn’t turned up it would’ve only been a matter of time until Luce fell for my charms.”

Ant laughed. “Sorry to have ruined your plans.”

“And what irresistible charms would they be?” Zoey asked.

Realising the conversation wasn’t going quite the way he wanted, he tried a different tack. “Anyway, you two freak me out. Look at the pair of you standing there like tweedle dum and tweedle dee. When we’re on the pitch in our kits, I don’t even know which one’s which.”

Zoey laughed. “You sound like Callie in work. Twins freak her out too. I told her we buy them matching jumpers for Christmas.”

“Matching jumpers, not a bad idea.”

“Adam! Don’t encourage her, it took us twenty two years to stop mum buying us matching outfits. If she could hear us now she’d be straight down M&S buying two of everything,” Ant mocked.

“Matching bloody jumpers, you’re all insane. There’s only me and Luce not getting involved in this madness. See babe, we could’ve been perfect for each other.”

“Edward, will you behave. She’s a married woman, off limits. Get that into your thick ‘ead.”

Zoey looked at Lucie, expecting her to be laughing, but she looked miles away with a strange expression on her face. Something was obviously bothering her.

“Err, right guys, teas ready.”

“And after tea, you can all sod off. Zoey and I need some baby making time.” Adam tried to lighten the atmosphere that had suddenly appeared.

“Still not up the duff yet sis?”

“Obviously not Ed or we wouldn’t need the baby making time would we?” she slammed a plate down in front of him with more force than she'd intended. Ed looked shocked.

"Sorry sis... I didn't mean..."

"Oh just shut up Ed, sometimes I can't believe we're even related." She stormed out of the kitchen and went straight upstairs.

Adam found Zoey on the bed, her legs pulled up close to her chest, arms wrapped round them. Her eyes were red and puffy from crying. He'd finally managed to get rid of the others after they'd stuffed themselves with scouse. She looked up at him, her green eyes full of sadness. His heart went out to his wife. She desperately wanted a baby. He hoped his swimmers would hit the back of the net soon. He sat down next to her.

"You ok, babe?"

She nodded her head slowly. "I keep telling myself not to get stressed about it. We haven't even been trying that long, but I just can't stop thinking about babies and then bloody Ed with his flippant remarks; he does me 'ead in."

"Listen, Ed hasn't got a clue about relationships or emotions. He wouldn't know where to begin if he met a girl he really liked."

"I'm just being stupid aren't I? Some people try for years to have a baby; we've only been trying for five minutes."

"We just need to relax about it. I mean we don't have sex anymore, we make babies," he grinned as he spoke. "Let's just get back to the fun sex life we've always had and that might take the pressure off."

"Yeah, I have been obsessed by it."

"So we're agreed? We'll just chill out about it."

"Ok, but just before we relax about the baby thing, just a few suggestions... don't have your bath too hot, don't keep your mobile in your pocket and for God sake don't even think about starting to wear Y-fronts, your sperm might get over heated and not as effective." She looked deadly serious as she said this.

He laughed. "You would never catch me in Y-fronts. Come here; give us a hug and from now on, it's cold showers for me."

Lucie drove home from Zoey's the long way round, which took her along the prom. Ant was dropping Ed off in his car so she took the opportunity to have some time to get her head together. She loved driving along the prom; she had Kings of Leon blasting out from the CD player. She tapped her steering wheel and sang along as she drove alongside the River Mersey that at some point became the Irish Sea. On nights like tonight when you got a beautiful sunset you could easily forget that you were in the North West of England and imagine you were somewhere else on the planet. She pulled into a car park that belonged to a pub; it had a great view across the bay. There were still some people sitting in the beer garden enjoying the sunset. She needed to think. She turned the music down slightly so as not to distract her. She remembered back to those first few weeks after she left the ship. It was the one and only time in her life when she could say that her heart may have been broken. She had cried every day for a month, not in front of anyone, at night on her own. The second month was tears every other day. This was mixed together with a rollercoaster of emotions; she knew when Nick went to bed he probably wasn't thinking about her (although now she knew differently). It was more probable that after twenty hour days he would just fall asleep as soon as his head hit the pillow. Then by the third month she'd started to think he'd probably found someone else to focus his attentions on. Their emails had become less frequent and before she knew it she'd met Ant. She hadn't expected it to get as serious as it had; she certainly hadn't thought she'd end up marrying him. When she and Zo had first met the lads, Zo and Adam were really into each other. Lucie thought it might be fun to date Ant for a while, help her get her mind of Nick. Before she knew it, she was down the aisle and married. She sighed as she reached across and turned the music back up. The sun was almost gone, if she didn't head back home now Ant would be wondering where she was. She was still in deep thought during the five minute journey home. It wasn't that she wasn't happy with Ant, she was – at least she had been till Nick turned up. Now she was just confused.com.

CHAPTER SEVENTEEN

After her conversation with Jake, Lucie felt guilty enough not to meet up with Nick on Sunday. She'd told Jake whatever had been started was finished. He'd looked at her sceptically, she knew he didn't believe her but then again she didn't believe herself either. She decided her only option for the moment was to stay as far away from Nick as possible, she knew she couldn't trust herself alone with him. They were still texting, which just felt like a harmless bit of flirting, although if it was so innocent why did she delete the texts straight away? Then there was the bracelet, Ant wouldn't notice it but Zoey would. Maybe she should just tell her about the bracelet, she could laugh it off as a joke, but then she'd have to admit to meeting up with Nick again without Zo knowing. She felt like screaming, this was just nuts. She'd pretty much decided the more space she could put between herself and Nick the better, if she couldn't trust herself around him then she shouldn't put herself in that situation. Her inner voice was very happy with that decision, all well and good until fate stepped in. The manager of the Chester shop had been signed off sick for a few weeks and Bushy, the regional manager wanted Lucie to cover the branch. Zoey commented on the convenience of it all. "You might bump into Nick, have you heard from him at all?"

"Oh y'know just the odd text. I think he's busy trying to find his land legs."

"Really? He sounded bored the other day when he texted me, said he's not used to leisurely days."

"He texted you?" Lucie failed to hide the surprise in her voice.

"Why not, we're all mates aren't we?" Zo raised an eyebrow.

Lucie was sure Zo was getting suspicious; she'd commented frequently that she seemed pre occupied.
She tried to make light of the subject. "I'll be so busy in Chester branch, I probably won't even have time to go to the loo," she tried to laugh.

From the look on Zoey's face she could tell she didn't seem convinced.

Now three days into her first week at the Chester shop, not only had she found time to go to the loo, she'd managed to meet Nick for lunch twice...so much for keeping her distance from him. Despite the guilt she felt, she knew it wouldn't stop her meeting him again in about half an hour for lunch number three. Chester felt safe, it was far enough from home to feel like she wasn't really doing anything wrong.

Zoey was having a bad day, she'd already had a couple complaining they didn't get the double bed they'd requested and had to push to single bed together, which were far too small. She'd managed to shut them up by making a joke of it... "Isn't it more fun in a single?"

Then Larry managed to make himself scarce when there

was a regional conference call, apparently Greggs were about to run out of pasties. So she'd spent fifty minutes listening to Bushy drone on whilst Larry sat in the office shuffling paper, drinking coffee and eating a pastie and a steak bake. She'd been busy trying to think up ways to get back at him, like hiding his holiday tickets to Skiathos or better still accidentally cancelling his holiday altogether, so she ended up missing some points on the call. After the call she'd got way laid with another problem, so it was about an hour later when she finally got the chance to call Luce to catch up on what she'd missed. She rang Chester only to be told by one of the girls that Lucie had gone for lunch with her husband. As she slowly put the phone down she tried to process that bit of information. *Lucie had gone for lunch with her husband*... Ant worked in Liverpool, so it would be pretty difficult to meet Lucie in Chester, unless he had a day off...yeah maybe that was it. The niggle wouldn't go away. She picked up the phone again and called Jake.

"Hey Zo, how's your day going?" he asked cheerfully.

"Not quite sure yet. Y'know the staff night out you had the other week, where was it again?"

Jake was caught off guard. "Err...The Nelly, no err Weatherspoons, yeah we went to Spoons."

"Spoons? Ok then."

"Why? What's up?"

"Nothing."

There was a moment of silence.

"You know don't you?"

"That Lucie is currently having lunch with some guy who may or may not be her husband?"

"You think it's Nick?"

"Jake, please tell me I'm wrong, please tell me I'm a terrible person for suspecting my best mate is cheating on her husband."

"Look, I know as much as you. She swears there's nothing going on..."

"Are you off tomorrow?"

"Yeah, why?"

"Fancy a trip to Chester?"

Blissfully unaware of what was going on Lucie was wandering happily along the banks of the River Dee sharing a portion of "Dave's chippy chips" with Nick. It was a beautiful September afternoon, the last few weeks had been like an Indian summer. They walked along the river, under the bridge and into Grosvenor Park, which was full of students taking advantage of the warm sunshine and supposedly revising outside. Most of them looked like they were sleeping off last night's beer session on their picnic rugs. Nick took her hand as they strolled through, he felt her stiffen slightly.

"Luce, it's ok. Everyone is oblivious to us. We could strip off and run round naked. and they wouldn't bat an eye lid."

"I'm sure they would."

"Well yeah, they probably would, I was just trying to tempt you."

"You tempt me far too much."

He pulled her closer, swinging his arm around her shoulders. Her arm was around his waist, she looped her thumb into the belt hole of her jeans. It felt so natural to be like this, just like when they were in St Lucia, they hadn't been doing anything wrong then. So why shouldn't it be ok now? *You're married...*the voice in her head was starting to piss her off.

Grosvenor Park was so beautiful, in an elevated position overlooking the river and full of all different types of trees. They were just coming up to a huge conifer Tree which was like a gigantic cone. Nick broke away from her and started running around the base of it.

"You nutter," she laughed.

"You'll never catch me."

She began to run after him, he was right, the base of the tree was so big and round she felt like she was chasing nothing, although she could hear him laughing, so she knew he was still there.

"Gotcha!"

She felt his arms around her waist. "Thought I was chasing you."

"Think it's me doing the chasing Luce." He spun her round and pulled her tight. "I know you wanted space and we agreed not to do this, but I can't help myself."

She felt her skin break out in goose bumps, how could one person have such an effect on her? The air between them felt heavy, like a thunder cloud and the electricity between them was the lightening. He let his fingers trail through her hair, then along her neck and just under the material of her blouse to her collar bone. He stopped as he reached the top button and toyed with it. She wanted him to rip it off right there and then, in fact she thought her buttons might just spontaneously combust, but she had to remind herself she was in a very public place, even though they couldn't be seen behind the giant tree. He grinned at her and winked, she knew he was reading her mind, although he probably didn't have to delve that far, her desire was written all over her face.

"I want you Luce and I know you want me." It wasn't a question it was a statement.

"I just wish it was that easy..."

"It is..." He took her face in his hands, closing his eyes as he gently pulled at her lower lip. He felt her body relax against his as she surrendered to his kiss. He let his hand wander up her blouse, stroking her skin with the merest of touches. She reached up, running her hands through his hair and pulling him closer to her; his stubble scratched her chin but she didn't care. She moved her hands down his back towards his bum which felt so tight in his jeans. She squeezed it and pushed her body closer to his. It took her right back to that first kiss all those years ago, he still gave her that same heady feel. She reluctantly moved away. "I have to get back to work."

"Mmm," he murmured as he trailed her neck with kisses.

"Nick!" she tried to tell him off.

He laughed. "Sorry, you know what you do to me." He shrugged his shoulders.

"I really have to get back."

"Ok, as I can't tempt you to throw a sickie this afternoon, how 'bout you come back to mine after work?"

She looked at him, taking in those cheeky blue eyes and the even cheekier grin, he could charm the birds out of the trees. She had to stop this before it got more serious. She loved Ant, but here, now in this park it was like he didn't exist...but he did. The only sensible and right thing to do was to say no.

"Ok, I'll meet you after work but I can't stay long." So much for sticking to her guns.

She wasn't sure how she got through the afternoon; she was a mixture of a ball of excitement and a bubble of nerves. She knew exactly what would happen in Nick's flat, she knew it was wrong but the sane, rational part of her seemed to have jumped ship the minute she saw Nick for the first time in five years. She was planning on telling Ant she'd got held up with a customer then stuck in traffic on the way home. She just hoped she didn't really get stuck with a customer. *Would serve you right if you did.* God that voice was really doing her head in.

So there she was at quarter to six standing outside the door to Nick's building. She took a deep breath and pressed the buzzer. There was no going back now.

"Yo. C'mon up."

She nervously climbed the stairs to Nick's first floor flat, each step sending more butterflies to her stomach. He was already standing at the door, dressed in jeans and a white shirt, left open. She remembered that chest so well and could quite clearly recall resting her head on it as they slept in the posh cabin on the final night of the cruise. She was also very aware that she was gawping, he looked damn hot. She suddenly felt very unattractive in her blue polyester uniform.

"Hey lovely you, welcome to my crib." He held his arm out and led her into the flat.

She loved nosing around people's houses and Nick's was no exception. It was a typical lads' pad, huge wide screen TV embedded in the wall, minimal furniture, no real décor, massive sound system an X Box...seeing that made her think of Ant, he always said that after her and rugby his X Box was the dearest thing to his heart. God Ant, her lovely husband with the cute dimple and fabulous thighs...why did she need anyone else? Truth was, she didn't, she just had unfinished business with Nick. This really would be closure, one more time with Nick and that really would be it, had to be. He came up behind her and wrapped on arm around her waist, his head resting on her shoulder. His other hand snaked around her front and snuck under her top. She let her head fall back onto his shoulder and closed her eyes, she felt like she'd been transported back in time. She could almost feel the heat of the Caribbean, although maybe it wasn't the Caribbean that was so hot, maybe it had been them all along. The feel of his fingers lightly stroking her tummy made the fine hairs on her skin stand up and yep, there were the goose bumps, as always. She didn't stop him as he slowly undid the buttons on her blouse and slid it easily away from her body. She gasped as her bare back touched his chest, the heat from his body seared through hers. He spun her round, taking her hands in his, holding her out at arm's length. She felt overdressed in her skirt and bra as he looked her up and down.

"Luce, babes, you've got too many clothes on," he winked.

What was it with him? Why could he always tell what she thinking?

"How can you always read my mind?"

"Coz' I know we both have the same thought running through our heads," he pulled her close. "We've wasted too much time." He whispered as he picked her up and carried her into the bedroom, kissing her.

CHAPTER EIGHTEEN

Sitting in Starbucks opposite the Chester branch of 'BOOK IT' were Zoey and Jake. Operation 'overboard' was in process. Jake shifted uneasily in his chair. They'd been sitting there since ten thirty and were starting to get glares from the staff who were getting ready for the lunchtime rush. Why he agreed to this. he didn't know. He didn't like the idea of spying on Lucie and this entire undercover lark. Operation Overboard? Operation Over the Top more like.

"Ok, it's T minus ten minutes to sandwich." Zoey checked her watch.

Jake glanced at his and translated that to mean, it's nearly lunch time. She really was taking this far too seriously.

"Ok, so here's the POA..." she saw the blank look on his face. "Plan of Action, J, c'mon getcha head in game."

He nodded his head slowly then saluted. "Yes SIR!"

She pulled a face. "Right, you keep your eyes on the shop door, I'll keep a look out for Sailor boy..."

"Zo, do we really have to stick with these stupid names?"

She ignored him. "When Sailor boy makes contact with the target we will follow discreetly behind, if they pause, we pause. Be prepared to jump into a shop door way, we don't want to get spotted."

"Where is my standard issue ear piece?"

"J, this is serious. We could be about to discover something terrible."

"Yeah, but sometimes isn't it better not to know these things? There's nothing we can do about the situation." He lifted his cappuccino to his lips.

"I can't stand by and watch Luce, I mean the target wreck her marriage for some fly by night Sailor boy who could charm the knickers off a nun."

He spat his drink back into his cup.

"Oh here we go, here comes sailor boy."

They watched as Nick strolled up to the shop window.

"Look, he's clever; see how he makes it look like he's looking at the window cards?"

"Maybe he is Zo."

They watched as Nick hovered by the door and Lucie came out. Zoey could hear her heart pounding in her ears. She couldn't take her eyes off the scene in front of her; it was almost playing out in slow motion. Luce looking up at Nick and smiling, him brushing her hair back behind her ear, linking arms as they turned to walk. It could all be so innocent but yet it seemed so intimate. She had almost forgotten Jake was there until she heard him shout.

"All units, go, go, go!"

She grabbed her bag and ran out of Starbucks with Jake in tow.

"Remember, first rule of surveillance, don't look like you're following." She slowed down so they were at a safe distant not to be spotted, but where they could still see them.

Nick and Lucie were deep in conversation as they walked. It didn't look like it was a serious discussion; she could see them both laughing.

"Hmm, since when was adultery funny?"

"We don't know that's what's happening yet," Jake said. Nick and Lucie stopped and were looking in a shop window. Zoey stopped suddenly and crouched down to tie her shoe lace.

"Quick, get down! What type of shop is it? Can you see? Please tell me it's not a jewellers or an estate agent."

"Relax, it's a café. They're looking at the menu. What the flip are you doing?"

"What does it look like? I'm tying my laces."

"Err Zo, you haven't got laces."

"I know! I'm stalling so we don't catch them up."

"Seriously, you have got to stop watchin' Spooks and Diagnosis Murder repeats."

"What's wrong with Dick Van Dyke?"

"They're on the move again." Jake held his hand out and helped her up. They carried on following them as they turned out of Bridge Street and headed towards the clock bridge. They were holding hands now. Zoey felt sick to her stomach, it was perfectly obvious to her what was going on. They stopped again as they looked in another shop window. With the reflexes of a cat but the grace of an elephant Zoey shoved Jake literally into the shop door of the Disney Store.

"OWW!" he rubbed his head.

A member of staff wandered over "Err, how can we make you dreams come true today?"

Jake turned to the bewildered shop assistant. "Don't worry, we're fine. Don't mind her, few too many drinks with her lunch." He dragged a glaring Zoey away.

"Thank you for visiting the Disney store, have a truly magical day."

"Err, we will."

"What are you playing at? I'm not pissed?"

"No, but you threw me into a shop, wanna get arrested for assault?"

"This is ridiculous and we've lost sight of the target."

Oblivious to the surveillance operation currently being undertaken Lucie returned back to 'BOOK IT' after yet another lunchtime meeting with Nick. They'd strolled around the shops, laughing and joking with each other and this time when Nick asked her to come back to his after work she had managed to find the willpower to say no. It hadn't been easy to turn him down, especially when he'd given her that cheeky smile and wink, like he knew she really wanted to say yes. There was the problem; she did want to say a great big huge yeah baby, but she'd told herself she was only going to let it happen once. Ant was the one she'd married and the one she'd promised to forsake all others for...there hadn't been a clause that said "I forsake all others except Nick Slater" - if there was she'd be sorted. Yesterday with Nick had been everything she thought it'd be and more. He was more passionate than she remembered or maybe it was just that she and Ant had lost some of their passion. Oh God, Ant would go ballistic at her for thinking like that. Actually he'd probably be madder at the fact she'd slept with another bloke. It was the strangest feeling, when she was here in Chester with Nick everything felt fine but as she drove home along the M53 yesterday and got nearer to home she suddenly realised what she'd done. She didn't want to lose Ant but Nick had been like an itch that needed scratching. She groaned, Nick wouldn't be impressed being compared to an itch. She didn't know how she'd managed to act normally around Ant last night, she kept telling herself that it was just a one off and now she and Nick could just be friends... yeah, friends who walked round Chester holding hands and having the odd snog outside M&S, that little voice in her head reminded her.

Lucie spent the afternoon trying to keep her mind off Nick, she stayed on the counter serving customers. She spent most of the afternoon with a couple booking their honeymoon to the Maldives, which funnily enough was where she and Ant had gone for their honeymoon. Although the wedding had been joint the honeymoons had been separate. Zoey and Adam headed off to New York and she and Ant went to a beautiful five star resort in the Maldives, they had a water lagoon "hut" as Ant called it. It was beautiful, they had their own pool and their "hut" was on stilts over the ocean. They spent the first night out on the decking watching the sun set in each other's arms. She found herself telling the couple how romantic the Maldives were and telling them about midnight strolls along the beach. She'd have to shut up before she divulged far too much information. The couple didn't seem to mind, they were pretty loved up and excited about their honeymoon. Had she been as excited about it as this couple were? She thought back. Zoey had done most of the wedding organising Lucie had been excited, but compared to Zo she probably didn't seem it. Flying out to the Maldives, sharing a bottle of champagne which Zoey had arranged she rested her head on Ant's shoulder, she loved his shoulders almost as much as his thighs and he draped an arm across her. She couldn't remember having any misgivings, she just felt happy, going off on honeymoon with her new hubby.

"Ooh, you so need to have champagne on the flight too," she told the honeymoon couple.

She suddenly felt the need to speak to Ant. "If you'll excuse me one second, I think I have a brochure in the back that has better pictures. I won't be a minute."

She nipped into the back and grabbed her phone out of her bag. She could see an envelope on it for a message. She pressed the button, it was from Nick.

Hey sexy, my lips are missing yours.

"OH God, don't do this to me, I feel guilty enough already."

She deleted the text without reading it again; hopefully she could delete it from her mind just as quick. She scrolled down to Ant ring or text?? Text was always safer, no chance of getting tongue tired.

Hey babe, jst thinking bout you...love you. What do u want 4 T tonite? X

She pressed send, God how to ruin a romantic text in one easy go, ask about boring mundane things.

As she put the phone back in her bag it beeped. She felt butterflies in her tummy, was it from Nick? She looked at the screen. Ant. She opened the message, he had replied with one word.

You. x

Zoey was home alone, Adam had another parent's evening so she'd planned on getting comfy on the sofa and watching the Diagnosis Murder she'd sky+ today, but her mind was racing, she couldn't get into the programme and solve the murder with Doctor Sloan, not even Dick Van Dyke's real life son Barry could lift her spirits. Hmmm, was it wrong to have a crush on Barry Van Dyke? She grabbed her mobile and text Suze that very question. Her phone beeped almost immediately.

> Get a grip Maxwell, if ur gonna have a weird crush then pick someone normal like Jeremy Clarkson.

Jeremy Clarkson? Yuk, no way. Suze would eat her words when Barry appeared in HEAT's top twenty weird crushes.

She was clearly going even more bonkers than usual. She paused the TV to give her a moment to get her head together and ran through what she knew. OK, so she'd seen Lucie wandering round Chester arm in arm with a guy, laughing away. Not unlike the many times she'd seen Lucie link arms with Jake and laugh when they'd all been on a night out and she had never even raised an eyebrow at that. So why should this situation be any different? Well, the guy was Nick for a start. She wasn't going to think about this anymore, she hadn't even spoken to Lucie about it yet. She probably had totally the wrong end of the stick and it really wasn't worth stressing about, when really she didn't have any idea what was going on, how could she possibly think so badly of her best friend? Nope, the best thing to do was get back on the case with Doc Sloan and solve the murder, watching tasty Barry would be a bonus until her sexy hubby got home. Yep, that was a plan. She flicked the play button and settled back down.

CHAPTER NINETEEN

Lucie and Zoey had a rare Saturday off, the lads had an important match and they'd promised to be there to support them. They walked across the field towards the pitch where a crowd was already gathered. Although they were only a small local team the Spartans had lots of supporters. They were still getting unseasonally warm weather, but that didn't stop Zoey wearing her woolly stripy scarf in navy and gold – the club colours.

"Zo. You're gonna boil in that."

"Its tradition, if they lost and I wasn't wearing my scarf, I'd feel well guilty."

"If they lose it'll be because they haven't scored as many tries as the other team, not whether you have your scarf on or not."

"Can't help it, you know I'm superstitious, Adam's the same."

"So that means you've had your 'pre match bonk' this morning and he's got his lucky boxers on."

Zoey grinned. "Too right, Ads always says if he's scored in

the morning he'll score on the pitch."

Luce shook her head laughing "Ed would kill you if he knew, you know he tells the guys that pre match sex is not allowed, puts them off their game."

"Ah what does he know, bet Ant would agree with me and Adam."

Lucie suddenly went quiet.

"Hey, what's the matter?"

"Nothing, you're right he probably would."

The girls reached the barrier to the pitch just in time to see the lads running out, led by Ed.

Zoey laughed. "Look at him with his serious face on, if it was up to him he'd have the whole team doing the Hakka to psych the other side out."

Adam and Ant ran past, Adam turned towards her and flashed her a big smile, well a big luminous orange gum shield smile. Ant's gum shield was yellow, just in case the guys got confused. The rest of the team ran past in a streak of navy and gold. Zoey watched Adam's retreating backside.

"God, he looks hot in those tight white shorts."

"Two of my favourite things about watching Ant play Rugby, the shorts and the fact that old Ma Maxwell never watches them play."

Zoey laughed. "Bet that Ref still has the scars when she hit him with her brolly the one and only time she watched the lads."

"Can you imagine the embarrassment of her storming the pitch to stop a scrum? She's totally insane."

"Got no arguments from me." She watched as Ant threw the ball to Adam, he stormed down the wing, leaving the other team for dust.

"GO ADDDAAAMMM!" She jumped up and down, he slammed the ball down behind the posts. "YAY!" She screamed.

"See I told you the 'pre match bonk' works, three minutes into the game and he's scored."

"Just hope he wasn't that quick this morning," Lucie quipped, getting her mobile out to see if she had any messages.

"Expecting a call?"

"No, just habit isn't it? Checking your phone."

"Mmm, Luce, I wanted to ask you..." Zoey got distracted by Adam running down the wing again. God that boy was on fire today. Maybe now wasn't the time to question Lucie about Nick, she was pretty sure he was the reason Lucie couldn't leave her phone alone.

The lads won the match easily and the cheering and their singing in the bath could be heard all through the club house. The girls sat in the bar waiting for them.

"Luce, is everything ok? I've been a bit worried about you."

"Everything's fine. Why wouldn't it be?" Lucie twisted a strand of hair round her finger as she spoke.

"I just wondered that's all. How are things going in Chester?"

"Fine, great."

"Don't supposed you've bumped into Nick at all?"

"Nick?" Lucie lifted her wine glass to her lips. She shook her head as she took a drink.

Was this the time to bring up the stalking episode? Zoey wondered.

"Oh, here come the boys."

Obviously not. She turned to see Adam, followed closely by Ant walking towards them. Adam looked gorgeous; he was in his club suit and his hair still slightly damp from the bath. He grinned at her as he came closer. He put his arm round her waist, lifting her up to him in one quick movement and planted a kiss on her lips. He smelt gorgeous too, a mixture of Hugo Boss and ralgex, so manly and sexy. She couldn't help a "Mmm" escaping from her lips.

"Right back at ya Mrs M".

"You had a storming game today babe."

"It was the pre match bonk," he turned to Ant

"Reckon you should try that too bro, might improve your game."

"Reckon I might, I was shite today," he draped his arm around Lucie's shoulders. "Shall we give it a go, hon?" Before she could answer Ed headed over and handed a pint to Ant.

"There you go Adam, man of the match today. Nice one mate."

"Err Ed, I'm Ant."

"Ah crap, you'd think I'd get it right by now. You two seriously should wear badges," he turned to Adam and handed him the pint. "So yeah, well played Macca lad, whatever you did pre match, keep it up."

"Every intention," he winked at Zoey.

"How you two girls don't end up with the wrong twin confuses me." Ed shook his head as he walked away.

"He's forgetting that you're not twins and we know who we're married too," Ant grinned.

"Hey, we've never gotten you two mixed up..." Zoey started.

"...Not that we know of anyway," Lucie laughed.

Ant manoeuvred Lucie over to the bar. "Don't tell Ed, but the real reason I played crap was coz' I was too busy looking at my beautiful wife. You're gorgeous, d'you know that Luce?"

She tried to laugh. "Don't blame me for your bad performance." Inside her stomach was doing a somersault.

How could she have done this to Ant? As much as she felt like Ant didn't exist when she was in Chester she was annoyed at Nick invading her thoughts when she was trying to spend some quality time with her husband. HA! Like the blame only lay with Nick. She looked up at Ant, why had she been so stupid? Here she was standing in front of her gorgeous husband, with his beautiful blue eyes, infectious smile, with that dimple and that was before she even got started on those shoulders and those thighs and yet she found herself in some other blokes bed. What was wrong with her? Not only was she keeping secrets from Ant, she was lying to her best mate, although technically she hadn't lied – it was just an involuntary shake of the head. This couldn't go on. She had to stop seeing Nick, she wasn't in love with him, well not much. There was still time to stop it going any further. Like it hadn't gone far enough already.

As the evening wore on Zoey watched Lucie closely, she had blatantly lied to her earlier on, although to be fair she didn't know that she and Jake had followed her. Even so, they were best mates, they told each other everything. Lucie was leaning against the bar, her legs in between Ant's as he stood in front of her. Everything looked ok, she was smiling at him and then he leaned over and kissed her on the cheek. Yeah, they looked fine. She suddenly became aware of Adam talking to her.

"Sorry babe, what was that?"

"I said I was gonna need a few more drinks down me before I do the moon walk."

"Oh God; no. I forgot all about the captain and the man of the match doing the moon walk. Your arse I don't mind seeing, but my little brother's? No thanks."

"Hey its tradition, you have to moon the other team."

CHAPTER TWENTY

Zoey had every intention of having a lazy Sunday as she lay stretching out in her king sized bed, she turned into Adam's back, his warmth instantly heating her up. She ran her hand along his muscular shoulders and along his toned arm until she reached his hand and linked her fingers with his. She brushed her lips along his neck.

"Mmm, morning honey," he whispered sleepily. He turned over, taking her in his arms.

"How about we spend the morning in bed, go for a wander to get the papers then head out for lunch?" She planted soft kisses on his chest as she spoke.

"Sounds like a plan. Bit sore after yesterday's game, so I could do with a massage," He grinned as he stroked her back. The James Bond theme began to ring on his mobile. Who needed Daniel Craig when you had your very own Adam Maxwell, she thought as she let her tongue trace his taught abs, she felt his muscles tighten even more as he reached over to the bedside table and grabbed the phone, checking the caller id.

"Hey ma."

Zoey groaned and flopped back onto her side of the bed, trust old ma Maxwell to interrupt a baby making session.

"No ma, I hadn't forgotten, no, no we're looking forward to it. Yep see you at twelve," he snapped the phone shut. "Ah shit, I forgot mum's coming over for lunch."

"What?" Zoey glanced at the clock, it was ten thirty. "Your mum is coming over in an hour and a half and you spring it on me now? I have to cook, get the house straight and look like a wife fit for her beloved son in ninety minutes." She sprang out of bed. "Humph, so much for a lazy morning." She stomped out of the bedroom.

"No chance of a quickie then?"

Zoey was in the kitchen when Old Ma Maxwell arrived, when was that woman going to drag her fashion sense into the 21st Century? She looked like the queen in her tweed skirt and mint green twin set, nobody had worn mint green since 1987 when it was in the "in" colour. Zoey watched her as she undid her rain hat…it wasn't even raining, just a bit cloudy but obviously the rain hat completed the look. Her mother in law certainly wasn't going to find herself on the front page of Vogue with that get up…People's Friend maybe. Zoey knew she was being mean thinking these things, but she knew it wouldn't be long before the mother in law got some thinly veiled insults of her own in. It didn't help the Zoey was in a particularly bad mood, first Adam springing this on her and saying goodbye to a lazy Sunday, then she'd tried to get hold of Lucie to see if she and Ant could come round, safety in numbers and all that, but Lucie's mobile was turned off. So she had no choice but to face Old Ma Maxwell on her own.

"Zoey, dear, you look lovely, black really is such a slimming colour."

She no longer felt guilty for her uncomplimentary

thoughts, at least she kept them to herself. Unlike her mother in law, she didn't want to hurt anybody's feelings.

"So what are we having for lunch?"

"Err, I thought chicken and bacon pasta."

"In my day a roast was a typical Sunday lunch, not all this new fangled foreign cooking."

"Well, I just thought twelve might have been too early for a roast..."

"Oh I'm in no rush dear, I can stay all day."

Zoey turned her back on her and attacked an onion with more vigor than was needed. She would kill Adam later, or at least ban him from sex for a few days, actually no, if she was going to get pregnant she kind've needed his body so she couldn't really ban that...she'd cancel sky sports! And how dare Lucie have her phone turned off? She was in the bad books too.

"Ooh and I bought my Earl grey tea with me...I know you don't have proper tea."

Since when was PJ tips classed as not proper tea?

Just let me get through the afternoon without doing her serious damage. Zoey thought.

"Did I tell you I have a nice trip planned to Chester with my Thursday club?"

"Oh, when's that?"

"Oh really Zoey! On a Thursday of course, otherwise it would be called the Tuesday club, or the Friday club," she laughed at her own joke.

"I know what you meant," she took a deep breath. "I meant what date as in this Thursday? Next Thursday? A Thursday in three months time?"

"Zoey, that's not like you to be so sarcastic, we normally leave that to Lucie."

At that moment Adam walked into the kitchen. "How are my two favourite ladies?" he grinned.

Zoey gave him a look, he may look incredibly sexy and he may be flashing that gorgeous dimple of his but he was soooo in trouble and she was soooo cancelling Sky Sports.

Lucie and Ant had been having the lazy afternoon that Zoey was craving, curled up on the sofa. Lucie had turned her phone off, determined not to let Nick into her head and even more determined to tell him tomorrow that it was all off. She planned on telling the girls in work that she had to leave early for a doctor's appointment, she'd go and see Nick and tell him she wasn't prepared to risk her marriage. Simple as that. So she was spending the day making it up to Ant, not that he knew there had ever been a problem, but that didn't mean she didn't feel guilty. From now on she would be the perfect wife; she would tend to his every need. She watched him as he lay on the sofa flicking through the channels on the TV looking for a film they could watch. She wouldn't even moan about Sky Sports being on all the time. She would be a domestic goddess - he'd love it.

"Babe, I forgot to tell you, it's my turn to clean the kit this week...can you shove it in the wash for me?"

Fifteen muddy shirts and shorts and the occasional wandering jock strap clogging up her washing machine? No way.

"Hon, just take it to the launderette, it's much easier, my machine can't cope with all that mud."

"S'okay, I'll get me ma to do it, she won't mind."

"I'm sure she won't and it will give her yet another opportunity to comment on my inability to be a domestic goddess."

"Eh? What you on about?"

"Like your mother needs any more ammunition, she's forever getting at me and Zo."

"Babe, she loves you...I know she's a bit over protective..."

"A BIT??? Jeez, any more over protective and she'd be managing director of a condom company."

He laughed. "She's not that bad, she's just lonely really. She always tells me and Adam that you are the daughters she never had."

"Yeah, whatever"

"What's got you in such a bad mood anyway?"

"I'm not in a mood."

"So that's your happy face is it?"

How had she gone, in the space of five minutes from thinking how lovely she was going to be to him, to now wanting to tell him to sod off? She glared at him.

He grinned at her. "Luce, I'm not bothered whether you're a domesticated goddess thingy or not. If I'd wanted a maid I'd have married one."

"So, now you're saying I'm crap at housework?"

He flung his arms in the air and sighed. "Can't win can I?"

Lunchtime the following day was the first chance Zo had to catch up with Lucie, she gave her a quick call in between customers.

"...And d'you know what time she finally went? Quarter past bloody seven, she totally ruined my Sunday and she made us watch Songs of Praise."

"If it's any consolation, she wrecked mine too."

"How?"

"I had a row with Ant over washing the rugby kit..."

"Clogs up the washing machine."

"Exactly! So he said he'd get his mum to do it and it just escalated from there really. Totally stupid argument and I still had a gob on this morning."

"Bloody mother in law hey! How's your day going?"

"Good, it's pretty busy. I'm err off to the docs later so I'm leaving early."

"Is everything ok?"

She could hear the concern in Zoey's voice. "Oh yeah, just a repeat prescription for my pill." She felt awful lying to Zo again, but she had to tell everyone the same story. Besides, this would be the last time. She was putting an end to it all today. So, yeah it would all be over after today, fineto, finished. So quite how she found herself in Nick Slater's bed yet again she wasn't too sure. Well of course she knew how she got here, she just didn't know what happened to her will power...oh yeah, that flew out of the window as quick as her knickers. Not that her knickers had actually gone out of the window, which would've been embarrassing, although where her knickers actually were, was a mystery. All she knew was they'd definitely been flung.

"So I thought this was where you came to tell me in your beautiful scouse accent to, what's that term...? Do one," he teased as he stroked her hot skin.

"I was..."

He pulled her closer to him, her body seemed to fit perfectly with his. If she believed in fate she would say they were meant to be.

"So what stopped you?"

"What d'you think? You of course," she sighed as she tilted her head towards his. "I thought it would be so easy to walk away..."

"But I'm irresistible and I bring out your sex goddess side."

There was that bloody goddess word again. "Bad influence more like."

"Luce, I've thought about this moment for years and now it's actually happened, well I'm not about to let you go without a fight."

"Nick, have you forgotten - I'm married."

He reached across her body to her left hand, he lifted it up so her wedding ring was in front of their faces. "His ring is on your finger, but your heart is wherever you let it go…balls in your court."

"Don't put pressure on me, I'm not taking this lightly y' know. When I married Ant I never ever thought I'd end up in a situation where I'd cheat on him. I never thought I'd see you again…"

"So does that mean if you thought you would, you wouldn't have married him?"

"You can't ask me that, it doesn't matter. I'm married to Ant."

"So why are you in bed with me?"

CHAPTER TWENTY ONE

Lucie liked the fact that on her days off she could spend the day with Nick without having to hide what she was doing. Ant just assumed she was shopping or at the gym or whatever it was she did on her day off. Zoey was working today so she had no one to answer to...but herself. She was just putting the finishing touches to her make-up when she heard the doorbell. Smacking her lips together to blot her lipstick she headed out of the bedroom, she wasn't too sure why she'd put so much make up on and made such an effort with her clothes. Within an hour her clothes would be off and her make up kissed off. She hummed to herself as she skipped down the stairs stopping mid- hum as she opened the door to Zoey.

"You look lovely Luce, off out anywhere nice?"

"I, err thought you were working today."

"Had to swap with Larry, he has an important golf tournament tomorrow."

"Larry and his golf eh!"

"So, are you planning on leaving me on the doorstep?"

Lucie looked at her watch, damn, She should be on her

way by now. “No, no, of course not.” She stepped aside to let her in.

Well, she’s definitely flustered about something. “Not keeping you from anything am I? You got time for a cuppa? I feel like I haven’t seen you properly for ages.”

“Well, I have an appointment, but I suppose I’ve can spare twenty minutes.” She brushed past Zoey and into the kitchen.

Zoey was tempted to turn on her heel and leave Lucie to it...after all these years of friendship Lucie could only spare her a quick twenty minutes before she went off with sailor boy, only for the fact she couldn’t be a hundred percent sure that Lucie was off to meet him, she stayed.

“So what’s the goss then Luce?”

“About what?”

“I don’t know... anything...life in general.”

Lucie filled the kettle up then plugged it in. She turned to face Zoey placing her hands on the worktop as she leaned against it. “Nothing really, just been busy in the Chester shop.”

“So where’s your appointment?”

“Appointment?”

“Yeah, you said you had one, that’s why you’re in a rush.”

“Oh, yeah, err opticians.”

The two girls fell silent. Zoey couldn’t remember ever feeling so on edge around Lucie, she was her best friend.

“I just need the loo, you ok making the tea?”

Zoey nodded as she watched Lucie get out of the kitchen as quickly as she could. She started to get the cups and tea bags out. This awkwardness between them had to go. She’d tell Luce about following her around Chester, she’d laugh and call her a nutter for even thinking there was anything going on with Nick and then everything would be ok again.

As she was about to pour the water into the cups she heard Lucie's phone ring, she'd left her mobile on the worktop. She automatically glanced at the caller Id, there was only a mobile number flashing up. Zoey was pretty sure who that number belonged to. She reached out for the phone and hesitated, did she really want to do this? Too late, the phone was in her hand, held up to her ear.

"Hello?"

"Hey, babe, where are you? I'm lonely in bed without you."

"Nick?" she whispered.

"Luce?"

Zoey stared at the phone in disbelief then pressed the call end button, she looked up to see Lucie standing in the kitchen door way, the colour totally drained from her face.

Lucie watched as Zoey slammed the phone down, her eyes flashing with anger as she moved towards her.

"Zo, I..."

"D'you know what? I don't wanna hear it. You're right about one thing, you do need to go to the opticians." She stormed past her and straight out of the front door. Lucie wasn't sure whether to go after her or not. She obviously wasn't in the mood to listen. Maybe she should wait till she'd calmed down. A though flashed through her mind and made her skin prickle with fear, what if she was going straight to Ant? No she wouldn't do that, not without speaking to her first. She didn't really know what had just happened then, didn't know exactly what Nick had said to Zoey. She may as well stick to her original arrangements and head off to see Nick; he could put her in the picture.

Lucie spent most of the afternoon with Nick and the majority of it in his bed yet again, she kept trying to justify it to herself, but Zoey finding out about Nick was making it all become a bit too real. Nick was blasé about the whole thing. "She's not gonna tell Ant is she? She's your best mate."

"It's not that simple..."

"Simple as you make it babe, besides which, maybe it's better if it comes out."

"You wanna see my marriage fall apart? See me unhappy?"

"If that's what it takes to be with you, then so be it...I've gone through enough storms, this will be a breeze!"

Lucie was trying to get her head together as she made tea that night, Nick wanted her, Ant wanted her, who did she want? She didn't have too much time to think about it, she heard Ant's key in the door. She turned round to see him walking down the hall with a huge bunch of flowers.

Great, this was all she needed.

"Hey kiddo, bought you these to cheer you up and to make it up to you over the rugby kits..." He held the flowers out to her.

"Babe, you didn't have to do this, it was just me being a bit sensitive that's all..." and the worst wife in the world she added silently.

"Let's just forget it. I'm nipping out for a quick pint with Ads, how about I stop off at the DVD shop and get some classic romance out? I'm thinking 80's classic here."

She smiled. "Mannequin?"

"Ah thought you'd have gone for Cocktail."

"Oooh yeah, get that...listen, think I'll pop over and see Zo while you're at the pub, text me when you're leaving."

Adam and Ant stood at the bar with their bottles of bud in the Nelson. Ant was finding it difficult not to laugh at the barmaids face as she looked back and forth from him to

Adam. They often joked saying they should wear badges saying "Yes we're twins!"

"Nice to see you smilin' bro."

Ant shrugged his shoulders. "I'm alright mate, things are just a bit weird with Luce at the moment."

"How d'ya mean?"

"I'm not really sure, she just seems a bit pre occupied...I think it might be something to do with you and Zo trying for a baby."

"Why would that bother Luce?"

"Well, that's the thing, we've never really talked about having kids and when we should try, I don't know how to broach the subject."

"Don't make a big deal out of it, just drop a few hints, see how the land lies."

"Yeah, better to get things out in the open," Ant took a slug of his beer

"I just hope it happens soon for me and Zo, it's really upsetting her."

Ant sighed. "Women eh mate."

"So, what are our chances of beating New Brighton on Saturday?" Adam asked going for the safer subject of rugby.

Taking a bottle of wine out of the fridge and grabbing the biggest glass she could find Zoey took it with her into the living room and flopped down onto the sofa. So that was it, she finally knew what Luce was up to with Nick. She took a big gulp of wine...urgh...she must have had too much in one go, it tasted like vinegar. As she mulled the situation over in her head her thoughts were interrupted by the doorbell. She heaved herself up off the sofa, she was tired. It had been a long day. She was more than surprised to see Lucie at the door.

"Can I come in? I need to explain."

"I don't think it's me you need to explain to..."

Five minutes later the girls were sitting on Zoey's living room floor, a bottle of wine and a whole lot of tension between them.

"So," Zoey began. "What are you gonna do?"

"I don't know, I love Ant, I really do but Nick...he's just Nick."

"How can you say you love Ant yet treat him and your marriage with such little respect?"

"It's not as black and white as that, if you'd have asked me a couple of months ago if I'd ever cheat on Ant, well it wouldn't have even entered my head...I'm not trying to justify it or make it ok, but well, I never thought I'd see Nick again." "It doesn't make it ok just because it's Nick. You promised to love Ant, to be faithful not just until Nick comes back on the scene again. You're messing with people's feelings, how d'you think Ant will feel when he finds out?"

Lucie's eyes widened. "You can't tell him".

"You can't ask me to keep this from Adam, we already had a huge row the day we met Nick in Chester. You can't ask me to jeopardise my own marriage, it's not like it's a little white lie we are telling here. Once Adam knows there's no way he'd keep it from Ant."

"I know I'm being selfish..."

"Having your cake and eating it more like."

"You make it sound so sordid."

"Affairs normally are Luce."

Lucie's phoned beeped, she glanced at it and sighed.

"It's him isn't it?"

Lucie just nodded as she pressed the button to open the message. "He just wants to know if I'm ok."

"How sweet, shame he didn't think to stay out of your life and not cause all this hassle," Zoey snapped.

"He's in my life 'coz I let him back in."

"I know. God Luce, what were you thinking? Didn't you for one second think what you were doing was wrong?"

"Of course I did, but it's Nick."

"You can't keep using that excuse..."

"Ok! So it never felt like me and Nick were ever over, seeing him again made me come alive, he's so passionate, exciting. He wears Calvin Klein boxers, Ant wears Bart Simpson..."

"It's what's inside that counts..." Zoey saw Lucie smirk and realised what she'd just said. "What I mean is, you can't base all this on a bloody pair of boxer shorts."

"I never thought what would happen if it got to this stage, I just thought I could have them both," she sighed, "I didn't want to hurt anyone, especially not Ant. Despite what you're thinking right now, I do love him."

"Of course people are going to get hurt, affairs never end well."

"I just don't know where to go from here."

"You need to tell Ant the truth, he deserves that much."

"But, it'll hurt him."

"You should've thought of that before you jumped into bed with sailor boy."

"God Zo, I hope you never find yourself in a situation like this and you want my sympathy, considering you're supposed to be my best mate I would've expected you to be a bit more understanding."

"Considering you're supposed to be Ant's wife I would've expected you to have been a bit more faithful."

The two girls stared at each other, the realisation hitting them that it wasn't Just Lucie and Ant's relationship that was about to be tested, it was their's too.

CHAPTER TWENTY TWO

Later that night Zoey sat up in bed reading her book, well attempting to, she'd re-read the same line about fifty times. Her head was spinning. Adam was downstairs watching Sky Sports headlines, she smiled slowly, he was such a creature of habit. She heard him switch off downstairs and come up the stairs.

"Hey, babe, you ok? You look really tired tonight," he commented sounding concerned.

"I'm fine, honey," she smiled.

He noticed the smile didn't quite reach her eyes, he hoped to God they got pregnant soon, he could see the stress was getting to her.

"Y'know babe, it will happen soon. We will have a baby, think Ant and Luce are planning one of their own too."

"What d'you mean?" she asked slowly.

"He says Luce has been acting a bit weird and he thinks she wants a baby, but they've never really talked about it – so he's not sure."

He couldn't quite work out the weird look on her face, "Don't worry babe, I'm sure we'll still be first!"

God, if that was the only thing she had to worry about, she'd be well happy.

At three O'clock in the morning Lucie was still wide awake, her conscience wouldn't let her sleep although she actually felt like she was having a bad dream and she'd wake up any minute. She knew whether she wanted to or not, she had a choice to make. Her marriage or her lover? Then a thought struck her, the choice may not be up to her, when she finally found the courage to confess all to Ant, he might not want her anymore, leaving her free to be with Nick. The fact that the thought of Ant leaving her filled her with dread only made the situation worse. It certainly wasn't clear cut. She wanted them both, she loved Nick's passion, his whole live for the moment mentality, his sense of humour, his cheekiness and yes even those cheesy lines that she once fell for and he was just so hot. Could passion and cheekiness be enough? What would happen when the passion died and the cheekiness got irritating? Ant, her gorgeous husband, well it went without saying how much she loved his fabulous thighs and his strong arms, being wrapped up in them felt like she was totally protected, her big rugby playing husband who had such a quiet and caring side that the thought of hurting him made her feel like her own heart would break. She loved how he always called her kiddo, she didn't even know why, it just sounded nice whenever she heard it. She seriously didn't know what she was going to do…it was her last day in the Chester shop tomorrow so whether she wanted it or not, there would be some space between her and Nick.

Three am at Nick's apartment and all was not quiet. It had worked out pretty well that Lucie had felt the need to go and see Zo, it meant that Nick could re arrange something he'd put off. Bendy gymnast Tara had also been in touch on Facebook, she forgiven him a long time ago for dumping her for Lucie. She was also off the ships and back home in Manchester. So, finding himself on his lonesome he took Tara up on her offer to meet up for drinks. She'd got the train from Manchester and they'd hit a few of the local pubs, before stumbling drunkenly into Nick's bed for "old times sake". Tara certainly hadn't lost any of her athletic talents, but sometimes old times' sake was better left in the past - and Tara was definitely something he should've left behind. What if Lucie had come to the apartment too? Threesome briefly fleeted through his mind, No. He was supposed to have grown up. He watched as Tara's head worked its way down his chest. He was prepared to throw Lucie away over a cheap fling? He didn't think so. Nope, it was time to be strong and prove that he could commit to one woman.

"Tara..." he said throatily.

"Yeah, baby..."

Actually, maybe now wasn't the time to make any hasty decisions, he'd think about growing up in the morning. It would be rude to chuck his flexible friend out onto the street.

Nick woke up alone, but knew he wasn't alone in the apartment, he could hear the radio humming in the kitchen. Lucie? He rubbed the sleep from his eyes, lifted his head from the pillow and glanced around at the clothes strewn all over the place. Nope. Not Lucie, shit! Tara. He shook his head, defiantly a mistake. Ah well, she'd be off back to Manchester today, best get rid of her as quick as possible. He got out of bed, pulling on his Calvin Klein boxers and headed out to the kitchen, to the image of Tara in his shirt making coffee.

"Morning sleepy head, did I wear you out last night?" she grinned as he sat down at the breakfast bar, yawning.

"I can take the pace."

"Made you a coffee, get that stamina going. I got no plans today..." she walked towards him, the swaying of the hips and the suggestive pout finishing off the sentence for her.

"Look Tara, as much as that would be nice, I do have someone err something I've got to do..."

The pout turned from sexy to pissed off. "Ah c'mon Slaz, you're always doing this to me. What could be more fun than spending the day in bed with me?"

"I have a thing going on with someone and well, I can't mess it up. It's kinda important."

"She seems to have slipped your mind last night..."

"Last night was a mistake."

"Thanks Nick, you really know how to make a girl feel special. You treated me like shit on the ship with that bimbo travel agent, I thought this time might be different. That's the last time I let you do this to me."

"Lucie's not a bimbo."

"It's her isn't it? God that girl's come back to haunt me.

So not only are you binning me off again, you're binning me off for the same girl. I am so stupid, why did I even think it was even worth bothering with you?"

He ran his hand through his bed head. "What can I say? You know my brain is in my pants sometimes."

"Sometimes? ALL the time. I bet you've got the poor girl falling for you all over again and that still doesn't stop you cheating on her. She's welcome to you. As soon as I'm dressed, I'm outta here." She stomped off to the bedroom.

Nick breathed a sigh of relief, well it could've been worse, at least she was going.

Tara yanked off Nick's Ralph Lauren shirt, not caring that the buttons were flying off. Would serve the bastard right. Didn't he know she'd always been in love with him? Now he'd overlooked her twice for the same girl. She hurriedly pulled on her clothes, well she had her pride and she wasn't going to let him get away with hurting her again. She grabbed her handbag, rifling through it she pulled out her lipstick and an old receipt. She scrawled on the back, *Tara was here*. Then placed it under the pillow she'd just slept on, dropping the lipstick to the floor for good measure. Next time the travel agent bimbo was in his bed, she'd get more than she bargained for.

Lucie's last day in Chester was a busy one so she hadn't really had time to give Nick much thought, although she'd sent him a text at lunch time asking him to meet her after work. Ant was playing in the semi final of the Cheshire Plate that night, she'd promised him she'd be there. She wouldn't have too long to spend with Nick, but she needed to see him, she didn't know when they'd get a chance to be together again soon. She also hadn't been able to speak to him properly since Zo discovered about them. Nick had texted back to say he'd meet her in Stabucks after work. He was already waiting for her with a frappucino by the time she eventually left work. She sat down opposite him.

"I can't stay long, I have to get back. I just needed to see you."

He winked at her. "I was missing you too babe." He reached across and took her hand, there was no reason to 'fess up and tell her about Tara. That little episode was best forgotten. He'd kicked Tara out, that counted for something- right? "So, how did it go with Zo?"

"Well, I don't think she's gonna tell Ant yet, she realises I need time to think."

"What's there to think about? I want you, you want me - sorted." He shrugged his shoulders as he lifted his cup to his lips.

"Yes, but what doesn't fit into that nice little equation is my husband, I love him Nick."

He slowly put his cup down, not taking his eyes of her. "I thought it was me you loved?"

"I love you both and that's why it's so damn hard."

"Always is when you're around," he winked again and grinned at her.

"Oh my God, you're never serious about anything are you?"

"Life's too short to get stressed, but I am serious about one thing - you."

She sighed. " I don't know what to do, I'm stuck between a rock and a hard place..."

"Literally," Nick laughed.

"D'you know what? I'm glad you can see the funny side of this 'coz I flippin' well can't."

He moved his chair round closer to hers, slung his arm around her shoulders and pulled her closer. He gently stroked the bare skin on her arm as he spoke. "Hey babe, I'm sorry, just trying to lighten the mood, y'know I don't do serious."

She was all too aware of the goosebumps breaking out all over her skin as he continued to stroke her arm with one hand and cupped her chin with the other hand as he tipped her face closer to his.

"I know you've got a choice to make, but you also know how I feel about you. We missed our chance once before, let's not make the same mistake again." He moved his head closer to hers, tugging at her bottom lip with his own lips before her pulled her closer, her mouth opening up underneath the irresistible pressure of his kiss. She let herself fall deeply into his kiss, even just something as simple as him brushing her hair behind her ear made her tingle all over. No one had ever had such an effect on her like he did, as he pulled away and grinned at her she knew he knew it too.

"I have to go, I'm late."

Zoey was leaning against the railing surrounding the rugby pitch, cheering the lads on. She glanced up at the church clock tower that was on the hill just behind the rugby club, they'd only played fifteen minutes, but already they were in the lead. Despite the game going well, it wasn't easing her bad mood. First of all she nearly broke the button on her jeans when she got changed out of her uniform before, she was seriously going to have to step away from the Wispa bars, which was just as depressing as not fitting into her jeans and now Lucie was late for the match and she had a pretty good idea where and who she was with. Lucie had promised her she'd be her in time for the start of the match, she'd obviously gotten distracted. She watched as Adam ran down the wing on the opposite side of the pitch, side stepping his opponent with ease he threw the ball out to another player who popped it straight over to Ant, he picked up his pace going for the try line. A player from the other team went in for a tackle, but it was too high, right around Ant's neck, knocking him off guard. Ant went flying into another player and hit the ground hard. Zoey heard some of the supporters close by gasp as he fell, but the sound was drowned out by the crunch as Ant's body hit the pitch. Adam, who had been one of the furthest away at the point of impact, was now crouching down by his brother's side. Zoey felt her heart fall into the pit of her stomach as she watched the physio and the coach run onto the pitch.

"C'mon Ant, get up," she whispered.

"Macca, lad, get up mate," A disembodied voice shouted from further down the side line.

She held her breath, Ant didn't seem to be moving at all. The coach was running back to the supporters.

"Someone call an ambulance."

Zoey ducked under the railing and ran across the pitch.

Lucie was stuck at traffic lights, indicating to turn left onto the road the rugby club was on, she tapped the steering wheel impatiently in time with the music. She glanced at the clock on the dashboard, she wasn't that late, only twenty minutes or so. She'd be there for the important bit, when the lads won. The lights changed, she turned the corner and headed towards the car park. As she drove in the first thing she saw was an ambulance on the pitch, with Zoey standing by it. She abandoned the car and made her way over to the pitch. She could see Zoey by the ambulance doors and Ant standing next to her. Oh God, it must be Adam. She started to run but came to an abrupt holt when she saw Ant give Zoey a kiss and get into the back of the ambulance, the doors closing behind him and the ambulance taking off, sirens blaring, lights flashing. It wasn't Adam it was Ant. She could see Zoey still standing there, staring after the ambulance her hands in front of her mouth, like she was praying. She turned her head and focused on Lucie.

Lucie wasn't sure who ran to who, but within seconds she felt herself engulfed in Zoey's arms. She could feel Zoey's wet cheek against her hair.

"Zo..."

"It's Ant, he's been knocked unconscious, he hadn't come round before he went off in the ambulance."

Lucie couldn't speak. She needed to be with him.

Ed appeared behind Zo. “C’mon you two, I’ll take you up to the hospital.”

Wirral General Hospital was only ten minutes down the motorway, but it seemed to take forever. No one spoke in the car, Ed concentrated on his driving, Zoey stared straight ahead of her and Lucie looked aimlessly out of the window, not really seeing what she was looking at. Ed dropped them straight outside A&E.

“I’ll park the car, I’ll see you in there.”

Zoey spotted Adam straight away, he kind’ve stood out on his navy and gold rugby top. He seemed miles away. She held Lucie’s hand, took a deep breath and made her way through the waiting room chairs to get to the corner and to Adam.

“Hey,” she whispered.

“Where’s Ant? Why aren’t you with him? Can I see him?” The questions tumbled out of Lucie’s mouth like a high speed train.

“He still hadn’t woken up in the ambulance, he took a real knock. They took him straight through to be seen and told me to wait here.”

“Oh God,” Lucie flopped onto the chair, sobbing.

“Hey, he’ll be ok. He’ll wake up soon.” He reached across and squeezed her shoulder.

“How d’you know?”

Zoey glanced up and saw Ed coming towards them.

“My head is killing, but the pain is easing, the pressure squeezing it is wearing off. I feel like a bad hangover is wearing off,” Adam said.

“Yeah mate, sorry you got a headache an that, but it was Ant who took the knock,” Ed said.

“Ed, you dick, it’s the twin thing. Adam’s pain in his head

is getting better, which should mean that Ant's is too," Zoey explained.

Ed shrugged his shoulders. "You know I don't get that twin psycho thing."

Zoey rolled her eyes.

"Luce, I promise you, he will be ok. I can feel it. Trust me," Adam said.

Lucie still couldn't talk properly, her head was spinning and she just wanted to see Ant.

They sat there in silence, drinking coffee from plastic cups, seeing the same headlines on loop as Sky news flashed across the plasma screen chained to the wall.

After what seemed like forever a nurse came over to them.

"Mrs Maxwell?"

Lucie stood up. "That's me, I'm Mrs Maxwell."

The nurse smiled. "You can see your husband now."

"Is he...is he awake?"

The nurse nodded and smiled again. Lucie looked at Adam who breathed a huge sigh of relief and grinned at her. "Told you."

Lucie pushed the door open slowly, the lights had been dimmed. Ant had a huge bandage wrapped around his head. She crept in; he looked like he'd fallen back asleep. As she got nearer to the bed he opened his eyes and a smile slowly spread across his face. He reached out for her hand.

"Hey kiddo," he croaked.

"Oh Ant, thank God you're ok. I'm so sorry." She bent down to kiss his lips.

"You didn't whack your head into mine."

"I...I should've been there, I'm sorry I was late."

"You're here now, that's all that matters." He lifted her

hand to his lips and kissed it softly.

She never would've forgiven herself if anything had happened to him. This was obviously her punishment for cheating on him. Big, fat, hot tears rolled down her cheeks.

"Hey, hey, it's ok, I'm fine." Still holding her hand he wiped the tears away.

"I just love you so much."

CHAPTER TWENTY THREE

Lucie had left Ant with Adam as she nipped out to the vending machine to get yet another coffee, she needed something to settle the sick feeling welling up in the pit of her stomach, Zoey walked along the corridor with her, neither of them quite sure what to say. Lucie rooted around in her bag for her purse.

"S'ok, I've got this." Zoey pulled some loose change out of her jeans pocket.

"Thanks," Lucie mumbled. "Just a coffee please."

Zoey turned her back on Lucie slightly as she put the coins in the machine.

"Sure you don't want something stronger? Adam said the outlaw's on the way."

Lucie groaned. "That's all I need."

Zoey punched the button for coffee, still avoiding eye contact with Lucie. "So, no prizes for guessing why you were late to the match."

"I tried to finish it Zo, I really did, but I'm just so confused and now I feel as guilty as hell that I wasn't there when Ant needed me..."

"Nope, you were too busy with your sailor boy. You're being so selfish Luce, it's all about you. Poor you, you can't make your mind up over who you want to be with. Well what about Ant, your poor husband, who is lying in a hospital bed, thinking you raced to his bedside when in reality you're throwing your marriage away and cheating on him with some Casanova."

"I didn't want it to be like this. Ant was never second best."

Zoey turned round to face Lucie, but found herself in direct eye contact with Adam, He looked totally deflated as he stood rooted to the spot. Zoey knew he'd heard their conversation.

"Adam..."

Luce spun round at the sound of Zoey's voice and stared into a premonition of Ant's face when he discovered the truth. It might be the wrong twin she was looking at, but the look on his face could've been Ant's.

She tried to open her mouth to speak, but she couldn't find the words.

It looked like Adam was also contemplating the words to say as he stood there, his hands deep in his pockets staring at Lucie.

"You bitch," his voice was barely above a whisper, he walked towards her. "What the hell d'you think you're playing at?" This time most of the corridor heard his voice as the anger seemed to take hold.

"Adam, ssh, calm down. This isn't the place to do this." Zoey tried to shove Adam and Lucie into a side room, but trying to shift her man mountain husband was proving quite difficult. "Please," she pleaded. "Just come in here, we can talk more rationally."

"Rational?" Adam followed his wife into the room; Lucie had already flopped down onto a chair. "There is nothing to be rational about."

The room fell silent whilst everyone seemed to take stock of the revelation. Lucie sat with her head in her hands, Adam stood with his arms folded across his chest looking like he was about to erupt again at any second. Zoey ran a hand through her hair and looked nervously back and forth between the two of them. Adam switched his attention from glaring at Lucie to Zoey.

"And you knew about this Zo?"

The hurt in his voice tore at her heart. "I...only just...I..."

"How could you keep this from me? From Ant?"

Zoey hung her head, why was she the one getting the shit for this?

"Adam, it's not her fault, I asked her to keep it to herself, while I...while I worked out the best way to tell Ant." Lucie lifted her head up to face Adam.

"Oh, so you were actually gonna come clean about this bloke you've been shagging? And you thought it was ok to drag my wife into your sordid little mess?"

"D'you know what? You don't know anything about this, you don't know what it's doing to me, being in love with two different guys and I wouldn't expect you too, what with your perfect relationship. I'd just appreciate it if you let me handle this my way and for your information..." she turned her gaze back to Zoey.

"Zo is on Ant's side...she would never condone what I've done."

If Zoey felt like her heart was tearing before, now she felt like someone had reached in and twisted it, she'd let Lucie down, plain and simple. Friends shouldn't judge and that's exactly what she'd done, instead of being there when she need her she'd flown off the handle and immediately thought the worst of her. Her eyes filled with tears, mirroring the tears forming in Lucie's eyes.

"I'm so sorry, Luce."

"Give me one good reason why I shouldn't go straight back into the room and tell Ant what you've done?"

"Adam," Ed's head popped round the door. "Your Ma's here."

"Ha," Lucie spat. "There's one very good reason."

"You got till the end of the week, if he doesn't know by then, you leave me no choice...I won't keep secrets from him." He looked pointedly at Zo, turned and left.

"There's me in the dog house," Zoey sighed,

"Just tell him to bloody do one, who does he think he is making you feel like shite? I'm the one that's caused all the trouble."

Zoey shook her head smiling sadly. "You won't let the out-law get a sly dig at me without pulling her up, you give Adam as good as you get, so why, when it comes to Nick d'you turn into someone I don't know? Why does he have this effect on you that makes you lose your mojo?"

Lucie tilted her head back, looking up at the ceiling as she contemplated the question "If I knew the answer...I probably wouldn't be in this mess."

Ant's head was getting another bashing, this time from his mother.

"...and really, it's no wonder people are ill in hospital, just look at those walls, enough to turn anyone grey. You have a head injury; they should at least put you in a room that hasn't got orange walls and you're over looking the car park what a dreadful view. The NHS has gone to pot. Oh boys, I wish you two would give up that silly game. You worry me sick, why can't you take up a nice sport like chess? Your Uncle Frank, God rest his soul was the champ three years running down the social club..."

Adam sighed. "Ma, uncle Frank choked on a bishop trying to cheat."

It fell on deaf ears. “Well I don’t approve, it does you no good. Adam, you look like the colours drained right down to your boots and you Anthony, lying there in a hospital bed with a bandage around your head...and where is that wife of yours? She should be here, by your bedside.”

“She’s just popped out for coffee. Ma, it’s not that serious, just a bit of concussion. It looks worse than it is.”

“Well, I’ll be having words with those girls; they shouldn’t be encouraging you in this ruffian sport. Do they want you to have camouflage ears?”

“Err Mrs Maxwell,” Ed butted in. “It's cauliflower ears, the lads won’t get them, they don’t go in the scrum.”

“What’s this about cauliflower ears?” Zo asked entering the room. Lucie was behind her, she went straight over to Ant, avoiding any eye contact with Adam.

“You girls really need to get the boys to stop this game. I never condoned it when they lived at home.”

“Listen Ma, come and get a coffee with me, give Ant some space. We’re overcrowding him.”

“Oh. Ok dear, that’d be nice.”

“I’ll come too,” Zoey said.

“No, its fine, you stay with Lucie.” Adam didn’t even look at her as he left the room. Lucie threw Zo a sympathetic look.

“C’mon sis, come with me, we’ll leave these love birds alone,” Ed suggested.

Finally alone Ant turned to Luce and smiled, he reached out for her hand. “I know me mum means well but I’ve got a bigger headache now than I did when I got hit.”

A tear slid down her cheek as she entwined her fingers with his.

“Hey, hey, don’t get upset. I’m fine; they’re letting me out of here tomorrow. Everything’s fine.”

She leaned over and stroked his cheek with her hand. “Whatever happens, whatever we might go through, please don’t ever forget I love you.”

“Bloody hell Luce, what’s brought this on? You sound like a Hallmark gift card. Has the doc told you something I don’t know?”

“No, no. Nothing like that...I just...I don’t know, I needed you to know.”

“I know how much you love me, I’ve never doubted it. You are everything to me kiddo, everything. God, you’re getting me all mushy now...take advantage while this knock on the head has sent me a bit loopy,” he grinned at her.

The one solitary tear had now multiplied and was falling down her cheeks. He reached up, his hand still holding hers and wiped them away with the back of his hand. “Don’t cry, I hate to see you cry.”

“I’m ok...you just scared me that’s all.”

“Maybe mum's right, I should take up chess.”

“Do chess players get to wear really tight shorts?” she smiled through her tears.

“I knew that was the only reason you watched me play,” he lifted her hand to his lips. “That’s better,” he said seeing her smile again.

“I wish they’d let you out tonight, I don’t like sleeping on my own.”

“Why don’t you go and stay at Adam and Zo’s, I don’t like the thought of you being alone either.”

“D’you know what, I’ll be ok...it’ll be nice to have some peace and quiet.”

He pulled a face.

“I’m only joking, I’ll miss you tonight babe.”

Zoey and Ed walked in silence along the corridor towards the café, with Zoey occasionally letting out a deep sigh.

"So what's going on with you and Adam, never seen you two off with each other like that."

"Oh it's nothing, well it is, he thinks something's my fault, when really all I tried to do was stop it happening in the first place, now it's come back to bite me on the arse and he's blaming me."

"That's about as clear as custard," Ed shook his head. "Look, he's over there with that flippin' battleaxe, I'll go and charm her over a cuppa – you go and sort things out with Adam. If he's still being an arse tell him I'll drop him from the next match." He walked off towards the table. "Hey, Mrs M, mind if I join you? Your conversation will be far more intelligent than anything I'll get off my sister."

"Great, just slag me off why don't ya. I'll never get in her good books at this rate." Zoey muttered, glaring at Ed.

"You talking to yourself Zo?" She hadn't noticed Adam come up along side her. She turned to face him, no doubt he was gonna have another go at her.

He looked around. "Let's go outside, we can't talk here." They wandered out to the car park, passing all the pyjama clad patients who were not only clogging their lungs up with cigarette smoke, but also the hospital entrance. They battled their way through the fug. As they came to a stop Zoey folded her arms across her chest and turned her head nervously to the side, waiting for Adam's rant.

"Before you say anything...I'm sorry."

She spun her head back round to face him, did she hear right? Did he just apologise?

"I was being a tit, I'm sorry babe. I'm so mad at Lucie and I took it out on you. I know you're just as disgusted with her."

"Yeah I am, but she's still my best friend, I won't turn my back on her and you need to take a step back and let her handle this her way."

"Zo, she's cheating on my brother!"

"Yes, I know...but I believe her when she says she wants to finish things with Nick..."

Adam pulled a face at the mere mention of his name.

"She shouldn't have started things in the first place."

"There's no point us arguing about this...I know you're protective of Ant and yes what Lucie did was...is wrong, so we're both on the same page. Just don't blame me for it all."

"You think I blame you? Babe, don't be soft. I was just angry. I'm sorry."

She looked up into his eyes, seeing the hurt in them...this was exactly what she'd dreaded when Nick got in touch again, it wasn't just Lucie's life she would be affecting, it was all of them. She wrapped her arms around his waist and let her head rest against his chest.

"Me too," she whispered as he squeezed her tight.

Lucie felt sick to her stomach as she sat at the bottom of her stairs, she'd been home about an hour and hadn't moved from that spot. She wasn't used to the house being so quiet, well apart from her mobile beeping every half an hour with another message from Nick. The last thing she felt like doing was talking to him. At least Ant would be coming home tomorrow, coming home to what? His lying, cheating wife? God, when she thought of it like that she couldn't believe she was describing herself. When she'd arrived at the rugby club and Zo had told her Ant hadn't woken up, she'd thought the worst and knew it was all her fault. She loved Ant so much, but Nick was fastly becoming an addiction she knew she had to give up. Now that Adam knew, things were certainly gonna come to a head one way or another. The one thing she wanted to avoid was Ant being hurt, but she supposed she should've thought of that before she so willingly jumped into bed with Nick. God, she'd hardly even tried to resist him...it was like Zo said, where Nick was concerned she was totally under his spell. Well it was time to break that spell and make a decision. Ant or Nick?

CHAPTER TWENTY FOUR

The rain pelting against the window woke Lucie the following morning. It sounded like the Indian summer was well and truly over. She'd slept surprisingly well last night; she was so exhausted she'd just flopped into bed, the stress of the day totally knocking her out. She'd woken up on Ant's side of the bed, snuggled into his pillow. Before she could even start to contemplate the day her mobile began to ring, she reached out and flipped it open.

"Hello," she yawned into the phone.

"Luce? Where the hell have you been? I've been worried about you."

"Nick, you need to give me some space. Ant's in hospital, his brother knows about us..."

"Is he err ok?" Nick sounded like he wasn't really bothered, but felt obligated to ask.

"Yeah, just a rugby injury. You need to give me time to think."

"What's there to think about? We've already had this discussion, I want you,"

"What about what I want?"

"Me!"

"Nick, please...my head's all over the place, I'll ring you when I've got it together."

"Ok babe, your head may be a mess, but I know where your heart is, it's been in my bed along with your sexy body."

"Now you're sounding like some freaky stalker."

She heard his laughter down the phone.

"Stop doing that, this is serious now."

"Sorry babe, but I love it when you get angry with me."

"Now you really are freaking me out," she tried to sound cross, but as usual he made her behave totally out of character. She tried to regain some sense of control. "Look, just don't call me for a few days, wait till I call you." With that she flipped her phone shut. She sighed as she flopped back down onto the pillow and flung her phone across the bed. How the hell had she got herself in such a pickle? How had she allowed herself to get swept away on memories of a romantic holiday? And why did Nick seem so sure it was him she wanted? If she didn't love Ant she'd have just left him when Nick showed up, not had an affair behind his back. However she tried to justify the situation, the result was still the same...she'd committed adultery and it looked like it wouldn't be too long before Ant found out. She had to speak to Adam, she couldn't let him tell Ant, he couldn't find out that way. She had to be the one to tell him, no matter how much it hurt her to do it. It was her own stupid fault. She should've known she'd never be able to say no to Nick.

After what seemed like no sleep at all, Zoey dragged herself out of bed to get ready for work, Adam was already in the shower. God, she wished today was her day off so she could crawl back into bed and under the duvet. She felt so tired, yesterday had been totally crazy, Ant's accident was bad enough but now Adam knew about Lucie and Nick, things where just gonna get worse. She was attempting to hide the dark circles under her eyes when Adam came back into the bedroom, normally the sight of her yummy husband with tiny droplets of water running down his perfectly formed body brightened her morning up, but not this morning. She could barely focus.

"You ok babe?"

"I'm shattered," she yawned.

"Well let's just hope, that if she has any conscience Lucie's had less sleep than us." He almost spat her name out.

"Oh God Adam, I can't do this now. I'm too tired, don't know how I'm gonna get any work done today."

He came up behind her and wrapped his arms around her waist. "Sorry honey, I can't help being mad at her."

By the time Zoey got to work she felt like she was asleep on her feet.

"Ooh Zo, you look rough. Night on the piss?" Callie asked.

Suze rolled her eyes. "Straight to the point as ever."

"Just a night pissed off..." She filled the girls in on the events of the day before, finishing with Adam's discovery of Lucie's fling.

"What?" Suze gasped.

"God that Nick must be fit, why would you ever cheat on one half of the tasty twins?" Callie asked.

Despite herself Zoey couldn't help but smile. "Tasty twins?"

"Oh c'mon Zo, you know your hubby and his brother are like, well hot."

Suze elbowed Callie. "Go an make her a coffee, she looks like she needs it."

"Oooh yeah, that'd be great." Zoey temporarily forgot she was supposed to be avoiding caffeine in case it hindered her chances of getting pregnant.

The following day Lucie could almost kid herself that everything was back to normal. After being let out of hospital the day before Ant had decided he was well enough to go back to work. He was never the type to sit hanging around and being in hospital had done his head in, he'd told her. So he'd tootled off to the office this morning and she made her way to work. Just like every other day really, except it wasn't. Ant may be unaware of the bomb shell that in the not too distant future was about to be dropped from a great height and possibly blow their marriage to pieces, but she wasn't and it was all she could think about. She so didn't want that, but she also couldn't work out what to do about Nick. She knew exactly what Zo and Adam would say, leaving the only other person she could really confide in, Jake, but she also knew what he'd say too.

So she sat at her desk searching her computer for some good deals to go in the window, maybe she should book herself on one of them. The shop was empty, it was still only early and the people of this town generally didn't surface till lunch time. Jake was in the foreign exchange booth, whilst her other two colleagues, Helen and Claire were out on the counter with her. She was trying to lose herself in the window offers, so she'd tuned the other's out. Jake's bellowing voice jolted her back into the land of the living.

"Oi, Maxwell, are you even on the planet this morning? We're gonna do the top ten tunes on the radio again, win a free lunch from the pastie shop. You got the hits book in your desk?"

"Some of us are trying to work," she glared at him as she pulled out the directory of every UK chart since the year dot from her desk. "We've won the lunch so many times, the radio station are bound to know we're cheating."

"Everyone does it, anyway it's using our initiative." Claire grabbed the book and began to leaf through it as the DJ played 'Barcelona.'

"It's defo an Olympic year 'coz they used this for the Olympics...can't remember which Olympics it was though," Helen said.

"Err, Hels try Barcelona," Jake rolled his eyes then without warning stretched his arms out and belted out "BAARRRCCEELLOOOONNNAAA."

Jake's antics brought a small smile to Lucie's face.

"You really are a misery today; I did that to make you laugh! C'mon Luce in the back, we'll leave these two to win us some lunch."

Reluctantly she followed him, she knew he'd have a pretty good idea of what was going on and she knew he wasn't gonna let her off easily.

"What d'you want me to say J? I told you so?"

"Might be best if you start at the beginning or at least after the little kiss that wasn't gonna lead to anything..."

"Well it did, it led to way more and now Zo and Adam know but Ant doesn't."

"Look Luce, I'm your mate, but you should've stayed well clear of sailor boy and if you're honest with yourself you knew it wasn't gonna end with a kiss."

"D'you think I did this on purpose? That I planned to have an affair?"

"No, you're not that calculated, I just don't think you've tried very hard to stop it."

She sighed. "Oh God, I don't know, it sounds stupid but I

just thought it wouldn't do any harm going down memory lane."

"Yeah, but there's a difference between going down memory lane and going down on it."

"Jake!"

He shrugged his shoulders. "Look it might sound like a cliché but you can't go backwards to go forwards."

"That's the whole point. We didn't get our chance to go forwards. He was stuck on the ship and I had to go home."

"If it was really meant to be, you would've found a way, he didn't have to stay on the ship."

"It's not a bloody movie, those type of things don't happen in real life. He had a job to do, he wasn't just gonna run after me and 'abandon ship'. I don't even know why you're having a go at me. It's got nothing to do with you."

"You're right it hasn't really, apart from me being your friend and the fact that Ant's a good guy and doesn't deserve this... AND you've put Zo in a bad position."

She held her hands up. "Ok, stop. I know all that you don't need to tell me. I know you're all disgusted in me, I'm the bad person and no one is on my side...well apart from..." she let the sentence hang in the air.

"It's not about sides, well ok maybe it is, its human nature isn't it?"

"What d'you mean?" she asked.

"OK, Brad and Jen?"

"Team Aniston obviously."

"Katie and Peter?"

"Surprisingly Peter Andre."

"Cheryl and Ashley."

"Obviously Chezza. Ok, ok you've made your point, there's always a bad one and in Lucie and Ant it's obviously me..."

"Well, in all fairness it's not Ant sleeping with Nick is it?"

Before she could reply Claire burst through the door. "Luce, Mrs Foster's here to see you, she's kicking off 'coz she's got building work at her hotel oh yeah, we've won the free lunch too!"

"Oh for God sake," she muttered as headed off towards the shop floor and plastered her happy travel agents smile on her face.

"What are you doing babe?" Adam came home from work to find Zoey already home and fiddling with the net curtain in their bedroom. "Oh Suze gave me this crystal, it's like a feng sui thing."

"Cool." He sat down on the edge of the bed and began to loosen his tie.

She'd only told him a little white lie, it was actually a fertility crystal, but they were supposed to be chilling out about the whole pregnancy thing, so if he knew what it really was he might get pissed off. Especially as their stress levels had risen hugely in the last twenty four hours. She also made a mental note to move all those pregnancy testing kits to work in case he found them, one or two she could explain, but thirty was a bit excessive!

She'd gotten into the habit of buying a few every time she did her weekly shop in Sainsbury's. She dreaded to think how much she'd spent on them. She just thought it was best to be prepared, just following what she'd learnt in Girl Guides! Whenever she did a test, she always did a few, just to make sure the result was accurate and of course she also did a few tests a couple of days before she was due on and some a few days after and maybe just one or two at random times of the month just in case. In her own mind she knew she was getting a bit obsessed, but she knew she wasn't alone. She'd read someone's pregnancy blog and that person couldn't even pass a chemist without buying at least three tests. Adam had no idea about her stash of tests; he really would start worrying then. Now she thought about it, she was sure she was overdue a test, all this stuff with Lucie was taking her mind off her pregnancy stress.

"How come you're home so early?" Adam's voice broke her train of thought.

"Larry sent me home; he said I looked like shit."

"That boss of yours has such a way with words."

"Yeah, but his hearts in the right place."

"I'm knackered, I almost fell asleep in my own class, never mind the bloody kids."

"I couldn't stop yawning in front of customers; I kept telling them the neighbour's dog barking all night keeping me up."

"You should've just told them it was your selfish best mate. D'you know how bad I've felt ignoring Ant's texts today? He must think I don't even care that he's just come out of hospital."

"Adam, it's not my fault."

"I'm sorry babe, I know. I just hate knowing something so bad and not being able to do anything about it. We've always been there for each other and now for the first time in our lives I don't know what to do."

"All you can do is help him through it when the time comes." She slipped her arms around his neck.

"What about you? Are you gonna be there for Lucie?" His tone was accusing.

"I really don't know," she sighed

Lucie wasn't aware she was chasing peas around her plate until Ant broke her concentration.

"Hey kiddo, you ok?"

She looked up and replied absentmindedly. "Yeah, yeah fine."

"You don't seem your usual self."

She stared back down at her plate and stabbed a pea.

"Just work stuff." She didn't look back up at him, how could she? He'd be able to tell in a nano second she was lying. Jake had been right earlier today, Ant didn't deserve any of this...she'd come home tonight to find Ant already making tea, he'd told her he'd been fine at work, just dosed himself up on pain killers and now he was pretty much back to normal. She instantly felt guilty, he was so lovely. She didn't deserve him, not after the way she'd behaved. Maybe she should just come right out and tell him.

"Luce, I think we need to talk, properly. I know what's going on."

Her head shot back up so fast she nearly gave herself whiplash. "You do?"

He pushed his plate to one side. "It's so obvious."

Lucie had a horrible taste of peas in her mouth. He knew? Adam must've told him. Well, here it was, time to face the music, 'fess up. "Ant, I can explain..."

"You don't need to, there's nothing to explain. It's a conversation we should've had a long time ago."

"We should?"

"It's natural for it to be on your mind, what with Adam and Zo trying, but if you're ready, then I am. Let's have a baby."

"WHAT?"

"I think it's time for us to start a family."

"What's brought this on?"

"Well, you've been so pre occupied lately; I thought that's what was on your mind. I mean we're married, financially we're ok, there's nothing to stop us is there?"

"I'm not ready, I'm too young," she protested.

"We're the same age as Adam and Zo."

"Oh for God sake, we don't have to do everything they

do." She was aware her voice was getting higher and higher.

"Ok Luce, calm down will yer," he took a deep breath. "What's the point of being married if you don't want a family?"

"I married you because of you, not because of any kids we may or may not have."

"I married you for our future, our future as a family, which includes children." He sounded defeated.

"Look," she sighed, this so wasn't the time to be having this conversation. "I didn't say I didn't want them, it's just now isn't the time." So not the time she added silently. "There's still things I wanna do before we have kids, places I want to travel to, adventures to have..."

He reached across the table and took her hand. "I'm sorry; I just thought that's what was bugging you."

"I really am fine."

"I just can't shake the feeling that something's not quite right between us. I thought it was babies..." He let the sentence hang in the air as he looked her straight in the eyes.

If she was gonna tell him, now was the time. She could see it in his eyes, the doubt, and the confusion. *Tell him,* damn, that voice in her head was back again.

"Ok here's the thing..." she took a moment to choose her words, as she did his mobile began to ring. "It's me ma, I'll get rid of her." He stood up from the table. "Hey ma, yeah I'm fine, no my head's not really hurting anymore..."

She sank back down into the chair, all her courage gone. How could she tell him? His head may be ok, but she didn't want to be responsible for breaking his heart.

CHAPTER TWENTY FIVE

Lucie had thrown herself into work. Jake was still giving her the cold shoulder after yesterday's row. So to avoid any further confrontation she'd stayed on the counter and hopefully out of trouble. If she thought back to her time on 'Oceania' with Nick it brought a smile to her face just thinking about the whirlwind of love, lust or whatever the feeling was that made her feel almost drunk when she was with him. Now adding Ant to the equation the whole situation just made her head fuzzy like she had a massive hangover. Did she regret letting Nick back in her life? If truth be told she didn't. Some part of her mind had always wondered about him. The sad fact was the timing was all wrong again and not only that, they had changed. Nick still had a carefree zest for life and his boyish charm. She had a mortgage for the next twenty five years, she was now officially a grown up. In which case she should start acting like one. She'd made a commitment to Ant, she wasn't willing to throw it away, despite her feelings for Nick. She'd arsed around for long enough. It was time to make a decision, Ant or Nick? She nipped into the back and pulled her phone out of her bag.

We need to talk.

She pressed send before she had time to change her mind. As soon as she put the phone back in her bag she heard it beep. She took it back out and opened the message. Jake appeared as she was reading it.

"Luce, I just wanted to check that everything is ok."

"J, I can't talk now," she pulled her jacket out of the cloakroom. "I've got to go."

"Go? Go where? What about work?"

"Tell Sal I'm sick or something, I have to go and sort this out."

"Where are you going?"

"To see a dog about a bone." With that she was out of the door.

Zoey was updating the cruise file in work; she hoped doing something she enjoyed might stop her feeling like crap. She and Adam had made a conscious effort last night not to discuss the Lucie and Ant dilemma they'd found themselves in. She'd turned off her mobile to avoid Lucie's texts. She and Adam needed some quality time.

"Zo?" Callie shouted over. Zoey looked up. "Mrs Woods balance on her holiday is a week overdue. She's on the phone now and wants to know if she can pay on Tuesday."

Zoey picked up the calendar, Callie told her the date of travel "I'll just work out the cancellation charges." She counted the days from next Tuesday to the date of travel, as long as it was within fifty three days the cancellation charges would be loss of deposit and they'd be covered so they could extend the payment date. "Seventy two days, we're ok, but make sure you tell her we can't extend it further than that."

"Will do, thanks."

"No problem hon." Zoey went to put the calendar down when a thought struck her. She pulled out her diary from her desk and flicked to the last circled date which singled the start of her last period. She counted the days between then and now, and then counted them again and once more. How the hell could she have been two weeks late and not realised? Obviously Lucie's problem had distracted her more than she thought. A ball of excitement welled up inside her – could it finally have happened? Could she actually be pregnant? What if it was just stress that made her period late? She'd pop next door to Boots and get a test or did she have time to nip home on her lunch? No she couldn't wait that long. She'd get one from Boots then use some of her secret stash when she got home. Just as she stood up the phone rang.

"Good morning, thank you for calling 'BOOK IT', Zoey speaking, how can I help you?"

"Zo, its Jake."

"Hiya mate, how are you?"

"I'm good. I just thought I should let you know that Lucie's gone AWOL."

"What d'you mean?"

"Well I think she's either gone to see Nick or Ant. She was messing with her phone before and then she said she had to go and sort it out. I've got a really bad feeling about this..."

"You're not the only one. I take it she told you what's been going on?"

"Yeah, we had a bit of a row about it..."

"Oh this is getting ridiculous, lots of people know and Ant doesn't"

"And she thinks no one's on her side except Nick."

"Which might just drive her straight into Nick's arms. Oh I don't know what to do."

"There's not a lot you can do Zo."

"You're right," she sighed. "I'll try her on her mobile. Thanks mate."

She immediately began to dial Lucie's mobile after hanging up from Jake, unsurprisingly it went straight to voicemail. "Luce it's me, call me. I'm worried about you."

She put the phone down and sighed, she had to put this out of her mind, she had more important things to think about.

Lucie tapped her finger tips on the table as she waited, she glanced at her watch, he was at least ten minutes late. Trust him to keep her waiting. She'd arranged to meet in Debenhams coffee shop, somewhere neutral and somewhere she was more likely to stay in control. She twisted her hair around her index finger. Five more minutes and she was off, her stomach was in knots as it was, any longer and she'd bottle it.

"I love how you do that."

She looked up. How did he do that? Just appear from nowhere.

"Love what?"

"How you fiddle with your hair, it's pretty sexy."

She smiled shaking her head slightly. "You never stop with the lines do you?"

"You make it easy for me, there's lots to love about you babe."

She sighed. Be strong Lucie, like you normally are, don't let him turn you to mush again. "Nick, we have to stop."

"Stop what? Meeting like this?" he grinned.

"Yes."

If he was surprised by her reply he didn't show it. He leaned back in his seat. "You see the thing is, I'd be really worried if I thought you actually meant that but I know you don't. What we have Luce, it's too strong to break. You want me."

"Wanting and having are two different things. I want a Gucci handbag, doesn't mean I can have it."

"Did you just compare me to a handbag?"

"You know what I mean. Yes I want you, but it doesn't alter the fact that this has to end. I have to decide between you and my marriage and I can't turn my back on it."

He lifted his hands up in exasperation. "There you go using funny ways to describe things again, you make it sound like it's the idea of your marriage that's important, not actually who you're married too..."

"I just want to leave Ant out of this."

"So you're just gonna go back to him and pretend none of this ever happened?"

"If Adam and Zo will let me, I don't want Ant to get hurt." She looked away.

"What happens in six months time when you realise you've made a mistake?"

She turned back to face him. "I haven't made a mistake Nick. Our time was five years ago, we should've made it work then, not now."

He reached across the table and threaded his fingers through hers, she could feel the tell tale sign of goose bumps again. Oh God no, Get a grip Lucie, he's only a guy, do not let him have this effect on you. It was no good, as if to mock her the bumps raced up her arms,

"Tell me one thing and I'll walk away right now."

She could barely breathe "What?"

"When he touches you, do you get goosebumps?"

She stared at him, he knew the answer to that question,

he knew he was the only one who could make her body react that way.

"We can't base a relationship on goosebumps..."

"Why not? Seems perfectly reasonable to me."

"Nick, please...you're not making this easy..."

"Because I don't want you to walk out of my life again Luce. I stupidly lost you once, don't let history repeat itself."

"I've made my decision."

"What if it's the wrong one? You know deep down it is."

"No, I don't."

"I will wait; I give it six months- max. I guarantee within six months you will be knocking on my door with your suitcases."

She smiled sadly. "So you want my marriage to fail just so you can get what you want, d'you know if it was the other way round and it was you with someone I'd want you to be happy."

"Look, I don't give a damn about him, it's you. D'you think I wanna see you walk off into the sunset with some guy, when we both know deep down you should be with me?"

She broke away from him. "We're going round in circles here. We have to end it and it has to end now." She stood up. He was out of his seat just as quick and in one step was right in front of her. "Why did you want to meet here? Why not at my flat?" he inched closer.

"I...I..."

He lifted his hand to the back of her head, pulling her face closer to his. "Was it coz' you thought I wouldn't do this?" he whispered, his lips millimetres away from hers. She didn't have time to answer, her arms were around his neck, his hands in her hair, holding her face to his as he kissed her. He moved his hands to her cheeks as he finally moved away, although still close enough that their noses were almost touching and she could see deep into his eyes.

"That was exactly why," she whispered.

"You can't leave me like this. If you want him I won't stand in your way but please, let's just have one last time together. One for the road," he winked.

She shook her head laughing. "I can't believe you've just said that. I almost said yes until the road comment."

"Forget I mentioned the road," he shrugged,

Against her better judgement and ignoring the voice that was now yelling at her to walk away and quit while she was ahead she said "One for the road."

Lucie had been so involved with Nick she paid little attention to the people around her in the café, apart from the few people around her who'd jeered "Put him down love" when she and Nick kissed. Had she been slightly less absorbed in him, she may have noticed, sitting in the corner with her Thursday club and her best peach twin set on, the dreaded mother in law.

Old Ma Maxwell watched her daughter in law in the arms of another man and then leave with him. Not one to cause a scene, especially not in front of her Thursday club, they were such gossips; she quietly took the view in. Quite frankly it put her off her cream tea and scone. She always knew her son was far too good for that Lucie one and now she'd been proved right. She informed her friend Beryl that she wouldn't be going to bingo that night, she had some family business to attend too. Not that she planned on having that girl in the family much longer. How dare she flaunt the Maxwell name like that.

Lucie and Nick were on the stairs leading up to his apartment. As soon as they got through the door they were kissing. Lucie wasn't quite sure how they managed to get up the stairs, they were messily kissing, noses bumping, teeth clashing, jackets being pulled off, balances being lost. In the end Nick scooped her up into a fireman's lift and marched her straight into the apartment where he swiftly dropped her on the bed, he yanked his top off and followed just as quickly. He landed almost on top of her, his arms either side of her shoulders pushing himself above her. She stretched out underneath him.

"Oh crap, I really shouldn't be here."

He leaned down and planted kisses on her face. "Yes. You. Should." He jumped back up. "I know just what'll get you in the mood. Back in a sec."

He sprinted out of the room.

She rubbed her face with her hands. Seriously what was she doing here? She'd just told him that she was putting her marriage first, that she'd chosen Ant over him. What kind've fool was she? She stretched her arms up, grabbing the pillow to put under her head. Her left hand brushed against something. She flipped onto her stomach and grabbed the paper ready to chuck into the bin He really was a messy bugger. She caught sight of something written on the paper. She straightened it out. *Tara was here*. Tara? Why did that name ring a bell? She sat bolt upright swinging her legs over the side of the bed. The gymnastic off the ship. She'd been here! She was a bigger fool than she thought. She quickly did the buttons up on her jeans and grabbed her jacket. She nearly knocked Nick over as he came through the door with a bottle of champagne and two glasses.

"Where are you going?"

She threw the paper at him. "I can't believe I fell for your crap."

Bombing down the M53 towards home Lucie was still bubbling with anger. She'd stormed out on Nick, he'd followed her, running out in just his jeans. The same stairs that ten minutes previously they'd been kissing on like their life depended on it, was now the stage for a full out row. She'd run down the stairs, he was right behind her, taking them two at a time.

"Luce, I know what I did was wrong, but it's no different to you...bet you're still sleeping with Ant."

She stopped at the small landing before the next flight of stairs, she spun round to face him and slapped him hard across the cheek. He instinctively lifted his hand to his cheek and rubbed it. "Hit a nerve there did I?" he raised an eyebrow at her.

"He's my husband, I should be sleeping with him, not you." It riled her how he always stayed so chilled.

"Which makes me free to sleep with whoever I want."

"Well, I hope your little gymnast makes you happy," she spat as she turned on her heel and bounded down the stairs. Again he was behind her. "Babe, I'm sorry, that was below the belt. You know I don't want her, I just want you." He jumped over the banisters and landed at the foot of the staircase, getting there before she did, making her practically fall on top of him as she collided with his bare chest. He put his arms around her, initially to steady her fall, but then he didn't let go. She shrugged his arms from her. "Nick, I don't want to speak to you right now. I need to get home."

He stood aside to let her past. "Can I call you later?"

"You can't call me ever. We're finished."

"So are you gonna pretend none of this ever happened?"

"If that's what it takes to stop Ant from being hurt then I will."

She looked at the speedometer, she better slow down.

The last thing she needed was being pulled over. She slowed right down then indicated to leave the motorway at the junction for Wallasey. She had to calm down before she got home. Ant was already suspicious about her recent behaviour. She pulled into her road spotting the mother in law's car parked outside the house.

"Great," she muttered. She took of her glasses and put them in the glove compartment until the next time she drove. Hopefully she was only here for a flying visit.

CHAPTER TWENTY SIX

Unable to get Lucie off her mind Zoey decided to take a chance on her being home rather than with Nick, so she headed over to her house straight after work.

Really she wanted to go home and see Adam but she knew he'd be at the rugby club. Thursday wasn't a usual training night but they'd won the game that Ant got injured in meaning the final was only weeks away, hence the extra training. She couldn't wait to show Adam what she had in her bag. As she pulled into Lucie's road she was relieved to see her car there, but also spotted the Mother in laws too. Ah well, at least if Old Ma Maxwell was there she and Luce would have to be civil to each other. When she reached the front door it was already a jar, she could hear raised voices. She found Lucie in the living room facing the window her back to the mother in law who was giving her an ear bashing.

"I could not believe my eyes when I saw you practically fornicating with that, that gigolo!"

"We were doing nothing of the sort...it was a goodbye kiss for a very old friend." Lucie spun round.

"What's going on?"

"It would seem, Zoey dear, that your friend has been having a fling behind my sons back."

Zoey looked over to Lucie. "She knows about you and Nick?" Too late she realised she'd said the wrong thing. The Mother in law almost pounced on her.

"You KNEW! How could you let this happen? I thought you were the sensible one. Obviously not."

Here we go again, me getting the blame – again. Zo sighed to herself,

"For Godsake will you leave Zo alone, you're always on her case. She tried to stop it, so just get off her back."

"I am not always on her 'case' as you put it at least I know she has Adam's best interests at heart and she actually wants to give him a child. Still, I suppose if you got pregnant we wouldn't know who it actually belonged too. We'd have to go on Jeremy Kyle for him to do a DNA test, oh the shame."

"You poisonous, crazy, lady."

Old Ma Maxwell squared up to Lucie. "Don't you dare speak to me like that, you are nothing but a little scrubber."

Zoey jumped in between them, she could see the anger in Lucie's eyes and knew this wasn't going to end well. "Stop it both of you." She tried to push them away from each other. She may as well have been invisible. Both women were still screaming at each other.

"She's nothing but a whore."

"She's an evil cow."

"I want her out of my sons' life."

"Over my dead body."

"What the hell is going on?"

The argument abruptly stopped at the sound of Ant's voice. He appeared at the door way, alongside Adam.

"Ant...I thought you were going to training..."

"I was, but they wouldn't let me train, said I had to wait till I was fully recovered from the knock I took. So I come home and find I've walked into the middle of a battlefield."

Zoey caught the look on Adam's face; he knew exactly what was going on.

"Oh Anthony, my darling boy, it's just terrible," Old Ma Maxwell grabbed Ant and pulled him to the sofa to sit next to her.

"Ma. What's happened...are you ok?"

Adam stepped in. "Ma. I really think you should leave this to Lucie and Ant."

"Not a cat in hells chance. I'm not leaving my son alone with that floozy."

"Mum! You're well out of order, that's my wife you're talking about."

"Yes dear, I know. You just ask your wife what she's been up to."

Ant turned to Lucie, she'd retreated into the corner of the room, her arms folded tightly across her chest, chewing at her bottom lip. He tried to decipher the look on her face, but it was an expression he'd never seen before. "Luce?"

"She's nothing but a trollop," Old Ma Maxwell still hadn't finished putting her two pence worth in. Zoey'd had enough. No matter what her own personal feelings were on the situation, the mother in law was practically gloating. If the shoe was on the other foot Luce would be the first one fighting her corner. Zoey marched across the living room and pulled her mother in law up off the sofa. "I think, *mum*. That you've said quite enough for now. I think it's time we left these two to talk things through without your interference. Don't you?" She carried on walking towards the door, taking the mother in law with her.

"But, but, he's my son, he needs me."

"What he needs is to have this conversation with his wife." She turned round glaring at Adam and through gritted teeth said "Back me up,"

"Come on Ma. I think you've said enough." Adam guided her out of the room.

They'd been alone for a few minutes, but hadn't actually spoken. Lucie could tell by the look on his face that he was expecting something bad, she knew he had no idea just how bad. She stayed standing, she badly wanted to go over and sit next to him but she had a feeling that in few minutes he'd want to be as far away from her as possible. She just wished she could find the right words, to stop him from getting hurt. He spoke first. "What's going on Luce?"

"I wish I knew where to start."

"The beginnings always good."

The beginning, all those years ago. It seemed like it'd had all happened to someone else. It had been so good then, now it had all gone wrong. "Ok, the beginning, but please let me say what I need to say. You can scream and yell at me as much as you want afterwards, just let me get my side out."

He leaned forward, his elbows on his knees and propping his chin up with his fists, "I'm not sure I wanna hear this, but I'm all ears."

"You know the story about how me and Zo first met, on the ship, well there's a bit more to the story than you know..."

"There was a guy right? Sorry, I'm not meant to be interrupting."

She nodded. "Yeah there was a guy. I never really told you how serious it'd been between us 'coz I thought it didn't really matter. It was in the past and then I met you and everything was good. I never thought I'd see him again."

"He's back?" He held his hands up gesturing that he wouldn't interrupt again.

"Yep."

"He wants to see you, right? I know I'm butting in, but I can't help it, you're telling me some guy from years ago who you had a fling with wants to see you?"

"It wasn't a fling, we fell in love."

"Like I need to know that."

"You do, it's important. There are only two guys I've ever loved you and...him."

"Why do I need to know that?"

She turned her gaze away from him. "So when I tell you the rest you'll know that...that this wouldn't have happened with just anyone." As she looked back she saw the colour visibly drain from his face.

"I think I can fill in the blanks...you've already seen him haven't you?"

She could only nod.

"Have you, have you," he rubbed his hand across his face. "God I can't even say it."

Again she nodded. "Babe, I'm so sorry," she whispered her voice cracking.

"When? Where?"

She looked down at the floor, tears stinging her eyes as she tried to keep them in. She couldn't look at his face, couldn't see the hurt when he realised just what she'd done. "It was at his apartment...but it was more than once, he says he still loves me..."

Ant jumped up from the sofa. "He still loves you? Loves you enough to have not bothered with you for the last five years, then the minute he's back you're dropping yer knickers. Of course he bloody loves you. What have you done? What about us? Didn't you even think about us?"

"Of course I did, I never stopped thinking about you. I

didn't want this to happen I love you, but I never stopped loving him either..."

"I can't believe you could do this. I would've given you anything you wanted, done anything for you..."

"I'm sorry...it's all over now."

"Oh well, that's ok then. I'll conveniently forget that you've been shagging some guy behind my back. So am I supposed to feel flattered that he still loves you, but you say it's over with him?"

"Oh God, everything's such a mess. To tell the truth, I don't know how I feel about him, he says he loves me...all I know is, I DO love you, although right now you probably hate me..."

"I can't do this...I'll only end up saying something I'll regret. I never ever thought you'd do this to me. One year we've been married, one year, do I mean that little to you that you could just discard me the minute someone better came along. I always thought I wasn't enough for you, I'm not like Adam."

"What the hell's Adam got to do with all this?"

"Coz' he's the confident one, he shower's Zoey with affection and big gestures."

"Yep and he can also be an arrogant arse. Ant, I have never ever wished you were more like him. I fell in love with YOU, your unassuming ways. Your..."

"Well, from where I'm standing it doesn't feel like you're still in love with me."

"Ant, I love you so much, I'm just confused, I know I shouldn't have feelings for another guy."

"How about I make this easier for you," he grabbed his keys from the mantel piece. "I'm getting off."

"Ant, no! Don't go, we need to sort this out."

He turned round "One question...you obviously got found out. Would you have told me if you thought you could get away with it?"

She stood in silence, contemplating the question, she didn't know what she would've done. She just looked at him.

"Wrong answer, kiddo."

With that he was gone.

So what do you do when your husband has just found out you've been having an affair? Lucie wasn't sure of the answer to that one, normally in a crisis she'd turn to Zo, but that probably wasn't an option at the moment so the only alternative she could think of was to crack open the bottle of white chilling in the fridge. So what if she didn't find the answer at the bottom of the bottle, it'd make her feel a hell of a lot better.

Lucie paced the floor of her living room while she gulped down a glass of pinot grigio in almost one go and automatically filled it straight back up. What did Ant mean about getting off? Just for tonight or forever? Had he left her? Not that she didn't deserve it. She didn't feel any clearer about her feelings for either of them apart from knowing she loved them both in different ways. How could Nick expect her to throw her marriage away if he couldn't even show he could commit to her? But then that was Nick all over, his whole life had been a lack of responsibility, no worries on the ship and away from real life. Yes, she might be special to him but that didn't mean it would ever work. Whereas up until Nick's return she thought she and Ant would be together forever. She knew Ant's insecurities and being in Adam's shadow but how could he even think he wasn't good enough? The second glass was almost finished and going straight to her head, she'd had no tea. It was making her feel both woozy and emotional. She grabbed her mobile and dialled Ant's number, it went straight to voicemail. Hearing his cheerful voice asking her to leave a message made her begin to cry. What was she supposed to say? She snapped the phone shut and started on that third glass of wine.

After driving around for a while unsure what to do Ant finally found himself in Adam and Zo's living room. Zoey had tactfully left him alone with Adam.

"I wanna go and kick his arse."

"He's not worth it bro," Adam said.

"Of course he's worth it, he's just broken up my marriage which was everything to me. That deserves a kicking of the arse."

Adam nodded his head "Yeah, you're right," he paused, looking up at his twin brother's face and seeing the hurt etched all over it. It made him wanna go and kick cruise guy's arse too. "So, is that it? Is it really over?"

Ant sighed. "I dunno mate, I really don't know what to think or what to do. I never knew I could hurt like this. I can't get the look on her face when she told me out of me 'ead."

Adam reached across and squeezed his brother's shoulder. He didn't know what else to say, there was a reason men didn't have deep and meaningful conversations and it was mainly 'coz they were crap at it.

Zoey was in the kitchen trying to keep herself busy shoving the next load of washing in, rearranging the tins in the cupboard but mainly just eating her secret stash of Wispa bars. She'd thought it was best if she gave the lads some space, also she felt guilty about knowing what had been going on. She couldn't quite look Ant in the eye. She sat on the kitchen worktop working her way through the second of her Wispa bars. She couldn't believe what a mess everything was. Tonight should have been so different and now she was keeping things from Adam, but she couldn't tell him now. She didn't want their news to be tainted by this. She wanted it to be perfect when she told him. The Diagnosis Murder theme tune started ringing on her phone. She looked at the caller ID. It was just as well her phone told her it was Lucie ringing, because from the noise of the whaling banshee down the phone she couldn't be sure.

What ever was being said down her phone Zoey couldn't make any sense of it.

"Calm down, Luce, I'm on me way over."

CHAPTER TWENTY SEVEN

In staff training the following morning the last thing Zoey felt like doing was role plays for the benefits of booking a car on your holidays, especially when everyone else seemed to be in a bad mood too. Larry was in the foreign Exchange, he'd been huffing and puffing away all morning, his long suffering wife, Janice had put him on a diet and he wasn't impressed. He was now trying to balance the till, he'd already counted it all once before but dropped it over the floor on his way out to the counter after he tripped over a left over pastie he'd inadvertently left by the safe. So now he had to do it again he was even more cantankerous than usual. The fact that they'd all laughed when he went arse over tit didn't help matters.

Callie had been out on the pop last night, so now she had a hangover that only a double egg Mcmuffin was solving. If Zo didn't like Callie so much she'd hate her, she was skinny, far too pretty and could live on Maccy D's, Vodka and blackcurrant, cigarettes and not put on an ounce of weight. Totally the wrong person for Zo to ever stand next to, especially when she was having a fatter than normal day, although to be fair she did have an excuse. She watched Callie unwrap another Mcmuffin, the smell was starting to make her feel nauseous. She half thought morning sickness must be psychological coz' she hadn't felt a bit sick until two minutes after she'd peed on the stick.

To make matters worse she'd hardly slept last night she'd spent hours with Lucie, not getting much sense from her drunken rant. By the time she'd flopped into bed it was gone mid-night, she'd tossed and turned most of the night worrying about Luce and trying to think of when would be the perfect moment to tell Adam. How could she be carrying this tiny little baby inside her and hadn't yet managed to tell the person she loved most in the world?

Suze came out from the back with cups of coffee. The smell hit Zoey's nose like a torpedo. Yep, that's gonna do it. She thought as she legged it past Suze to go and throw up in the loo.

Suze raised an eyebrow at Callie "Hmmm, d'you think our Zo might have something to tell us?"

"Like what?"

"Like she might finally be preggas?" Suze lowered her voice.

Larry had radar when it came to maternity leave. "What was that?" he boomed.

"Err nothing boss man, just err Cheggars..."

"Cheggars?" he asked.

"Yeah Cheggars on the radio."

"Hmm, didn't know he still had a radio show, he's much better than the crap you girls listen to oh and by the way I'll be having the radio in the Foreign Exchange on Saturday, Everton are playing the red shite, the Manc red shite not the scouse red shite that you lot all support, although they're both shite."

"D'you know what boss, it comes as no surprise to me that Jim Royale is your hero," Callie said.

"My arse!" he laughed, pushing his glasses back up to the bridge of his nose.

Suze and Callie rolled their eyes. Larry had taken Jim Royale's catch phrase as his own.

Zoey reappeared from the back looking an off shade of green.

"You ok chick?" Suze asked concerned.

"Err yeah, just a bad curry last night or something."

"Zo, you don't like curry."

"Well, this is obviously why I don't eat it isn't it? Now come 'ead lets get a move on with this car hire training."

Lucie had gone to work that morning but Sally had sent her straight home. She said she didn't know what was going on, but it was obviously something serious and she couldn't have her on the counter serving customers in the state she was in.

She didn't know what to do when she got home. She hadn't been able to get hold of Ant since he'd walked out last night. She didn't even know if he'd gone to work, she could ring his office, but didn't want the embarrassment of having to speak to any of his colleagues. If he'd gone to work they probably all knew what she'd done. So she carried on ringing his mobile, leaving messages, texting him but he hadn't replied. She was also getting inundated with messages and texts from Nick. Never mind a love triangle; it was like a vicious circle. Most of Nick's texts just said he was sorry and to call him, his voicemails were a bit longer. She had three new ones since leaving work. She had no choice but to listen to them, what if one was from Ant? She put her phone on speaker and lay it down on the table in the hope that she could distance herself from the message.

"...Luce. Babes. I'm sorry, I should've told Tara where to go...It's you I love...I know you love me too, just let me prove it to you..."

And the next message..."Babe, we are so good together, you know we are. I know I've been a dick, but I can change...just give me one more chance..."

She held her breath hoping message three was from Ant, but all she got was Nick pleading with her again. "It's me again, look if you stay with him, you know you're making the wrong choice...he can't..." she reached over and pressed the end call button. She'd heard enough. She flopped down on the sofa, what a mess. Nick sounded really desperate, but probably no more desperate than she sounded on the messages she'd left for Ant, messages that were met with a wall of silence. The house seemed so empty without him and sleeping alone last night had been horrible. She suddenly felt guilty for not answering Nick's messages; he was obviously feeling as miserable as she was. Maybe she should go and see him. *Bad idea Luce.* If she'd listened to that inner voice to begin with things might have turned out differently, on the other hand if she hadn't acted on impulse Nick would've always been at the back of mind. Nothing was going to get sorted if nobody was speaking to each other. Ant was obviously MIA at the moment, but Nick did want to speak to her. She grabbed her phone, bag and began scrolling for his number as she head out into the hall. She opened the door and spoke to him as she tried to lock the door at the same time.

"Nick it's me, you're right we do need to talk...no it's ok, I'll come to you. See you in about half an hour." She flipped the phone shut and turned round. Ant was at the gate. The look on his face, the hurt in his eyes spoke volumes. "It's not what you think..." She was aware how lame that sounded.

"Tell me what I'm supposed to think? I listened to all your messages, you sounded so sincere. I thought maybe I'd been a bit harsh walking out on you last night, I didn't give you a chance to explain." He shook his head in disbelief. "Turns out I should've trusted my instincts. The minute my backs turned you're crawling back to him, d'you know what Luce? He's welcome to you." He turned to walk away. She ran down the path after him.

"Ant! Wait!" She grabbed his arm and pulled him back round to face her. He shrugged her off.

"Please," she pleaded. "Just give me chance to explain. You wouldn't answer my calls, he did...I need to talk to someone I'm going crazy."

"You're going crazy? You should try being in my head for the last twenty four hours."

"Please just come back inside, we can't leave things like this..."

"You've got five minutes."

Zo was wandering around Sainsbury's with Adam doing their weekly shop after work. She still hadn't told him their news and looking at him now she wasn't sure when the right time would ever present itself. His rugged profile was dominated by his knotted eyebrows and clenched jaw, his broad shoulders were about an inch higher than usual and she knew if she touched them she'd feel how tense he was. Even as she glanced down his arms, his shirt rolled up at the sleeves revealing the remains of a summer tan, she could see the strain in them as he gripped the trolley, he was pushing it round like The Stig. He rarely got stressed out but she knew he felt helpless in his ability to make things right for Ant. She wanted to take his mind off it all, he normally liked the silly stories she told him from work so she'd give that a try.

"Oh my God, it was so funny today in work," she started as she chucked some loo roll into the trolley.

Adam nodded his head slowly. "Go on then, tell me," he sighed

"Well Janice has put Larry on another diet, so he was in a proper bad mood and then he dropped the counter cash all over the floor so when we all laughed it got him even more knarked. Anyway, he'd supposedly forgotten his lunch so he popped out to get a couple of pasties. In the meantime Janice calls in with the egg salad he'd left at home and catches him walking in with two pasties. She did her nut and he just looked like a naughty school boy." She managed to get a small smile out of Adam. "That'll be us in years to come when I've stopped playing rugby and I'm going grey."

"Yeah right, you're gonna be one of those blokes who still look hot when they're grey, you'll be like George Clooney or Phillip Schofield."

He threw her a look. "Phillip Schofield, really?"

She grinned. "He'd deffo get it. Anyway it'll be me still trying to get my arse into shape when we're old."

This time he did laugh. "Nah, you'll be a MILF."

"Hmm, on the subject of MILF's."

"I like the sound of where this is going..."

This wasn't quite how she imagined, in the middle of the fruit and veg aisle at Sainsbury's but she was bursting to tell him. "Yeah it's more to do with the mum part of that abbreviation."

He turned to face her, the frown lines instantly gone and a smile starting to spread on his handsome face.

"D'you mean? Are we?"

She nodded her head as tears sprung from her eyes.

"Yes, we're having a baby." She couldn't keep the smile from her face.

"We did it, we bloody did it!" He pushed the trolley to one side; almost taking out a carefully stacked display of melons then picked her up and swung her round.

"Careful!" she giggled.

"Oh God, sorry." He put her down but still held her close. "I can't believe it finally happened. How far gone are you? When are we due?"

She was a ball of emotion, tears, laughter, happiness. "I don't actually know, didn't feel right going to the doctors without you knowing."

"But you are sure? When did you find out?" He was oblivious to the weird looks they were getting from other shoppers.

"Yeah, I've done like a million tests." Not too far from the truth, she had to use up all those spare pregnancy test she had stashed. "I found out the day it all kicked off with Luce and Ant...I didn't want to say anything then..."

"We bloody did it! You're amazing,babe."

"You did have something to do with it too y'know," she grinned, tears of happiness streaming down her face.

"I bloody well love you Zoey Maxwell." He took her face in his hands planting kisses all over her face. She caught the eye of an old dear behind him and as she trundled past with her trolley asked her, "What aisle did ya get him from lovey? I could do with one of him at home."

Lucie had succeeded in getting Ant into the house, but things hadn't really moved on from there. They'd hardly spoken a word. She could see how hurt and angry he was, she knew what it must've looked like when he turned up before and she was on the phone to Nick. Trouble was, she didn't know what to say to make it right. Could she even make it right? She needed a drink.

"I'm getting a drink d'you want one?"

"If I want one, I know where they are, this is half of my house after all."

She stood up, shaking her head as she walked past him, this obviously wasn't going well.

He called after her. "Actually, bring us in a beer, think I'll need it."

Her phone kept beeping, she knew it was Nick; she pulled her phone out of her pocket and shoved it in the kitchen draw. Out of sight, out of mind. She took the lager into Ant, he barely looked at her as he took the can from her.

"Ant, this is stupid, I can't stand this silence…I know I've hurt you really badly. I'm so sorry, I never meant it to happen?"

"You never meant to hurt me or you never meant to sleep with that dick?"

She looked down. "The truthful answer is both…I tried to stop it before it started but…"

"But you just didn't care enough about us to stop it."

"That's not true! If it had been that easy I'd have just walked away, told you it was over before anything even happened with Nick."

Ant laughed spitefully. "So you're saying you only cheated 'coz you love me? God, you sound like a bloke d'you know that?"

"Look, I know there are no excuses for what I've done and I know I should've been honest from the start, told you all about him and said I needed some space to work out what I wanted."

He stood up, slamming the can down on the fire place. "You are unbelievable…work out what you wanted? So you expected me just to take a step back while you decided if you wanted to be with me or cruise boy? You're my wife Luce…marriage doesn't work like that. Forsaking all others, remember?"

She nodded her head in shame. "That came out wrong. I just don't know what I want..."

"Really the question should be, what do I want? Do I still want you after you've treated me like this? You might take your wedding vows with a pinch of salt, but I don't? Sailor boy still wants you? Well he's gonna have a fight on his hands. I'm not ready to walk out on us yet."

CHAPTER TWENTY EIGHT

Lucie hadn't got very far with her clear the air conversation with Ant, they'd spent the majority of the evening either glaring at each other, moving from the sofa to the lazyboy chair and drinking endless cups of tea. They'd managed to waste almost four hours doing this.

"What's happened to us Luce? Were things so bad that you couldn't talk to me about it?"

"I honestly didn't think it would get to this stage, I thought I was over him a long time ago, or at least I hoped I was..."

"And I wasn't enough for you?"

"Oh babe, it was never about how I felt about you."

"Doesn't feel like that; imagine if it was the other way round and I'd gone off with one of my exes."

He had a point, she mused. If he'd done to her what she'd done to him she'd go ballistic and then some. God if he turned up with Sasha, that skinny bint he'd been going out with for years before they met, she'd do her nut and it totally would be her, 'coz that was the ex that pissed her off the most, the one he'd nearly moved in with, the one who was the actress with her bit parts in Hollyoaks, and it was her bits that got the most exposure, bloody Sasha, it would so be her.

"Are you trying to tell me you still love that skinny bint Sasha?"

"What the hell are you talking about? Don't turn this around on me...I'm asking you to empathise, see how it looks from over here. What's Sasha got to do with it?"

"Coz' she's the one you never got over."

"Me and Sash were over a long time ago...funnily enough when I met you I realised what I'd been looking for. Shame it wasn't the same for you."

She didn't know what to say to that, three months ago he was everything she'd been looking for, but now Nick had stuck his oar in...she'd tried to explain to Ant how if felt with Nick, like it wasn't real, like she was in a movie. It hadn't gone down well.

They sat in silence again, she looked up at the clock on the fireplace, God she hated that clock; it was one of those gold carriage types, a present from the outlaw. It looked like it belonged on the antiques road show (along with her). It looked so out of place with the modern décor of the living room, but what could she do? The outlaw would throw a hissy fit if the clock was relegated to the bathroom or even worse the utility room. The minute hand ticked onto the ten, the small hand also on ten. Time really had flown tonight, but not 'coz they were having fun, far from it. She was seriously losing the plot, what the hell was she doing giving a flippin' clock so much thought time? The doorbell rang, interrupting her thoughts.

"Who the hell is at that at this time of night?" Ant got up to answer it.

With a jolt Lucie realised exactly who was at her door at eleven minutes passed ten at night, someone she was supposed to meet hours ago and whose texts and calls she'd ignored. "Shit!"

"What?" He asked as he reached the living room door.

She jumped off the sofa. "Nothing, nothing. It's ok I'll get it."

"It's nearly the middle of the night, I don't like you answering the door this late at night, you never know what nutters are about." He looked at her as if he was about to say something else, but he'd already let slip enough, he did care. Unfortunately she knew exactly what type of nutter was on the other side of the front door and she didn't think Ant's compassionate moment would last much longer.

She ran down the hall and wedged herself between the door and him.

"Oh I don't bloody believe it…it's him isn't it? Nick the bloody prick. Right outside MY house."

"Look, its ok. I'll get rid of him."

"Who does he think he is coming round here? I'll bloody well sort him out."

She could almost feel the aggression oozing out of him, he had his rugby face on, this wasn't gonna be pretty.

"Calm down, calm down, let me sort it out, you're too mad."

There was hammering at the door. "Luce, it's me, are you ok? Let me in."

The red mist descended over Ant's face. "That's it, the little shit." He flung the door open.

Nick's reservations about turning up unannounced where reinforced when he saw the man mountain standing in front of him. Lucie's husband was at least three inches taller and a hell of a lot broader, those shoulders were like built like a tank… what the hell; he could probably still take him if he had too.

"I err, I just came to see if Luce was ok..." he was not impressed that his voice sounded a few octaves higher than normal. The trick was not to let this hulk know he was intimidated, not that it was working out too well for him at the moment. C'mon Slaz, step it up, he told himself.

"She's fine, we're fine and we'll be even better if you just piss off back under whatever rock you crawled out from."

Nick held his hands up. "Hey, I'm not here to cause an argument, I was just worried, she was supposed to meet me and never turned up."

"Doesn't that tell you something? She's not interested *mate.*"

The patronising intent behind the word mate wound Nick up.

"Oh she so is interested MATE,"

"You little..."

"Ant! Stop! Both of you, just stop, you'll have the neighbours out in a minute." Lucie tried to get in between them, but just ended up peeking over Ant's shoulder.

"He's just leaving," Ant glared at him.

"I'm going nowhere till I've spoken to Lucie."

Ant stood down from the doorstep and squared up to Nick. As Nick looked up at him he re-evaluated his first thoughts, he was probably only two inches taller, he could definitely take him.

Nick relied on his usual bravado to try and get him out of this situation, but his mouth kicked in before his brain. "Come and have a go if yer think yer hard enough." He groaned inwardly as soon as he said it and steeled himself for the punch that he was sure would come flying his way any second. Instead he heard Ant laughing.

"What the hell did she see in you? You're just a cocky little shit."

"I'll tell you what she sees in me, passion, excitement a guy who makes her blush, a guy who gives her goose bumps every time I touch her, a guy who gives her the best sex…" He didn't get to finish the sentence, the delayed punch landed right on his chin. Ant rugby tackled him to the floor.

"That's my WIFE you're talking about."

Nick tried to scramble out from underneath him. "Yeah your wife who wants to be in my bed," he panted as he tried to get to his feet, Ant took him to ground again. Nick tried to give as good as he got but he just connected with pure muscle.

"STOP IT!" Lucie shouted as she tried to pull them apart, she managed to separate them. Nick staggered backwards trying to straighten his clothes, he'd definitely come off worse, his lip was cut and a bruise was starting to form on his cheekbone.

"You ok?" she asked.

"Oh yeah, just great, didn't realise I'd be stepping into the ring with bloody Rocky tonight."

"What did you expect? Was hardly gonna ask you in for a beer and compare notes was I?"

"No worries mate, I'm sure my notes would've been better."

Lucie winced as Ant stepped forward again to launch another punch at Nick. She stepped in his way.

"Right, this stops now. Ant stop chucking your weight around and Nick stop being a dick. You're both doing my head in and right now I'd be quite happy not to see either of you. Nick just go home and Ant, do whatever you have to do, come back inside or go to Adam's. I've had enough." With that she turned and walked back into the house.

"Right well, I'll be off then." Nick certainly wasn't gonna hang around for round two, he scarpered pretty quickly.

With Luce back in the house and Nick gone Ant stood in the front garden alone, did he want to go back into the house? Did he really want to speak to her after Nick's little outburst? He thought what he and Lucie had ran much deeper than just sex, but obviously not. He spotted his nosy neighbour over the road peeking behind her curtains, he shoved his hands in his jeans pockets and headed back into the house, kicking the door shut behind him. He sat down on the bottom step of the stairs, he felt like he'd had the wind knocked out of him, that dick had totally gone for the jugular, what guy wants to hear that his wife wants to be in bed with some other guy? It wasn't just that though, it was Lucie. She had broken his heart. He tried to blink away the tears that were forming, tough guys don't cry. Evidently he wasn't as tough as he thought, he couldn't stop them from falling, he wiped them away with the sleeve of his rugby top and took a deep breath.

She'd heard Ant come in so she went off to face the music, seeing him sitting on the stairs crying tore her apart. He never cried. Not even when they watched all those soppy films together, she always cried buckets, he never did. He used to say it was sweet that she cried at the films, even if it was a happy ending she'd still be crying. Would they get their happy ending, or did that only happen in the movies? She stood in front of him. He shifted his gaze up to hers. All she could focus on were his beautiful blue eyes swimming in tears.

"Is it true what he said?"

"What d'you mean?" she asked quietly trying to stall for time.

"You know...that whole goose bumps thing. Is that what he does to you? Is that how he makes you feel?" he gritted his teeth as he spoke.

"That's not important, it's just a...a reaction."

Ant laughed bitterly. "Yeah, a reaction you should be getting from me. D'you know what...I thought we had so much more going for us, but it turns out that when it comes down to it, that's not enough is it?"

She crouched down next to him, taking his hands in hers.

"What are you saying?"

"There are so many things I loved about you Luce, not just the obvious stuff of how gorgeous you are, but the little things, the everyday stuff, like how you always watch me play rugby even though you don't understand the rules, how, if I get in your car, there's always some cheesy pop CD in there and I can't help listening to it, how you've never told anyone how much I love romantic films...and now I don't know what's gonna happen to all those things, 'coz I don't know what's gonna happen to us."

"Don't say that..."

He shrugged his shoulders. "What else is there to say? You say you love us both, you have to choose. I love you Luce, but I don't know if I can forgive you for this, so maybe that doesn't leave you with you a choice, maybe just a lack of options." he stood up, grabbing his jacket off the banister.

"Are you leaving me?"

"I don't know...I'll be at Adam's, I need to think."

"Ant...I love you too, and you're wrong, it's not just about sex, those little things are important to me too... I love how you call me kiddo, I love how you never laugh at me for crying at all those films, I love your quiet nature and I'm sorry I've messed everything up."

"So you don't love him?"

"Just in a different way."

"Yep he made that clear tonight exactly which way," he shook his head. "I can't do this anymore tonight." He opened the front door.

"Ant wait, please don't go. We can stop talking; I'll sleep in the spare room if you want."

"No, I need space. I need to work stuff out," he walked back over to her and kissed her on the cheek. "I'll speak to you tomorrow."

She watched him walk out of the door.

CHAPTER TWENTY NINE

There were many good things about being a twin, Ant reflected as he stood under the shower the following morning, the hot water sluicing over his shoulders in an attempt to loosen the knots formed across his upper torso. The whole twintuition thing meant Adam had been sitting up waiting for him last night as he had a "feeling" he was gonna call.

One of the other bonuses meant he could borrow his brother's clothes to go to work. As he'd walked down his garden path last night he'd been in two minds whether to turn back and go back to Lucie. He knew she was hurting just as much as he was. She hadn't cheated on him out of spite, she had genuinely found herself stuck between her past and her future. Not that it made it ok. What would he do if his "one that got away" turned up again? Despite what Luce thought Sasha had never been the great love of his life, it had been Mel a girl he went to uni with and the first girl to ever break his heart, the second being Lucie. What would he do if he ever bumped into Mel again? He'd often wondered how her life had turned out, was she happy? He'd like to think if he ever did see her again it would be nice to catch up, but that would be it. Obviously that hadn't happened with Lucie. He meant it when he said he wasn't sure he could forgive her, but he didn't want to let her go either. What to do? The pressure of the water on his back was starting to ease the tension from his body.

"ANTHONY MAXWELL, GET OUT OF MY BLOODY BATHROOM!" Zo yelled through the door as she banged on it.

"Two minutes Zo."

"Open the door now, I can't wait two minutes."

"I'm naked in here." Jeez, couldn't she wait two minutes to have a wee.

"I don't care, it's nothing I haven't already seen on your *identical* brother, just grab a towel and open this door NOW!"

He pulled the shower curtain to one side; the towels were too far away so he grabbed one of those fluffy things girls used to wash with to hide over his manhood. He reached across and undid the lock. "Where's the flippin' fire?"

She didn't reply, her head was straight down the toilet and he pretty much got his answer straight away. Adam arrived in the bathroom about ten seconds later.

"Babe, are you ok?" He knelt down next to her and stroked her hair. She shook her head and threw up again.

"Err, everything ok bro?"

Adam turned his head towards Ant, who was looking slightly awkward with a purple puff hiding his bits. Adam just grinned and nodded. Ant tried to discreetly get out of the shower and managed to grab a towel, just as Zoey looked up from the toilet. Fortunately he'd managed to whip the towel round him in time.

"Zo, are you ok? Sorry I wouldn't have hogged the bathroom for so long if I knew you were sick."

"Don't worry," she mumbled.

"She's not ill, she's got morning sickness," Adam couldn't keep the big grin off his face.

"Glad you can smile about..." her head went back to the loo.

Adam ushered his brother out of the bathroom.

"Oh my God mate, that's great news. I'm so happy for you." He slapped Adam on the back. "I'll get out of your hair; you don't need me hanging around with all my crap while you've got this going on."

"Its fine mate, stay as long as you need and yep, we're well chuffed."

Zoey emerged from the bathroom. "Zo honey, I'd give you a huge big hug, but I'm half naked and you've just been sick...let's hug it out later. Just said to Ads, I'm well pleased for you both."

Adam pulled her close to him. "Babe, you can't go to work like this."

"I'll be fine, like you said, I'm not ill...I'm sure by lunchtime I'll be fine."

By lunchtime Zoey was anything but fine and trying to keep the pregnancy to herself had lasted about five minutes, during which she'd been sick twice. To give him his due Larry had been concerned. "You can go home if you want Zo." She felt quite touched by this, Larry normally only sent you home if you were missing a limb or had the plague.

"It's ok boss man, I'll be ok, besides I can't take the next few months off with morning sickness can I?"

"You're bloody pregnant?" he rolled his eyes, but then a smile spread across his face as he gave her a hug.

"Congratulations kid, haven't you got a TV?"

She laughed knowing that was the best she was gonna get from him.

"I haven't told the others yet..."

"Don't worry, my lips are sealed."

She went back onto the shop floor, just as a load of brochures were being delivered. She signed for them as Larry's voice boomed from the Foreign Exchange as he counted his Euros.

"Suze, Callie, move these brochures," he stopped counting as he peered at them over his glasses. "Zo can't do it in her condition." He pushed his glasses back up the bridge of his nose and carried on counting.

"Argh!!! I KNEW it!" Suze squealed as she jumped up from behind the counter to hug Zo, Callie wasn't far behind.

"How exciting!"

"When are you due?"

The poor brochure man was caught up in the middle of all the excitement. "Err, that's nice news love, but I need me order form back."

She handed it back to him. "There you go." The brochure man escaped as quickly as he could, they were mad in that shop.

She turned her attention back to the girls. "I only told Adam yesterday, what with everything going on with Luce, I needed to find the right time...I don't even know when I'm due yet, I'm going to the doctors later."

"But you're deffo preggers?" Callie asked.

She nodded her head. "Yep. I wasn't gonna tell you till I'd been to the docs, I knew I'd have no chance of keeping it a secret till three months, you can't even fart in this place without someone knowing."

"Bet you've cheered Lucie up with your news," Suze said.

"Err, she doesn't know. I haven't had chance to speak to her...things aren't looking great. Ant stayed at ours last night."

"D'ya think they'll split up? Ant's proper fit," Callie said.

"I don't know, I hope not..."

"Let's stop talking about that, we've got baby news to talk about."

Zo felt the nausea hit her again. "Something I have to do first." She dashed off back to the loo.

Lucie was finding work a welcome distraction, as much as she'd wanted to stay buried under her duvet, she also couldn't wait to get out of her bed, her bed that felt so lonely without Ant. She'd checked her phone as soon as she got up. There was no message from Ant, but there was one from Nick

Sorry 4 being a dick last nt...meet me?

She hadn't replied yet, she didn't know what to do. She wanted to see him, but last night, seeing Ant's reaction...it made everything feel so raw. Maybe Ant had the right idea trying to put some space between them, perhaps she should do the same. It might be easier to work out what she wanted if she wasn't being influenced by either of them.

"Luce, you've just put Mr Rowlands tickets in the bin."

She turned to Jake and then looked in the bin. "Ah crap," she fished them out of the bin, along with a flight invoice.

"Funny filing cabinet you've got there," Jake said.

"Sorry, didn't sleep much last night. I think Ant's left me."

"WHAT?"

"He went last night and said he'd call today, he needed some space and I haven't heard from him yet."

"He actually said it was over?"

"No, but that doesn't mean it isn't. God I've made a right mess of this haven't I?"

"Well at least now that's it's out in the open it's made you realise its Ant you want."

"That's the thing; I still don't know who I want to be with."

"Excuse me for talking out of turn here, but get a grip.

The Lucie I know wouldn't get herself all in a state over some bloke. Stop sitting on the fence, you either want Ant or you don't and the same goes for that Nick bloke. If you can't make a decision then maybe neither of them are right for you and maybe you should walk away from them both," he passed her a piece of paper. "This came down from head office today; I think this could be the answer you're looking for." He stood up and left her to read the information. Once he'd gone in the back she screwed it up and tossed it in her 'filing cabinet'.

Zoey couldn't wait for the day to be over so she could get back home, crawl into her favourite pj's and snuggle on the sofa with Adam. She'd have to check with the doctor later how long this morning sickness thingy lasted for and while she was at ask him when it was called "morning" sickness when it lasted all feckin' day. She hadn't even been able to eat her lunch never mind the emergency Wispa bar in her bag. It was getting on for three o'clock, she only had to get through one more hour before she could get off to go to the docs and then it was home. The huge bouquet of flowers that arrived at lunchtime from Adam had cheered her up and reminded her that no matter how rotten she felt right now, it would all be worth it in a few months. She answered the ringing phone on her desk.

"Good afternoon thank you for calling Book it, Zoey speaking."

"Hey Zoey speaking, its Jake speaking, you sound rough."

"Thanks mate, what can I do you for?"

"Just a quick call to let you know Miss White has just paid some money off her honeymoon, sending a receipt over to you guys."

"Cheers me dears, I'll put a note on the system….how's Lucie?"

"She's not good; she said Ant's left her."

"I don't know if…uh, hold on…I'll be back in a minute." She flung the phone at Callie as she made another sprint out to the loo.

"Hey J, its Callie."

"Where'd Zo go?"

"To upchuck City again."

"Again? Is she ok?"

"Yeah, just this morning sicknesses palaver."

"Ah fab! She's finally pregnant, ah that's great news. I'll bloody kill Lucie for not telling me."

"I don't think Lu…"

"Soz Cal, gotta go mate, customer."

For the next hour Jake's time was taken up with sorting out an All Inclusive to Turkey for a family, it was pretty easy, he booked them to the beautiful resort of Olu Deniz and the fabulous Lykia World complex, seventeen pools, nine bars, twelve restaurants, amphitheatre, water sports, what more could a family want? So as soon as his very happy customers left the shop he legged it up to the office where Lucie had taken herself off to for the afternoon.

"Lucie Maxwell," he barged into the office. "How could you not tell me? We're still mates aren't we? Just 'coz I don't agree with your love situation at the moment, doesn't mean you can with hold this important info from me."

"What have I done now?" she spun round on the office chair. "What are you talking about?"

"Zoey, of course."

She took her glasses off and nervously pushed her hair behind her ear. "Zo? What about her? What's happened?"

He could tell by how high her voice was going with each question that she didn't know. "She didn't tell you?" he whispered.

She stood up now. "Tell me what?"

"She's pregnant."

She sat back down on the chair as if someone had pushed her down. "Pregnant? She didn't tell me."

"She probably hasn't had chance, y'know with everything that's been happening."

"I'm her best friend, how can you know before me?"

He shrugged his shoulders.

"God, I've ruined everything haven't I, my marriage and my friendship with Zo, before Nick came back I'd have been the first person she'd told and now I find out via office bloody gossip." Tears stung her eyes.

"I'm sure she didn't mean for you to find out like this." She stood up again and ran out of the office, down the stairs and straight to the filing cabinet formally known as the bin. She rummaged around and found the piece of paper she was looking for. Sometimes the answer was right in front of you.

Six O'clock and Zo still hadn't got into her longed for pj's. She'd met Adam at the doctors and since then it had been pretty hectic. The doctors had been fine. He confirmed she was eight weeks pregnant. She'd asked him what she could do about the morning/ all day sickness, he said not a lot, she could try ginger biscuits; it would pass by about twelve weeks. Adam had come out of the doctors grinning like a Cheshire cat. She, although very happy was extremely tired. So when she'd got home to find the outlaw waiting for her she wasn't best pleased. Ant was also there, he'd obviously decided he wasn't going home yet. He was really apologetic as they walked down the hallway.

"Sorry guys, I let slip to mum, she was round here before I'd even put the phone down to her."

Zo smiled tiredly. "Don't worry, we'd have to tell her sooner or later."

"Cooee, Zoey, come in here and put your feet up dear." She walked into the living room, the smell of Vanderbilt making her immediately turn on her heel and head for the bathroom.

"Oh the poor thing, I was terrible with sickness when I was having you two. Couldn't keep anything down. Bet she's having a boy."

By the time Zoey made it down stairs Ed had also arrived. Ant apologised again. "Sorry Zo, he texted me too ask why Ads wasn't going to training tonight, it err..."

She rolled her eyes. "I know, just slipped out."

"It just nice to have something else to think about..."

She leaned across and gave him a hug. "I know, honestly its ok, just glad we can help take your mind off it all."

"Bloody hell sis, thought Macca lad might have been firing blanks for a while there. Thought I'd never be an uncle."

She spotted the mother in law shooting a dirty look at Ed. She tried not to smile.

"Zoey dear, I knew you were trying for a baby. So I've been busy," she handed over a bag. "Those ones are all white, but I can knit some more in blue, you're just like I was when I was pregnant with my boys."

Oh God, this was gonna drive her nuts. Where was Lucie when she needed her? Crap! Lucie. She had to tell her before Ant inadvertently took out an announcement in the Liverpool Echo. She'd call her now, she went into the kitchen to try and have some privacy to make the call. She could see an outline of someone at the front door. She opened it. It was Lucie.

"Congratulations Zo."

As if she wasn't feeling sick enough, the hurt in Lucie's eyes made her feel ten times worse.

"I was gonna call...I've only just found out...who told you?"

"Jake."

"Jake! Didn't even know he knew. I'm sorry Luce, you should've found out from me."

"Well, things are different now aren't they?" She turned to walk away.

She ran after her. "Don't go, this was never how I imagined it would be when I told you I was pregnant."

"You see Zo, there's the thing. You didn't tell me, I never imagined I'd hear it from someone else. Look don't feel bad, I know it wasn't on purpose. Bet the old dragon's made up though hey," she tried to laugh.

"She's driving me crazy already, knitted booties and apparently I'm having a boy!"

Lucie smiled. "Certainly won't miss her."

Zoey's face fell. "You've made a decision?"

She nodded. "Ant needs to be the first to know."

"Oh Luce, what have you done?" she felt her heart sink.

"You'll find out soon enough. I've gotta go, now is not the place for me to talk to Ant." She walked back up to Zo. "I really am happy for you chick," she hugged her. "I love you lots."

Zo watched her best friend walk away.

CHAPTER THIRTY

Lucie had managed to get a Saturday off work, it had been a few days since she'd made her decision and as yet she'd told nobody. She'd been busy sorting out what she needed to so that everything was in place before she spoke to either Ant or Nick. She hadn't even spoken to Zo, her friendship with Zoey had been an unexpected casualty of her fling with Nick and something she'd taken into account when making her choice. If she was going to get her friendship with Zoey back on track then she needed to do this.

She'd been home alone the other night, hating being by herself. She wandered over to the DVD collection. They were all arranged in alphabetical order, apart from the first five, their top five romantic films. She picked up the first one and put it into the DVD player. She settled down on the sofa with a glass of wine and some Doritos. She was trying to prove to herself that she could watch this film on her own. Her resolve didn't last long; she reached for her phone to message Ant.

Watchin r fave film....

She wondered if he's reply and if he did his answer would be one of two options, Love Actually or... her phone beeped.

10 things I hate about u.

She sent a text straight back.

Yep, how d'you know? Sure u can think of more than 10 things you hate about me right now.

She tried to get back into the film, he might not text back, she might have gone a bit far with the ten things comment or he could be compiling a huge list of all the things he hated about her. Her phone beeped again.

We only watch Love Actually at Xmas...

she smiled to herself, he was right, never felt right watching that film without Christmas decs up. She read the rest of the message.

Could never hate you...although it might be easier if I did...

She didn't reply, she stared back up at the screen, Heath ledger was serenading the girl he'd fallen in love with. It took her straight back five years to Nick, she remembered telling him about this part of the film. God, she'd felt like she was in a film herself on that ship, the clandestine meetings, driving along Antigua's coast road in a jeep, romantic walks along the beach, fabulous sex, it was almost too good to be true.

Apart from those few texts, contact between the guys had been minimal. Ant had asked for space, she'd tried to give it to him. She knew he'd popped in to get his post and she'd rang him to ask where he'd put the window cleaners money. She'd asked Nick to give her time to think and for once he seemed to understand the seriousness of the situation, almost as if he knew the next conversation they had would be make or break.

So now, on her Saturday off she found herself parking her car up by the rugby club. What else would she do with a Saturday afternoon off than watch her husband play rugby? She didn't know if she'd get a chance to watch him again. She shook her head; she was letting her thoughts run away from her.

She could hear the cries of "Go Spartan's" from the other side of the field, from the cheers it sounded like it was good match. She felt slightly nervous as she crossed the field; this was Ant's first proper game since his injury, what if he got hurt again? As she reached the barriers she was surprised to see Zoey, it must've been her day off too. It made her feel sad, a few weeks ago she would've known automatically what Zo's days off where.

"Hey, how ya feelin'?"

She turned round and smiled. "I'm good, fresh air helps...you?"

"Yeah, not so bad." God they sounded like two people who only vaguely knew each other, not two friends who knew each other better than they knew themselves. Lucie hated it. She hated herself for what she'd done to the people she loved most in the world.

"Ant didn't mention you were coming down, day off?"

"Yeah, he err, he doesn't know I'm here."

"Oh right..."

"Look Zo, one way or another this will all be over soon."

"What the hell are you planning? You're being so secretive and mysterious, you've got me worried."

"Don't worry...oh Adam's just scored."

Zo turned back round to the game. "Damn, I missed it."

"Please don't worry about me hon, everything will be fine, it'll work out for the best...I just can't tell you yet."

"You're gonna break Ant's heart aren't you?"

Lucie looked down at the ground. "Think I've already done that."

They stood mostly in silence for the rest of the game, apart from joining in with the rest of the crowd with the cheering. When the final whistle went Lucie turned to leave.

"Aren't you coming into the club?"

Lucie shook her head. "Best not, just tell Ant I was here will you?"

Zoey nodded, on impulse she reached across to hug her friend. "You're still my best mate you know."

Lucie smiled. "I know babe, your still mine too, sorry for all this mess."

"God I'm gonna puke."

"Sorry, didn't think that was too soppy..."

"Not you, baby sickness."

Lucie smiled to herself as she watched Zo race into the clubhouse. She was gonna miss watching her through her pregnancy, it would be more than comical. Tears pricked her eyes, she'd made her choice and she couldn't change her mind now. She slipped away before Zo had chance to find her again.

Zoey collared Ant in the bar before Adam came out of the changing room.

"I don't know what she's planning, but I think if you don't want to lose her you need to go back home. You are welcome to stay at ours for as long as you like, but I think you need to start talking to her."

"D'you think she's chosen him?"

"I don't know, all I know is she seems different, like she knows where her future is...I'm not saying it's him she wants, but maybe she feels you've given up on her. If you still love her, don't give up on her because of your stupid pride."

"You think we belong together don't you?" He asked as the barman passed him a bud.

She nodded her head. "Course I do, and if I was a fairy Godmother, I'd be waving that magic wand like crazy, but life 'aint like the movies."

"Zoey Maxwell, I love you," he pulled her close and hugged her. "You are so right, life isn't like the movies." He kissed her on the top of her head.

"Alright Ads mate, cracking game again, you're obviously lighter on yer feet now you've got our Zo up the duff," Ed interrupted.

Zoey rolled her eyes. "Ed, this is ANT."

"Oh for Christ sake, he's hugging you and telling you he loves you, how am I supposed to know it's not Adam...come to think of it, why are you kissing my sister?"

"Because, your lovely sister is my fairy Godmother, she may well have just saved my marriage, tell Adam I'll catch him later." With that he dashed out of the club.

"What. The. Crap. Was that all about?"

She shook her head smiling. "I don't know but I'm hoping it's gonna be all good in the hood."

"Freakin' nuts you are sis, totally looped. I obviously got the sane gene."

She gave him a dig in the arm "Whatever loser."

Lucie was halfway home when her mobile rang; she pulled over and checked the caller ID. This was the call she'd been waiting for. The call took less than two minutes and in that time her decision had been finalised. No going back now. She took a few more minutes to get her head together. Well she'd gone and done it now. She just had to tell Ant, it was gonna hurt like hell, but this was the right thing to do. She turned the ignition and headed off home. She'd have to text him; tell him she needed to speak to him. As she turned into her road she saw his car was parked outside the house. She felt sick, she wasn't ready, but she couldn't let it go on like this.

"Ant?" she called out as she came through the front door.

"In the living room," he called back.

She pulled her bag over her head and hung it on the banister; she went into the living room. "What are you doing?"

He had all the DVD's out in piles. Oh God, please tell me he isn't dividing our stuff up and he's started with the bloody DVD's.

"It was something Zo said about life not being like the movies and something you said the other night about feeling like you were in a film with *him."*

"You've lost me..."

He picked up Bridget Jones. "Great film, but fundamentally flawed, they have a row and Mark Darcy leaves her to walk home on her own in the dark, as if I would ever do that to you. We could have the biggest row ever and I'd still make sure you got home ok." He flung the DVD box on the floor. "Four Weddings and a Funeral, she finally falls so much in love with Hugh Grant and doesn't even notice its bloody raining. Now that's wrong on two levels, A. because it's Hugh Grant and two. Who the hell would not notice a torrential downpour, not matter how loved up you were?" he threw that DVD on top of Bridget Jones.

She was trying not to smile as she watched him get more worked up, although she wasn't sure where this rant was headed.

"The Proposal. So they hate each other to begin with, then two weeks in Alaska and they're loved up, too farfetched," he went to throw that DVD as well but she grabbed it.

"It's not farfetched, it's bloody Ryan Reynolds, any woman alive would fall in love with him in five seconds flat. What is your point with all this?"

"My point is...we get caught up with these romance stories, but that's all they are, stories. It doesn't show real life. I love you, but if we were kissing in the rain, I'd notice, I wouldn't let you walk home alone in the dark after a row," he paused then gave a sarcastic laugh. "Although you did fall in love with someone after two weeks so what the hell do I know? I was just trying to make you see, the movie ending isn't always the best." He stood over the DVD's over the floor to get to her.

"I love you Lucie Maxwell, as much as I'm hurting right now, the thought of losing you to him would be even worse. I can get over this pain, in time, but if I had to live my life without you..."

"Babe, please don't..."

"Whatever decision you've made, you can change it. We can make this work."

"I've hurt you too much, I can't forgive myself."

"So that's it, you're leaving me for him..."

She watched his face crumple. "I love you Ant, I love you so much, but we can't work like this, you'd end up resenting me, hating me even, you need time to heal and I need time to forgive myself." She was trying to sound strong, but the emotion cracked straight through her words and the tears wouldn't stay away, she reached up to stroke his face. He put his hand on top of hers.

"What are you saying?"

"I'm leaving."

"You can't. I love you, kiddo."

CHAPTER THIRTY ONE

After a hugely emotional Saturday afternoon which went long into the early hours and a massive heart to heart with Ant, Lucie now had to let Nick know her decision. She woke up late into the morning on Sunday and alone. She didn't know where Ant had gone. She felt drained after the previous day; they had both cried, lots. But it was done now. She reached for her mobile at the side of the bed. She scrolled down to Nick. He answered almost immediately,

"Luce?"

"Yeah, it's me."

"Everything ok?"

"We need to talk can I see you?"

"Course you can, where d'you wanna meet up?" he sounded nervous.

"Err, your apartment?"

He paused for a moment "Yep, no probs." She could hear the confidence come back into his voice.

"Give me an hour or so."

"I'll be waiting."

Forty five minutes later she pressed the buzzer to Nick's apartment.

"Yo. Come on up."

With each step up the stairs a strange feeling of déjà vu swept over her. When she reached the top of the stairs he was already standing at the door, his shirt left open.

"D'you always answer the door like that?"

He winked at her. "Only when it's you babes." He moved to one side to let her pass.

Be strong Luce, she told herself. She could be in a room alone with Nick and stay in control. She nervously began to fiddle with her hair. He sat on the arm of the sofa, his shirt falling away even more. It was like a reflex action, his bare chest and tight stomach drew her eyes like a magnet. She could see him grinning. He stood up and walked slowly towards her.

Find your voice Lucie, the voice in her head told her. Quick *before he kisses you and you lose your bloody mind again.* The voice was now shouting at her.

Nick pushed his hand through her hair, cupping the back of her neck, tilting her head towards his.

QUICK!

"Nick, I..."

"We can talk later, let's just enjoying being together."

She took a step back. "You see that's the thing..."

"I know, you've left him. Why else would you come here? If you hadn't you'd be telling me over a coffee in Starbucks, you know you can't trust yourself alone with me," he winked.

"I'm here to tell you my decision."

"Yeah I kinda gathered that babe. I know it must've been difficult, but you've made the right choice. It's always been you Luce, I've never been able to get you out of my head. I just wish I hadn't left it so long. I wish when I realised I loved you after you left the ship that I'd done something then, but y'know we were obviously meant to be."

She ran her hand through her hair, she stood looking at him. She had a very surreal moment like she was a judge on X Factor or something, about to make or break someone's dream and tell them if they were through to the next round or not. She was Insania, God now she was quoting Peter Andre, things were going from bad to worse.

"Babe, were you listening then? You've got a weird look on your face. I was sayin' that we were obviously fated to be together."

She stepped forward. "Actually Nick," she closed her eyes. "I've come to say goodbye."

"WHAT? He doesn't make you feel like I do."

"It's not about that. The twenty three year old Lucie fell head over heels in love with you, and then you come swaning back into my life and think we can just carry on and for a while I thought it might be possible too but the twenty eight year old Lucie has grown up. As much as I love you, you're still the same guy I met five years ago, Lucie Scott fell in love with you, but I don't think you're ready for Lucie Maxwell. I'm not the same girl you met."

"So this is it? It's over? Babe, I can be whatever you want me to be, just don't walk out on me again."

"I'm sorry Nick."

"Let me prove myself to you...I can be the guy you want me to be."

"Can you wait six months for my answer?"

"I waited five years for you, I'm sure I can wait another few months. You're worth it."

Driving back along the M53 to Wallasey she felt like a weight had been lifted from her shoulders, well almost, there was one person still left to talk to, Zo. Strangely enough it had been finding out about her friends pregnancy that had spurred her decision on. She'd hurt too many people and she realised there was only one way to fix it. She pulled up outside Zoey's house. Adam answered the door to her. He was understandably off with her.

"Look Adam, I won't stay long, there's just something really important I need to tell Zo."

"Make it quick, I don't want you in my house any longer than you need to be."

She felt like crying as soon as she saw Zo, she'd miss her so much.

"What's wrong?" Zo asked getting up from the sofa and straight to her side.

"It's all over."

"You and Ant?"

She nodded "Me and Ant, me and Nick."

Zoey stared hard at her. "I don't understand, I thought Ant was trying to sort everything last night."

"He tried, he was too late."

"Luce, you're talking in riddles now, too late for what"

"He missed the boat, literally."

"Right, I have about a five minute window before I'm due to throw up again, stop talking shite and just bloody well tell me what boat you're talking about."

"Oceania. I'm going back on it."

"For a holiday? With Nick?"

She shook her head. "Neither, I'm going to work on it for six months."

"Six months? Six months? Why would you do that?"

"I've caused too much heartache. I need to distance myself and give people time to forgive me."

"Ant will forgive you."

"Not just him, you. It breaks my heart the way our friendship has changed. You are my best friend in the whole world I don't want you to hate me. So I thought if I went away for a while...time heals all wounds and that."

Zo flopped back down on the sofa. "Chick, I don't hate you, I could never hate you. Please don't go. I don't want to go through my pregnancy without you."

Lucie smiled. "You've got Adam to help you."

"But he's a boy, he'll be no use, he's done his bit now. How am I supposed to get through this and deal with the outlaw without you," she burst into tears. "Damn hormones."

"Zo, please don't cry, look you've started me off now," she wiped her eyes with the back of her hand. "Honestly, this is the best thing for me to do right now."

"But you are coming back?"

She nodded. "The contracts only for six months. It's a position head office managed to secure. I'll be doing future cruise bookings. It's to help strengthen the relationship between our two companies, and they decided I was the right person for the job. Oh the irony."

"So what happens when you get back, what will you do about Ant and Nick then?"

"Well, they've both told me they'll still be waiting for me when I get back; I'm hoping over the next six months I can get back to being me again and help me make my choice."

"You seriously wanna drag this out another six months?"

She shook her head. "No, it could be that they both find someone else in that time or I realise I'm happy on my own."

"I think this is crazy, just follow your heart, go with your instincts."

"That's the problem, everything's so messed up, I can't even decide what to have for tea anymore, let alone who I want to spend the rest of my life with. I've always felt that I gave up on adventures too soon and I think this will get it out of my system and everything will be ok in the end."

"I'm gonna miss you so much Luce," she reached over to hug her friend.

"I'm gonna miss watching your tummy get huge," she smiled through her tears. "Oh God, I really wish you could come with me. You know I'll get lost on that bloody ship everyday without you."

Zo jumped up. "Oh no, I need to be sick again, back in a minute."

She stood up and wandered over to the fire place, the pictures that she'd looked at so many times where still in pride of place. She looked so happy in all of them. She wanted to be that girl again and the only way to do that was to go and find her. She picked up the photo of her and Zoey, she wondered if she'd let her borrow that photo to take with her.

"When d'you go?"

She spun back round to Zo. "God that was quick."

"Got it down to a fine art now."

"Three weeks time."

"That soon? Can't I change your mind?"

Lucie walked over to her and hugged her. "Just don't be finding another best mate while I'm gone ok?"

"As if."

Three weeks later and Zo was driving Lucie to the airport. It was a forty five minute drive to Manchester Airport; Zo wanted it to take forever. She didn't want to say goodbye to her friend.

Lucie had said her goodbyes to Ant and Nick, both very tearful, she promised that before she came home she'd email, it didn't seem the best way to tell someone she wanted to be with them and she hoped they still wanted to be with her, but she would be on the other side of the world practically, what else could she do?

"Tell me truthfully, do you know who you're hoping you'll be coming back to?" She spotted the sign for the airport and came off the slip road.

"I'm kind've sure, but I need to sort my head out first, if it's meant to be, it's meant to be. Six months is nothing in the grand scheme of things."

Zoey nodded. "Yeah it's not like its five years or anything..."

"Anyway, it's not just that, if we're gonna repair our friendship then you need time to forgive me too."

"We would've sorted it out; you didn't need to jet off to the bloody Caribbean...without me. Yeah, just leave me here, while you're sunning yourself on MY ship, I'll be stuck here getting FAT." She pulled into the Terminal car park

"Zo, babe, you will look amazing, you'll bloom and I promise it'll probably be shit weather, you know what the rains like in the Caribbean, you'd hate it."

"Yeah right. Bloom? Burst more like, I'm eleven weeks pregnant and look at my tummy already. You won't even be back before the babies arrive."

"Yeah I will, you're almost three months, I'm back in six, three and six make nine. I'll be back just in time. Hold it right there missus...did you say babies?"

She flung the car into a space and turned to Lucie with a big grin on her face.

"I had the scan yesterday. Its twins...you're the first to know, obviously Ads was with me so he knows..."

"Oh my flippin' God...twins!! Oh now I really don't want to go."

"The doctors reckon I probably won't get passed eight months."

"I'm gonna miss the birth," she cried.

"Just get you're arse back here as soon as you can."

The two girls got out of the car and walked towards the terminal.

"Zo, I can't do goodbyes."

"Me neither."

They hugged each other, tears streaming down their cheeks.

"You just stay safe and when you get back I'm gonna need all the help I can get with these babies."

EPILOGUE

SIX MONTHS LATER...

Lucie wandered around the deck early in the morning, so early it was just after sun rise. It was her favourite time of day. The deck was deserted apart from a few early morning joggers. She liked to start her day off like this, it helped to clear her head. The ship had arrived back in Barbados, it was turn around day so it was gonna bedlam later on. She had two weeks left on the ship, the last few months had flown by. Her work on the ship had kept her days busy and night times were always hectic, there was so much going on.

She almost felt like coming back on the ship had taken her full circle, her journey was almost over and in four hours time the first of the newbie passengers would be arriving and there was one in particular she couldn't wait to see. She leaned against the railing watching all the commotion going on dockside, new supplies being loaded, suitcases being taken off. She'd miss all the hustle and bustle but she was more than ready to go home. She had missed Zoey like crazy and now she had two baby girls, Lily and Poppy who she was desperate to see, they were only two weeks old but the minute she'd seen the photo that Ed had emailed to her of Zo and Adam with their tiny bundles of pinkness she knew it was time to go home.

Although she knew she'd done the right thing getting away for a bit, she was starting to feel nervous about the imminent arrival. She couldn't wait till she got home so she'd emailed him a few weeks ago saying if he still wanted her, she still loved him. She'd arranged some flights and he was coming out to join her for her last two weeks on the ship. She couldn't wait to see him. She'd missed him like crazy. She checked her watch, time to get back to work.

She was waiting in the atrium when the first coach load of passengers arrived, she was part of the welcome aboard team. She'd checked on the passenger manifest what flight he was due on and what time he was expected to arrive portside. For the millionth time that day she checked her watch. He was due any minute. She'd tried to time a break so that she could show him straight to the cabin. She kept trying to look down the gang plank to see if she could see him but it was just so busy she couldn't really see much. Then there seemed to be a break in the crowd and there he was. He spotted her straight away and grinned at her, flashing off that dimple she smiled back, she felt the sudden urge to run up to him and fling herself in his arms but she'd suddenly lost the power of movement. Seeing him after all this time had the strangest effect on her. He walked towards her, the next thing she knew he'd picked her up, engulfing her in his arms. Tears streamed down her face as she wrapped her arms around his neck, taking in the familiar smell if him.

"Oh my God. I can't believe you're finally here. I've missed you so much," she said through happy tears,

"Me too kiddo, me too."

He put her back down on the ground, then taking her face in his hands he kissed her.

As long as he was by her side she was home. He'd been right all along; the movie happy endings were over rated. She wanted a happy beginning, middle and ending and she wanted it all with him.

Bev Dulson has written stories since she was old enough to hold a pen, she lives in a constant dream world and genuinely thinks her characters are real. She lives in the North West of England, where sometimes the sun actually shines. She's married to her ex-rugby playing, hubby and two adorable, well behaved (sometimes) daughters.

As well as writing she loves reading, whodunnits, dancing around a disco ball in her friend's kitchen, anything purple and chocolate oh and pink wine.

Find Bev on:

Facebook : Bev Dulson (Books)
Twitter : @thebevster25
Website: bevdulson.weebly.com

Lightning Source UK Ltd.
Milton Keynes UK
UKOW051803310712

196861UK00001B/1/P